CONTENTS

DERAILED

CHAPTER ONE

I couldn't really say that it was one specific event which caused me to have my epiphany. It was more of a collection of happenings that led to my 'moment on the road to Damascus', as it were. When the dam walls burst and spilled out all over my life and I suddenly turned into a person I didn't really recognise who didn't know her place in the world.

It was a bit of a shock, I can tell you. There you are, minding your own business and then one thing happens after another and it all starts to go awry. And as your life begins to change, so does the vision you have of yourself.

My name is Philomena. My parents had a shy flirtation with the mysteries of the Catholic church around the time that I was born and thought that if they endowed their darling daughter with the name of a saint, then perhaps some of those saint-like qualities would be passed on as well. Wishful thinking on their part, but everyone loves a dreamer.

I don't really mind it. Especially when I found out that it also means 'daughter of light'. I quite liked the idea of that, I could imagine myself surrounded with bright, clear light, softening my physical edges. A halo shimmering around my whole body, rather than just my head. A protecting force which could buffet away negative influences. And, of course, it could be a useful superpower at night, when making a hazardous sortie to the bathroom with my luminescence lighting the way.

They do say that if you have an unusual name that you are supposed to do one of two things. Either grow into it and become that name ("She really suits that name, it's just so *her!*") or else shrink away from it until it becomes a ridiculous moniker which can leave you open to ridicule, or at the very least a few sniggery remarks.

In my case, I tried to get round that problem by adapting my name into something which seemed a bit more run-of-the-mill. Not that my name is too outlandish, none of your PizzaTin-Fairycake business for me. But still.

As far as I could see I had three obvious options. I could shorten my name to Philo, Philly or Mena. I quite liked the Philo option until I realised that it did make me sound like a block of pastry. While I like filo pastry, I'd rather not be synonymous with a flour-based product. And Philly made me think of cream cheese or brought to mind a misogynistic landed gentry fellow bellowing, "Fine filly, eh?"

So, I became Mena.

I really do think, though, that I was meant to be one of those people who fall into the 'grow into their name' category. I'm not a complete shrinking violet. Unfortunately though, my bursts of confidence are few and far between and any long-term attempts to become an assured person ultimately tail off in an embarrassed fashion, like someone who has found themselves in front of a packed auditorium and then realised that – oops! – they have forgotten to wear their trousers.

It was just as well that I went down the 'Mena' route, considering the married name I ended up with. Frisby. Seriously. Imagine if I had come Philo Frisby. Or Philly Frisby. That was a narrow escape.

Anyway, about my epiphany. I blame circumstances. But then everyone finds someone or something to blame these days, don't they? Nothing is ever anyone's personal responsibility, or even just something that happens by chance.

Perhaps it would be fairer to say that I blame fate. I'm a big believer in fate. Even when really nasty things have happened to me, a few years down the line I can look back on that experience and say that it had its place in how things mapped out.

Circumstances and fate, a potent combination.

For a person with social anxiety, family gatherings can be a complete and utter nightmare. Especially family gatherings where you don't actually belong to the family and only slightly know the main players involved. There's always the problem of deciding what to wear for a start. You don't want to look too ostentatious, as if you are saying 'look at me, I'm high up in the family hierarchy and a main part of this event'. Unless you actually are of course. So that rules out the wearing of hats and feathers in your hair unless you are an attention seeker.

You also don't want to look too casual, as if you're implying that you only turned up because you *had* to and not because you really want to be a part of the occasion. I was brought up with manners drummed into me from an early age and the thought of insulting the hosts in such a way – and causing askance looks and caustic comments – turned me clammy with horror. The last wedding I'd been to as a peripheral guest, I'd heard one lady comment in scathing tones to her friends about a young male guest, "Well, in *jeans* if you please. At a wedding. (Sniff). You can take the boy out of the council estate but you can't take the council estate out of the boy!"

I didn't know either of the parties involved in this exchange but felt a prickle of embarrassment ripple through me which led to me dashing to the ladies to double check that my own attire was suitable. I stayed in there until I managed to convince myself that my outfit was sufficiently down key and yet smart enough to avoid notice.

It's a very tricky and tiring business.

Somehow one weekend I managed to find myself at a christening in a Sheffield suburb. I had had an unexpected phone call the week before from a girl I used to work with a couple of years ago. We were never particularly close, but used to chat regularly on a superficial basis until she left to move to Sheffield with her husband. You know the sort of conversations, what you've been up to the weekend before, what you thought of the new girl in HR, where did you get those nice trousers from and so on. But to be honest, Joanna wasn't really my cup of tea. She was very touch-feely, constantly finding a reason to touch your arm, pat your shoulder or give you a reassuring hug. She liked to sit just slightly too close to you and leaned in just a little too much when listening to what you had to say.

And to be honest, her eating habits were frankly quite revolting. If you'd ever seen her eat a plum with her mouth open, it could make you feel quite nauseous. I always had to find something to do away from my desk when she was eating fruit as I didn't think it would be good for my career prospects if I was sick in the wastepaper bin. She did mean well, but I have to say that I was secretly pleased when she announced that she was going, particularly as she had been on an all-fruit diet that week so that she could fit into a 'posh frock' for her husband's works do.

On her last day, Joanna asked a few people from work to the local pub for a quick lunch and farewell. It was a dark little place, with heavy mahogany furniture and swirly carpets which you knew would be a completely different colour if the years of grime were removed. Stuffing spilled out of brocade benches like split sausages on a grill and an unappetising aroma of stale beer and hint of dog hung in the air. A tattered piece of lino circled the bar and it stuck to the soles of feet and made a slight sucking noise. I had wondered if this lino was for the benefit of patrons with visual impairments to alert them that they had reached the bar. Perhaps not.

Over a plate of cheesy chips, Joanna chattered away happily about what she was going to do in Sheffield and how it was going to be a new start. Something about starting up her own business with her husband and working for themselves. I have to admit that I was starting to drift away from the conversation as I was trying to remember if I'd taken my pre-made chilli out of the freezer that morning. I did remember thinking that I must do it, but did I actually open the freezer door…

"And of course you must all stay in touch!" Joanna said brightly.

I clicked back into the conversation and smiled politely, looking around at the others who were nodding their heads and wearing polite smiles. In my experience, once a work colleague has left, it only takes a few months at most before the ties are dissolved and it's almost as if you never knew them at all. Of course, you may have conversations about them and remember them fondly ("Remember the time she sent that email to the whole company instead of just her boyfriend and got bollocked?" etc) but once the common ground is removed it isn't often that you feel the need to stay in touch anymore. Maybe harsh, but it's true. Even when the most key work colleague leaves that you couldn't imagine work without, everyone shuffles around a bit, readjusts and moves on. Not many make the transition to full friend status.

So I didn't actually have any intention of staying in touch with Joanna. I'd be sorry to see her go and would wish her well but that was it.

Except that as we left the pub, Joanna laid a hand on my arm and said very earnestly, "I really do hope we will stay in touch, Mena. I have enjoyed our chats and I hope you think that we are more friends than just work colleagues."

I blinked and then swallowed.

"Of course we are, I've enjoyed our chats too!" I said, slightly too chirpily.

Well that sounded fake.

I cringed inside.

"Keep in touch and I'll let you know how we're getting on."

Immediately I felt as though I was the meanest person around for even thinking that I wouldn't bother to stay in touch. Of course we would. How nice to be singled out in such a fashion. I felt a glow that Joanna thought enough about me from our chats to want to carry on our acquaintance. And WhatsApp messages were quite easy to keep up with, it wasn't as though we'd see each other very often. We chatted cosily all the way back to the office and parted company on the fondest of terms.

Anyway, Joanna had phoned me at home out of the blue the other week and after a few cursory 'how are you doing' questions had asked me if I was available that weekend to attend the christening of her young son, Joshua. I didn't really want to make the journey for a family occasion, particularly when I didn't know anyone aside from Joanna, but you try saying no to something when the other person is either a) right in front of you looking at you hopefully or b) on the phone and blindsides you so that you don't have a chance to think up a good enough excuse without it *sounding* like an excuse.

"Um, I'd love to. Thank you for asking me!" I replied after a slight pause. See, manners again. They are responsible for getting me into a lot of situations I could have avoided if I was a bit more assertive.

"Great, it's at two o'clock at St. Peter's church. I'll send you the address. We're having a bit of a reception at the local Community Hall after – hubby is friends with the man who runs the bar and he said he'd do us a special deal. I know it's just a Community Hall, but it's just been refurbished and spruces up quite nicely."

Who refers to their husband as 'hubby' in a conversation instead of their name?

If you hadn't realised already, this is my inner voice. My constant and very critical companion. It helps me to acknowledge some of the frustrations that I would never dream of saying. Not even if I was drunk and at the stage of drunkenness where I tell people that I think they're wonderful. It also acts as a constant jukebox, playing irritating earworms on loop at the most inappropriate times.

"Brilliant, just send me some directions and I'll be there."

I hung up the phone and frowned. I was a bit surprised that I had been invited to a family occasion when I had never so much as met her husband or new baby before. It wasn't as though we were that close – it wouldn't even have crossed my mind to invite her to a family occasion of mine.

"Who was that and where do we have to go?"

Paddy Frisby sat in his favourite chair, sipping a cup of coffee and checking his phone. In my opinion, he drinks too much coffee. I can't do much about it in the week when he's at work and can make his own, but at home I make sure I substitute several of his coffees with decaf. Except for the first one in the morning because that would be plain cruel. I thought this was quite cunning until I realised that on a Sunday he really is quite grumpy which is probably my own fault.

I summoned up my 'won't this be fun' smile on my face and

told him about Joanna's invitation to the Sheffield christening. Paddy looked puzzled.

"I thought you didn't know her very well? Isn't that the girl you used to work with with the fruit fetish?"

"Well, not fetish really, she just has an interesting way of eating fruit," I replied, wondering what I had said. The last thing I wanted was for Paddy to be smirking at Joanna at the reception if she picked up a plum.

"You said that she ate fruit like a washing machine with its door open and it's one of the most revolting things you've ever had to watch."

Ah, so that was what I had said.

"Yes, well," I fumbled. "Maybe so, but she's a nice enough person and it is nice to be asked."

"Really," said Paddy, a touch sarcastically I thought.

"Yes, really!"

"Nothing to do with her asking you on the hop and you not being able to come up with a good excuse?"

The knowing smile on his face was particularly irritating.

"How rude of you, of course not. If I didn't want to go I would say so. If you don't want to come that's fine, I'll go on my own."

Oh dear, there we go. How well Paddy knew me. He always managed to play on my little foibles to get exactly what he wanted. Instantly I knew that he didn't want to go – and to be fair, why would he? – and that he also had me pegged about the excuse.

"Oh good, that's great because there's a match on and I'm not trekking over to Sheffield from Manchester for someone I don't know, just to make up the numbers."

He saw my crestfallen face. I always seem to find it easier to talk to strangers when I have back-up.

"Unless you want me to come with you," he half-heartedly volunteered.

"No, no, that's fine. I'll go on my own. No point both of us wasting our weekend."

I picked up my magazine so that I could have something to slam down again in a petulant manner and stomped out of the room in a huff.

"It might be fun!" Paddy called after me as I crashed up the stairs.

I dutifully made the hazardous journey over the tops to Sheffield that weekend and managed to find the church with about twenty minutes to go. Joanna, her husband and baby Joshua stood outside the church. Poor Joshua was wearing some sort of satin sailor suit with a matching hat. He'll never live that one down in years to come, I thought to myself. Perhaps I should take a photo so that I could have one for blackmail purposes. Might be quite a good money earner, I thought to myself.

I sidled up and said hello.

"Oh, hello Mena, how good of you to make it. This is my husband Simon."

I smiled and nodded at Simon, who simply looked back at me with a vaguely puzzled expression.

"Thanks again for inviting me, I love christenings."

Dear god. You love christenings? That's what you came up with?

What a liar I am! At what point do 'good manners' mean that

you can tell outrageous fibs? I don't intend to tell lies like that, but sometimes they do just pop out before I can scoop them up and push them back in my mouth like an errant malteser when you're having a 'see how many maltesers you can fit in your mouth' competition.

"You're welcome. It's nice to see you."

There was an awkward pause. I never could bear pauses in social situations, I always break first.

"Paddy is sorry he couldn't make it, he had some work to catch up on."

I twiddled with the object in my hands.

"I've brought Joshua a gift," I said, helpfully holding up a blue package that I'd wrapped up that morning.

"How lovely," said Joanna, not moving to take it from me. Simon was holding the baby so I wasn't sure what to do next.

"I'll take it to the reception shall I?"

"Yes please," she said. And smiled.

Simon just stared at me and didn't say a word. I began to wonder whether he had been let out for the day. There was another pause.

"Perhaps I should have bought him a toy boat to go with his outfit!" I laughed in a jovial way.

Nothing. Just a social smile.

Oh, just give it up.

"Right," I said after a moment. And then gave up.

I sighed and headed off into the church and sat somewhere near the back. I had a dilemma about whether I should sit on the left or right side – do christenings run on the same rules as weddings? But then seeing as I couldn't remember which side the bride's friends and family sat on anyway I just plonked myself down as far from the front as I thought I could get away with without seeming disinterested. I didn't want to usurp a real family member, although looking around there didn't seem to be that many people.

The service was mercifully short and one of those where the vicar tries to be very jolly and produces a cuddly toy part way though the proceedings. The toy always has a name and some obscure reference to church or being good and is often missing an eye or limb. Well, you have to make sure you are politically correct at all times. Joshua was christened – so was the teddy, although that certainly wasn't part of the arrangement, more the result of a small over-excited cousin and the effects of a tube of smarties – and we all shuffled in an embarrassed manner out into the churchyard.

I looked over to Joanna for some sign as to where to go next. She was busy playing the dutiful wife and mother and making over-exaggerated gestures and did not seem capable of meeting my eye. So I stood with a fixed, slightly desperate smile on my face and tried very hard not to look like a spare part. That isn't easy when you clearly *are* a spare part. I felt very uncomfortable.

You see where saying yes to things you don't want to do gets you?

I loitered for several more minutes. In the end, I managed to follow a relative to the reception – not by arrangement as Joanna and Simon hadn't been over to check that I knew where I was going. I'd decided to follow an elderly aunt and uncle, although that had meant driving at well under the speed limit (unusual for me, I always try to keep to it at least) and resisting the urge to overtake or mouth obscenities which could be seen in the rear-view mirror by the car in front. I've done that before in a moment of temper and it's very embarrassing for all concerned when I've encountered the driver at my destination.

I parked up in the Community Hall car park and sat for a moment. I could just leave. No-one would miss me and there were plenty of other things that I could be doing at home. I had an old Hollywood musical to watch on DVD that had arrived and I could curl up on the sofa with a pizza and a glass of wine.

Make a stand for goodness' sake.

Yes, enough was enough, I was going to make a stand and make my apologies. I would offload the present onto another guest and make a swift exit. I turned to open the door when a sharp rap on my car window made me jump.

I turned my head to look out of the window – it was the elderly uncle. I opened the car window part-way down until there was a sizeable gap.

"Hello!" I said, brightly.

He eyed me suspiciously, as one does a suspected burglar or unstable person. He was probably right about the latter.

"Who are you?" he asked, peering into the car. "Were you following me? What do you want?"

His tone was quite aggressive and it threw me for a moment.

"Me?" I quavered. "Oh yes, I was following you, I hope you don't mind but..."

"I haven't got it any more if that's what you're after," he snapped, some spit landing on the window. Thank goodness I hadn't wound it down any more than I had.

"Sorry? I don't know what you mean. I'm here for the christening..."

His creased brow cleared and he seemed to relax a little.

"Oh. Well aren't you coming in then? Instead of sitting out here like some kind of strange person."

I flinched. That was a bit rich coming from a paranoid old man who goes around accosting strangers.

"Erm, yes I am. I was just taking a moment to reflect before I..."

Oh do shut up.

I trailed off.

He stood watching me. I could tell that the only way to get him to leave me alone was to get out of the car. I picked up the present from the passenger seat and held it up as proof.

"Well, come on then," he growled and stood waiting.

"Righto!" (suddenly I had now become an Enid Blyton character) and I stepped out of the car and made my way up the steps to the front door.

I could feel his eyes on me all the way up. What did he think I was going to do? Did he think I had wrapped up some explosives and was about to lob them into the room before doing a runner? Perhaps he was an old James Bond-type spy and he might be thinking just that. I decided to get away from him as quickly as possible.

Inside, small pockets of guests milled around talking to other people they knew. No-one caught my eye and I didn't get the impression that any of the groups would welcome me shoe-horning my way in amongst them. I spotted Joanna over in the corner and waved the present. She pointed to a table in the corner and I went over and laid mine next to the others. She bustled over with baby Joshua.

"Oh Mena, would you mind holding Joshua for a moment? I have to do the rounds and he's being a bit fractious. Thanks very much."

And before I had chance to say yes or no, the star of the day was deposited into my arms and Joanna dashed off.

I hadn't really had much experience of babies and so decided to sit down so that there was less chance of dropping him on the floor. That wouldn't do at a christening, to end up seriously injuring the main attraction.

I found a seat by a coat stand and settled myself down. Joshua was looking distinctly unhappy and his satin suit was sticking to his skin. I tried pulling faces at him to cheer him up. He began to look faintly alarmed.

"What is it?" asked a voice in a very put-out fashion.

I turned round carefully and looked over the sailor hat to see a very old woman sat in a wheelchair that was partially obscured by the coat stand. She had a fetching purple pork-pie hat pinned onto her head – I'd always wanted to see what a pork-pie hat looked like - and also had the most amazing whiskers I'd ever seen. They were several inches long and drooped down either side of her mouth, giving her the look of an ancient Chinese sage. I was very impressed.

"I'm sorry?"

"What is it?" she barked again, a thread of spittle connecting her upper and lower lips.

What is it with guests at this christening and saliva?

"Erm, what is what?" I tried to sound polite but it came out slightly frantic. I felt like I was failing a test.

She sighed and pointed a twisted, bent finger at Joshua.

"What's that?" she said, punctuating each word with a jab at Joshua. He was no longer looking alarmed, he was starting to look terrified. Poor kid. I gave him a reassuring jiggle on my knee to pacify him.

"Erm, a baby?" I hazarded. I wasn't trying to be facetious, I had no idea what she was talking about.

She looked at me as though I was an idiot, perhaps understandably.

"Boy or girl?" she snapped.

"Oh, I see!" I said in relief. "It's a boy. Joshua."

Wasn't she at the church service? And I know that the satin sailor outfit could raise questions about his gender identity, but he was still quite clearly a boy.

"Humph."

She settled back behind the coats. I was feeling quite perplexed. Thankfully, Joanna reappeared and swept Joshua off my knee.

"I see you've met Joshua's Great Aunt Alice. She does dote on him you know!"

Rubbish. She doesn't even know he's a boy!

"Thanks for holding him, must dash, I must take him for photos."

And off she went again, Joshua's hat slipping precariously off his head. Poor thing, to be immortalised in photographs looking like an infant member of the Village People. Still, now she was gone, I had no intention of being stuck in this corner with the barking Great Aunt Alice. I stood up, brushed my skirt down and announced brightly that I was off to the ladies. Great Aunt Alice couldn't have cared less, she simply glared at me, her whiskers quivering. Wouldn't you have thought that one of her relatives would have trimmed those for her? I wondered. Perhaps they had tried and their remains were now scattered around Sheffield with tyre marks where she had run her wheelchair over them for good measure.

I made a break for the ladies and hid in a cubicle for a few moments. I decided that I would have to get out of here, I was clearly not needed or wanted. I was about to emerge and gallop for the door when a couple of ladies came in together and each went in a cubicle on either side of me and continued their loud chatting. I was in a toilet conversation sandwich! I stood quietly so as not to draw attention to myself.

"Isn't Joshua a hideous name though?" said one of them, stupidly I thought. I had been in too many situations where I had said something ill-advised in the toilets only to realise that that very person (or a close friend of that person) was in the toilets as well. That's a horrible feeling when you realise what you've done and the mortification slowly creeps up your entire body. And then I always embarrass myself by trying to backtrack instead of standing by what I've said, so that no-one ends up with any respect for me at all.

I felt smug that I knew this and they didn't.

"Not my cup of tea," said the other lady, audibly hitching down tights before letting loose a stream of urine which sounded as though it was being unleashed from a great height, so thunderous was the noise. "Mind you, it could have been worse, Jennifer only went and called her boy Sheridan Theodore."

He'd have a tough time in the playground with a name like that. And I should know about names.

"I see," chuckled the other lady, pulling off reams of toilet tissue. "He'll have trouble at school with that name!"

I bridled. *I thought it first!*

"It isn't just that though," continued the first, accompanied by a vigorous flush. "His surname is Dennis."

There was a moment as a blanket of confusion descended upon the toilets.

"And..." prompted the first lady. It was like a test at school.

"And?"

"Well, think of his initials! He'll be an STD for the rest of his life!"

And with that she broke into a hoot of laughter and flung back the door with gusto. Lady number two giggled obligingly, but I wasn't entirely sure that she knew what she was laughing at. It was like the time I had listened to a school conversation about Mars Bar parties and had thought they were discussing something similar to a Tupperware party, but involving confectionery instead. Good idea, I had thought. It was a good job I hadn't tried to participate, I'd never have lived that one down.

They left the toilet and I slipped out and washed my hands. The soap was disgusting, a misshapen rectangle with thick grimy cracks all through. I wasn't convinced that my hands were any cleaner once I'd finished. I have a bit of a thing about washing my hands, I can't bear it if I see someone leave a toilet without washing first. I am always tempted to run after them and expose their shame by announcing loudly to those around that "She didn't wash her hands!" I imagine that there would be a shocked intake of breath and hundreds of accusing eyes would turn towards the culprit. In reality though, I bet no-one would care and would carry on as before, which is why I have never done it. That and the fact that I'm a huge coward who can't bear confrontation.

My favourite hand wash is that lovely foamy mousse you find in some shop and restaurant toilets. It usually smells of lavender or jasmine and leaves your hands fragranced for hours. I like to pretend I'm a doctor scrubbing in for surgery when I find hand wash like that and give my hands a good sudding.

The reception was still ticking along as I came back into the room. Joanna was stood ahead of me talking in the sort of voice a person reserves for social occasions where they feel they need to be larger-than-life and overly entertaining. She was doing exaggerated hand gestures and I could hear her from the doorway. She would have looked right at home in a twin set and pearls talking about the next village fete ("Oh you *must* come, darling!").

"...but then there was that awful stomach bug that went round," she was explaining to her captive audience of one. "We should have had at least another thirty people coming, but they were all taken ill in the week and I didn't know *what* to do. I ended up trawling through my address book to get in some emergency contacts otherwise there would have been no-one here at all!"

Ah. There you have it, I wondered why I'd been invited. No wonder Simon had looked so puzzled, he probably didn't have a clue who most of these 'extras' were. I glanced around the room and noticed that there were in fact a number of guests standing on their own, awkwardly clutching a drink in one hand, a nicely-wrapped gift in the other and a tangible air of 'I don't want to be here'.

Stuff this.

Right then, I was off. At least I had the excuse of needing to get back over the tops to Manchester before it got dark. I breezed up to Joanna.

"I'm sorry, I'm going to have to dash off, I could do with getting back before dark."

"Oh," said Joanna, a slight frown creasing her forehead. "But we haven't cut the cake yet and the buffet will be opening soon."

That gave me pause for thought. I'm a bit of a food fan and a complete sucker for buffets. I keep putting in requests at work to go on training days, simply for the buffets that are provided. I have extensive experience of which training companies do the best buffets and which ones to ignore and target my training needs accordingly. My manager thinks I'm the keenest employee around.

Joanna spotted my hesitation and gestured towards a table over to one side.

"Simon's mum has been working on it all morning. She's done her special fruit salad just for me!"

Oh no, please spare me the sight of Joanna working her way through a bowl of fruit salad. The horrific memories of her squelching away open-mouthed, eating a satsuma at work, while telling me about her new kitchen were only just beginning to fade and I couldn't bear the thought of replacing them with a new fruit-related episode. I could swing by a drive-through McDonalds on my way home.

"No, you're all right thanks," I said hastily, beginning to back away. "But thanks for asking me and I hope Joshua enjoys his day."

I quickly turned and caught a glimpse of the woman Joanna had been talking to looking horrified. I heard her faintly mutter "Not fruit?" before I headed determinedly towards the exit.

It mustn't have been just me then.

CHAPTER TWO

I felt slightly ruffled in spirit by the time I pulled up outside our little terraced house that evening. Not least because I'd had the usual panic about whether there would be a parking space left for me. That's the main problem with living on a street of terraced houses – the subject of parking becomes a huge issue for everyone concerned. "Number three has parked an inch past her threshold tonight, that's our bit!" and "Whose car is that over there? If they think they can have visitors and then park in my space, they've another thing coming!"

One of my neighbours has actually painted a dustbin red and yellow and has somehow managed to use a chain and padlock to secure it to the drainage grille in the road. It's very entertaining watching him trying to unlock it and manoeuvre the bin out of the way before pulling into the space. He has lost a number of padlocks down the drain. Serves him right. Everyone knows that on-street parking is a lottery and you take the rough with the smooth.

I also felt ruffled because it isn't particularly nice to discover that you have been invited to an event solely because you make up the numbers. It happens quite a bit with me, probably with me being such a pushover who can't say no. Perhaps I should set up an agency "Have body, will travel to your event for a small fee." Mind you, I suppose that that is starting to veer towards escort work and I don't think I should be getting involved in any of that. Not with me having the same name as a saint. What would the original Philomena think?

I was definitely in need of that pizza and a comfort film, particularly as I had missed out on the buffet and hadn't bothered to stop on the way home. I managed to manoeuvre into a tiny space outside my house and wearily exited the car.

I love my little terraced house. It's only small, but it's perfectly formed. Well, to me anyway - I'm not sure that too many builders would agree as spirit levels don't seem to correlate with the ceiling lines. But it is home and it is technically ours so long as we keep up with the mortgage repayments.

As is usual with terraced houses, my front door opens straight into my lounge which can cause a few draught issues. I'm not good with the cold as my hands and feet seem to be perpetually freezing cold.

I entered the room and plonked myself down on the sofa, throwing my keys onto the side-table. They scrabbled for purchase before disappearing down the back into oblivion. That would be a five-minute job to retrieve them, probably when I'm in a rush and don't have time. I sighed in disappointment at the world. Paddy must still be in the pub watching the match as I could feel the house was empty.

This is the point where I should pick up the telephone and call my camp and amusing gay friend who would laugh about the day and make me feel better before offering to come round and make me over and take me out on the town for cocktails and all sorts of fun. Only I didn't have a gay best friend. I'd often thought about getting one as it seems to be the thing to do in various chick-lit novels and films, but I wasn't sure where to start. Plus, I also didn't want to perpetuate any stereotypes. But I did feel that I was missing out.

There was only one thing for it. It would have to be an old film. I loved the old Hollywood musicals and black and white films, they seemed to hark back to a time when people didn't have so many stresses over ridiculous things. I could just imagine myself as an MGM starlet, I was definitely born in the wrong era. Philomena would have been a great starlet name, perhaps they could have come up with a suitable surname and a fictional story of how I had been discovered whilst riding on a hay cart during a clam bake or something similar. I could have swanned around in beautiful gowns, dripping with diamonds and been squired around town by gorgeous screen idols (who would then turn out to be gay). That's it! I need a time machine and a whole new vocation to get that gay best friend.

My new purchase was waiting on the shelves. I wandered over and picked up the case. It was "On Moonlight Bay" featuring Doris Day. I *loved* Doris Day. She was so quirky and funny and had an amazing voice. I wasn't sure I was in the mood for a comedy though. I looked at my old film shelf to see if there was anything else that was calling out to me. Paddy and I have an arrangement over our Billy bookcases from Ikea. He has his action film sections, I have my old film sections and the middle bit is common ground. I refrain from alphabetising and categorising his sections as long as he promises not to put his DVDs and general detritus on my shelves. It works quite well.

I ran an eye over my collection. Gone with the Wind – no, I didn't have the time to watch it now. The same for Imitation of Life. My eye caught Waterloo Bridge and I paused. Vivien Leigh was another brilliant actress and the dialogue between her and Robert Taylor was so engaging. It was a classic and it would suit my melancholy mood. I pulled the case off the shelf and clicked out the disc.

The television flicked on and I kicked my shoes off so they cartwheeled across the lounge and bounced off the wall. My stomach growled and I headed for the kitchen. I was feeling very hungry.

The tiled floor was a shock to my warm feet and I hopped

across to switch the oven on. I didn't need to consult the cooking instructions for my favourite pizzas anymore, they were ingrained in my brain. I popped one in.

The evidence of Paddy's lunch was scattered across the worktop over and around the bread board. He was so untidy, but there was something comforting in knowing that he always left a trail around the house. It reinforced his presence in some way. He would leave change scattered around in various rooms, piles of magazines by his chair, tools beside jobs he had completed, wrappers in a heap on the floor. It did get annoying sometimes that I had to be the house fairy who put everything back in its rightful place, but I had become used to it over the years.

I inspected the remnants of the meal like a seasoned forensic specialist.

"Hmmm. Looks like we have a crusty white tin loaf sandwich here with grated cheese and..." I dipped a finger in a smear on the board and sucked the tip. "Some brown pickle. By the hardness of the breadcrumbs I would suggest that the sandwich was made, ooh, three hours ago. This is also reinforced by the warmth of the water in the kettle which," I laid a hand on the side, "is not at all warm."

Yes, I was actually saying all this out loud. Still, it was important to practise for my role as an English detective in a golden-age Hollywood film when I did find that time machine.

My favourite red wine bottles are ranged next to the fridge so I can see at a glance when they need to be replenished. I don't drink to excess, only the occasional glass in the week and a bit more at weekends but I like to know that I have some available when I want some, usually after an irritating day at work.

There is something very special about the sound of red wine as the first glass pours out of the bottle. White wine just doesn't make the same noise. It is a rich, deep sound that 'glug, glug, glug, GLUGs' and surges into your glass bringing with it the hope of warmth and contentment. I could be quite happy sitting pouring out wine for hours at a time, I wouldn't even have to drink it.

I wonder why Paddy thinks I'm a bit odd sometimes.

The smell of the pizza was beginning to waft around the kitchen resulting in another stomach growl. The oregano on this particular pizza was a definite feature and I couldn't wait to dive in. Only another ten minutes to go. I opened the fridge door and removed my bar of Dairy Milk. I liked it chilled but not *too* chilled so always took my bars out at least half an hour before eating. Otherwise I would have to gnaw the chunks off with the possible danger of damaging my sensitive teeth. This preference also meant that I had to use self-control and not eat a piece while I was waiting for my pizza, which showed impressive strength of character, I thought. I laid it next to the sofa within reaching distance of my arm. Very important to get everything set up properly so I wouldn't have to stop the film at all, except for an emergency. Chocolate, mobile phone, pizza, drink and controllers for the TV. Perfect. A quick trip upstairs to put on my slouching clothes – joggers, over-sized fleece jumper and huge fluffy socks – and I was nearly ready.

The buzzer sounded on the cooker as I came back down the stairs and I flipped the pizza out of the oven and onto the bread board. In the old days when I was new to pizza cookery I would stick a finger in the middle of the topping to check that it was done, but now I can tell by sight. This is a very valuable skill, particularly as I was running out of fingers without scar tissue on the tips.

I carried the pizza platter back into the lounge and set it on the sofa to prepare myself for the piece de resistance. A wearable chunky fleece blanket hoody *with arms and a hood*. I had been told about this by a fellow fleece blanket devotee and could not believe that I had not thought of this before. For years I had snuggled under my fleece blankets to watch television and had had to suffer the inconvenience of sneaking my arms out to reach for my glass/mug/snack/remote. But now I could still feel as though I was snuggled under a blanket on the sofa and remain functional. Genius! Paddy preferred it too as it meant he didn't have to keep pausing films and programmes as I struggled with my arms and tried to keep covered whilst reaching for things. If only I had thought of this wonderful product, I could have given up my day job and spent all my time road-testing my invention.

Paddy is the complete opposite to me when it comes to keeping warm. Whereas I am usually freezing and can justify my fleece blanket hoody for at least nine months of the year, Paddy is definitely more hot-blooded. In the depths of winter when I have been ensconced under several layers of clothing, fleece blankets, fluffy socks and hot water bottles, Paddy will quite happily sit in his armchair in a t-shirt and shorts and *no socks or slippers*. It quite boggles my mind. However, it is wonderful to have your own hot water bottle in bed that is life-sized and never cools down but only gets warmer. Perhaps I should tout Paddy out as a professional bed-warmer as I'm sure he'd be popular. But there we go again, just one step away from the escorting business.

I was all settled. I pressed 'play' on the remote and took a big chunk out of my pizza and chewed slowly to allow all of the flavours to filter through. The film title filled the screen and the orchestral swell brought reflexive tears to my eyes and the film hadn't even started yet. The evocative power of music never ceases to amaze me.

The sound of the landline phone ringing cut rudely into the orchestral score. Dammit! Who on earth could be calling at this time. It's as if some people know exactly when it is the most inconvenient time to call, they have a knack for it.

I stifled my sigh of utter exasperation, paused the film and leaned over for the phone, carefully balancing my pizza on my knee and avoiding the full glass of wine on the table.

"Hello?"

Go away, go away, go away!!

"Patrick?" enquired a voice which managed to sound tremulous and imperious at the same time.

I mean, honestly, who could mistake my voice for a male voice on the phone. I'm sure that people who pretend they can't tell Paddy and I apart on the phone are just saying so to be annoying. I knew exactly who this was, Paddy's grandmother Evelyn who lives five minutes away and the only actual real person to use it to contact us, rather than our mobiles.

I refrained from saying I was Paddy's new boyfriend who just happened to be answering the phone in his absence.

"No, it's Mena."

"Oh, it's you dear," said Evelyn, managing to sound surprised. "Phone me back," she commanded and I heard the sharp click of the phone being slammed down to save precious seconds.

Evelyn was notoriously parsimonious (there seem to be a lot of 'ous' words to associate with her) and she begrudged paying anything more than she absolutely had to and that included phone calls. It was a standing family joke that quite often the gifts you gave her for Christmas reappeared through the year as birthday presents, but I didn't have a problem with 're-gifting', it was a bit like an annual tombola as long as I didn't get the present I originally gave her.

I didn't have Evelyn's phone number committed to memory so it took a couple of moments for me to reach for my mobile and find the number before calling back.

"I'm sorry," I mouthed to Robert Taylor on the big screen, "I'll be with you in a minute."

Robert looked disapproving. He clearly wanted to get on with the film.

"Yes?" answered Evelyn on the second ring.

"It's Mena, you asked me to call you back? Patrick is out at the moment," I explained. "Is everything all right?"

"Yes, why wouldn't it be?" she sounded perplexed.

"Only you just phoned and said you wanted me to call you back."

I paused. Evelyn was clearly also pausing as there was a silence. As usual, I broke first. Perhaps she just wanted a chat.

"What have you been up to today, anything nice?"

"This and that, keeping busy," she replied. "I don't mean to be rude, dear, but I am watching the Mentalist at the moment. It's a good one about a murder. Did you want anything in particular?"

I was flabbergasted. Surely Evelyn had phoned me in the first place?

"Oh. Would you like me to get Patrick to call you back if it's not too late when he gets in?"

"That would be nice dear..." There was a pause as though Evelyn was waiting to see if I had anything else to say.

"No, no, that's fine. Sorry to have bothered you," I said and put the phone down.

"You called *me*!" I huffed in the direction of the phone.

I picked up the glass of wine and took a big gulp to soothe

my jangled nerves. If I hadn't felt genuinely ruffled before, I certainly felt ruffled now.

Still, no real harm done. I sighed, bit into my pizza again and pressed play.

I had very nearly reached the grand finale when I heard the key in the door. I swallowed down my frustration and pointedly paused the film on a close-up of Vivien's face as she walked along Waterloo Bridge. Paddy sauntered into the room whistling, with a bag of fish and chips in his hand.

"Hello gorgeous," he said, coming over to give me a beery kiss.

"Hello, how was the match?" Straight away I showed how thoughtful and interested I was by asking about his day.

"Not so bad, there was a dodgy penalty but they can't complain as they usually get those decisions in their favour."

Unlike most of my female friends, I actually follow football and know about the teams, players and the offside rule without needing to have it explained in shopping terms (the handbag in the sale explanation, for instance, that I have heard bandied about which I find quite insulting to the female intelligence as if we can't grasp the rule in any other way). So I was actually vaguely interested in the result. I sat and waited.

"Many people out?" I asked, as Paddy emptied the change from his pockets onto two different shelves on different levels on the Billy bookcase.

"Most of the usual crowd," he replied, rustling in his carrier bag for his fish and chips. He glanced at the television. "Waterloo Bridge again?"

I bridled defensively.

"Yes, you know it's my comfort film," I said with a slight stress upon the word 'comfort' to see if he would pick up on it.

"Doesn't end well you know," he said with a grin and then he walked into the kitchen.

I sighed. He said that every time I mentioned the film. I had made him watch it with me when we first moved in together and as a result he knew the plot and characters and could even recite parts of the dialogue to me. He had that sort of memory.

I could hear the clatter of plates and cutlery in the kitchen and then the fizz of an opened can. He came back in a moment later with a loaded tray and took a seat in his armchair.

"Aren't you going to put it back on?" he asked, spearing chips with his fork.

I gave up waiting for him to ask me how the christening had been and so put the film back on.

"Oops, there she goes," he said a moment later at the most moving part of the film. I refrained from throwing the remote at him, which was a noble gesture of restraint on my part.

As the credits came up I switched the television onto standby and turned to look at Paddy. He smiled at me and continued eating his takeaway.

I cleared my throat and continued to stare pointedly.

"What?" he asked, genuinely puzzled.

"Don't you want to know how the christening was?" I asked, in injured tones.

"Not really, but how was the christening?"

I sighed again. I honestly don't think he means to be disinterested, it just doesn't occur to him to ask these things. I had spent whole evenings waiting to be asked how my day was until I realised that I either had to prompt him or just tell him. I get in with the question about his day as soon as I see him to see if he can be trained, but I've just about given up on that now as it never seems to work.

"Pretty awful. Most of her guests seemed to be strange or suffering from some form of delusion..."

"That's why she asked you then," he interrupted.

"...and it turns out she only asked some of us because half her guests had been struck down by some stomach bug."

"Oh dear," said Paddy, mopping up the last of the salt and vinegar from his plate with some bread and butter. "Can I have the remote?"

I handed it over without argument. He was the acknowledged keeper of the remote in our household. He was much better at navigating through all the menus than I was. When I fast-forwarded through adverts I always went too far and had to rewind for several minutes, much to Paddy's vexation.

"Oh, by the way, Evelyn phoned and she said she'd appreciate you phoning her back."

I explained the strange conversation I had had with his nan and he laughed.

"She probably forgot she phoned you."

"She isn't forgetful, she's perfectly canny," I replied.

"You are the only person I know who would use the word 'canny' in a conversation," he said. "That's why I love you."

"Just for that?" I asked, pretending to be outraged.

"And other things," he said, throwing a chip at me.

"Wow, you must love me if you're throwing me one of your chips," I laughed, picking it off the floor.

"It had a black bit in it, I wasn't going to eat it," he replied with a smirk.

I threw the chip back at him and watched in satisfaction as it bounced off his forehead.

"Right, I'm off to bed," I said, disentangling myself with some difficulty from my blanket hoody. "Don't forget to call her."

"Yes, yes," he replied.

I knew he would.

CHAPTER THREE

I travel into work on the train as I find it less stressful than negotiating my way into Manchester in my little car and having to face the general rudeness and ignorance of my fellow drivers. I much prefer to walk to our local train station and then sit on the train in my own little thought bubble, looking out of the window and shamelessly eavesdropping on other people's conversations. It's amazing what people will discuss on a train, as if no-one else can hear what they are saying. It isn't just the people on their mobiles who feel the need to shout, friends and acquaintances can be just as bad.

Today I was sat opposite two late middle-aged women who were engaged in their daily commute. The carriage was packed with passengers, with several stood in the aisle, swaying comically from side to side with an occasional lurch to recover balance. One of the ladies was still power dressing in an eighties style with a boxy jacket and short skirt, chunky gold jewellery and a long bob with blonde highlights. The other had clearly given up on her work attire and had short straight hair, a long flowing skirt of an indeterminate dark, muddy colour and a shapeless grey-white shirt that had seen better days.

"Well you know, if he'd caught it earlier, it wouldn't have been half so much of a problem," the frumpy one was explaining to Miss Eighties.

"They don't though these days, do they," replied her friend. "They aren't specialists in anything, they just have a rudimentary knowledge of run-of-the-mill complaints and are useless with everything else."

She looked quite pleased at having used the word 'rudimentary' at this early time of the morning. I guessed that she probably recorded Countdown each day to watch back at night.

"But it was so obvious!" exclaimed Frump. "It was big enough to start with but then it started to go green."

"Did it really?" asked Eighties, genuinely interested.

I could feel the male passenger next to me shifting in his seat in a subtle signal that certain conversations should not be had in public first thing in the morning when most people had only just breakfasted.

"Well, because of where it was, I had to use a mirror to check, but I got Noel to look for me and he said it was definitely getting worse. In the end, it was affecting my walk so I had to go back and demand that something was done..."

This conversation was amusing me, but even I had to admit that it was a bit much. Male passenger had a bout of exaggerated coughing. Eighties looked up to give him a baleful glare and muttered something to her friend about some people needing to use handkerchiefs if they were going to cough their germs about.

"Anyway," continued Frump. "I had it drained in the end and got a week off work so that was quite a bonus I suppose."

Older ladies fascinated me. As a child I had been a huge Enid Blyton fan and had come to think of the world as defined by her terms. As a result, I honestly believed that all old ladies were kindly, had a twinkle in their eyes and baked their own bread. Until I was rudely disabused of my misconceptions by a few encounters with the most astonishingly rude and obnoxious old ladies I have ever met who returned verbal insults for well-meaning acts of kindness. It took me years to get over the shock. Enid has a lot to answer for.

I started to daydream, which is one of my favourite pastimes. That is the benefit of having a vivid imagination, you can act out all sorts of scenarios in your head to keep yourself entertained. Just as I was about to get started, a thought popped itself into my head. Had I remembered to take the pork chops out of the freezer to defrost in time for tonight? I didn't think I had.

"Oh, pants!" I exclaimed, louder than intended.

Miss Eighties looked at me and raised an eyebrow. I flushed.

"I've forgotten to get them out," I explained, quite rationally I thought.

Miss Eighties looked disgusted, looked down at my lap area for some reason known only to herself and pointedly turned back to her friend.

What was her problem?

I work within the Admin section of a financial company in the centre of Manchester. I'm actually the supervisor of the accounts section and as a result I have to oversee another person which I had thought would be quite enriching and a career boost. I have since realised that having to manage or supervise another person is my idea of hell. I don't have the skills required to strike the fine line between being friendly with my staff and having to pull them up when they need it ("they won't like me anymore!") It causes me no end of stress and worry as I manage to take all work-related incidents very personally. I would be so much happier if I could just turn up to work, get on with my job and go home without having to mess about with other people.

The other person within the Accounts section is Naomi, a lean, perfectly groomed girl in her twenties. She is the sort of person who will always make you feel unkempt and unattractive. You just know that she has got up particularly early to choose her outfit, straighten her hair and *paint her nails* in the morning before coming in to work. It was all I could do to get out of bed, pull a brush through my hair and make sure I'm wearing clothes that are not inside-out. If it was the choice of having an extra ten minutes in bed or getting up to groom myself, I know which one I would choose every time.

Unfortunately, Naomi is also very good at taking advantage of other people's weaknesses i.e. mine. She always knows just how far to push things and I will be just on the verge of 'having a word' after gearing myself up to it for several hours – and sometimes days – when she knuckles back down again. I then feel weak and pathetic for not tackling the problem and it irritates me that I feel she has got away with her behaviour yet again.

Not surprisingly, Naomi was not at her desk when I arrived. Our 'Accounts Office' is little more than a patch of carpet in one corner of the Admin section that has been fenced off in a slapdash manner by screens on wobbly legs. As we are in the corner which is furthest away from the windows, we have no natural light and are bathed all day in the anaemic fluorescent glow of the strip lights above.

I had tried to cheer the space up a bit with a pot plant. We were onto the fifth incarnation already this year as they kept dying, which probably tells you something about the atmosphere within the office. We had also tacked up some postcards and posters onto our side of the screens. I had stuck to inspirational messages and uplifting images; Naomi had a large poster of Daniel Craig in his small blue shorts coming out of the sea. I was quite mortified when she had first stuck that on the screen and tentatively mentioned that it might be classed as sexism, or at the very least bad taste to have such an image in our workspace. How would Naomi feel about scantily clad females on the wall in the Compliance department? Naomi had looked at me witheringly and simply picked up her phone to make a personal call and that was the end of the matter, at least as far as she was concerned.

As a result, I am always on pins when a senior member of management comes to visit as I fully expect to be bawled out about sexism in the workplace. I have discovered that if I leap up to intercept the visitor and stand at a certain angle, they can't see the poster unless they walk all the way into our cube – and why would anyone want to go in there unless absolutely necessary? Although I do have to say that I am quite a fan of peak Bond Daniel Craig myself and it is quite pleasant on a quiet afternoon to have an imaginary conversation with him and stare into his piercing blue eyes.

My phone rang and I slung my bag down into my bottom drawer and seated myself before picking up the receiver.

"Hello Accounts admin department, Mena speaking," I said in my 'work voice'. I think I am a closet actress as I am quite good at impersonating how confident people do things. If I could only do it as second nature so it isn't completely fake, I would go a long way.

"Hello Trumpster, just got in?"

"Paddy! Don't call me that on a works phone, you never know who is listening in!"

"It's a direct call, I doubt anyone is listening in to you, it's not as if I went through reception," he sighed, clearly thinking I was paranoid as ever. "Your mobile went straight to voicemail."

"Still, it doesn't do much for my professional outlook to be called that while sat at my own desk," I complained, re-arranging my desk tidy so that all the same size pens and pencils are in the correct cylinders. Someone regularly messed up the order and I had my suspicions that Naomi did this just to torment me.

"Keep your hair on," he replied.

"I don't suppose you took the chops out the freezer, did you? Or did you see if they were in the fridge?"

There was a pause whilst the bafflement could almost be heard on the line.

"No, why?" he asked.

"Just a long shot," I sighed. Our meals were always down to me, it would be so nice for Paddy to take charge once in a while.

"What's up then?" I asked, keen to get him off the phone before Naomi came in. I spent enough time telling her that personal calls should not be taken in the workplace aside from dire emergencies, I would be very embarrassed if she came in to hear me having my own personal call about pork chops.

"Can I play out tonight? Tony's asked if I'm free and I said I'd check with you. It'd be for a drink after tea."

I pulled a face but spoke normally.

"Fine, just bring me a raisin and biscuit Yorkie home to make up for abandoning me again."

"Great, will do, see you later!"

I hung up the phone and looked at Daniel. I wondered if he ever called his wife 'Trumpster'. Somehow I doubted it.

Naomi wandered in, looking as manicured and maintained as usual.

"Morning," I ventured, with direct eye-contact and a slight smile.

"Hmm," she replied.

"Nice weekend?" I continued.

"OK," was the sighed response, as if speaking was just too much effort.

I paused, waiting for her to ask me if I'd had a nice weekend. The moment passed and she dropped her designer bag on the floor and powered up her PC. Good grief, it was like waiting for Paddy to ask me about my day. Surely it is quite common in life for people to follow the established rules of conversation, such as 'How are you', 'I'm fine thank you – *pause* - how are you?' Or was I such a nonentity that no-one thought of asking me as they thought I had nothing of interest to say?

I gritted my teeth. The week was starting well. I was already irritated and I hadn't even logged-on yet. I pulled open my top drawer to reach for one of my cereal bars. If I didn't have much time for a proper breakfast I always topped up with a cereal bar when I got in, a strawberry one if I was pretending to be virtuous or a chocolate one if I had already abandoned hope for the day. My grasping fingers scrabbled around in the drawer.

"Oh, for goodness sake!" I exclaimed.

"Problem?" asked Naomi, barely glancing up from her screen.

"Have you seen my cereal bars? There are none in here and I know I had some on Friday."

"No idea," she said in a sing-song voice which immediately made me suspicious.

I stood up and from my vantage point looked across into the office bin. Scrumpled at the bottom were two wrappers from my cereal bar stash. I hadn't eaten them on Friday and the bins hadn't been emptied since Friday morning.

The cow.

I bit my lip and sat down again, busying myself with a pile of invoices that I was going to go and copy.

Say something, challenge her, goaded the needling voice in my head.

I took a breath, my heart was racing and I was feeling flushed.

She knows you know, just say something and stand up to her!

I shuffled the papers some more. I really should say something, she was going out of her way to be provocative. What kind of feeble manager can't even manage to challenge unreasonable behaviour?

"I'm going to go and photocopy," I said, a note of weary resignation at my own feebleness evident in my voice. Technically, I should be sending Naomi to do the copying, but to be honest it usually wasn't worth the hassle. Kevin the Teenager had nothing on Naomi sometimes in response to a menial work request. I'd much rather do it myself properly.

Naomi didn't even bother to turn around. I could tell she was smiling to herself.

Pathetic. I knew you wouldn't say anything.

"You need to get on with the stationery account supporting information, it needs to be in today," I snipped. I stopped myself from adding a grudging 'please'.

Not really a confrontation, but I suppose it was a start.

There's something quite soothing about a photocopier churning out sets of copies. It's as if all is right with the world when set after set is neatly parcelled together, stapled and deposited for you like a little present. It's almost possible to hear a kind of music in the rhythmic whirrings and clickings. That isn't as fanciful as it sounds by the way, I do have a friend who claims you can actually groove to the 'beat' of their office copier when it's on a long print run. But then again, this is the same person who preferred to dance to the noise of a generator at a music festival rather than the bands on the stage, so I take that statement with a pinch of salt.

I quite often escape to the copying room to get a bit of peace and quiet. To draw a deep-breath and mutter through any irritations I may have which I don't have the balls to address. Such as Cereal Bar Gate.

"Hello Mena."

I leapt a good few inches in the air and threw in a startled 'Ooh!' just for good measure. How embarrassing. In a few years' time I can see I'm going to be one of those types who has 'the vapours' and needs reviving with smelling salts.

"Did I startle you?"

I turned round to see Sarah, the Head of Finance – and my line manager - in the corner stepping out from behind an open cupboard door.

"Sorry, yes, I hadn't seen you there," I muttered, before turning a faint pink colour.
Thank goodness I hadn't been talking to myself or doing a little dance to the rhythm of the copier (heaven forbid!)

Sarah smiled.

"There's no need to apologise."

I stopped and thought for a moment. She was right, why had I apologised? I felt a flare of irritation, what an idiot, why did I always do that? I really must stop apologising at every opportunity.

"No, of course not, sorry."

Oh, for goodness sake. I am clearly a hopeless case. Sarah looked pitying.

"Did you have a nice weekend?" she asked conversationally.

Finally, someone with social skills.

"Yes thanks, did you?"

"Not long enough!" she smiled. "Will you be able to have the stationery account ready for me today?"

"Absolutely," I nodded to emphasise the point. "I'm doing the main figures and Naomi is working on the supporting information now. I'll review it all before I send it to you this afternoon."

"Great, I need it for the heads of department meeting this evening. By four o'clock ok?"

"Fine, I'll make sure it's done."

"Brilliant." Sarah stepped forward and considered me for a moment. "How are things working out for you in your department, everything going ok? We haven't really had a chat about your team recently."

I paused. Was this the moment to bring up Naomi's attitude, the personal calls, the refusal to do routine jobs, the petty thefts, the provocative behaviour, her many casual sickness absences...

"Fine thanks, we're muddling along!" I said instead, with a bright laugh to underline just how much fun it was to work in my department.

"Glad to hear it," replied Sarah. There was a pause. "How come you're doing the photocopying this morning?"

This took me by surprise, I wasn't ready with a response. I tried not to show how flustered I was. The last thing I wanted to do was tell her that Naomi was so awkward about 'menial' tasks that I could rarely get her to do them.

"I'm helping out today," I eventually managed. "All hands to the deck to get the stationery figures finalised."

Hopefully this would show what a good manager I was, being so prepared to muck in when the pressure was on.

"I see," Sarah said. There was a pause. "Well, I'd better get on."

"Bye!"

The door clicked behind Sarah and I was left stood by the copier. My shoulders slumped.

She knows! She knows that you can't control your one and only member of staff.

I fed the remaining invoices into the top feeder and pressed the copy key. The churning and clicking noises began in earnest.

She must think you are pretty pathetic.

More parcelled copies began to shoot out of the copier in neat little bundles. I would have to do something about the Naomi situation. I resolved to have a think about it and be more assertive. Next time.

The rest of the morning passed by quite uneventfully. Naomi seemed to be busy with the accounts and I was busy simmering at her behaviour. The stationery figures were more challenging than I had thought as there was a kink in the spreadsheet which needed ironing out before I could collate the reports.

Just before noon Naomi started to get ready to leave our cubicle.

"How are the supporting documents coming along?" I asked, my head still down as if I was too busy and important to engage in proper dialogue.

Naomi picked up her bag and swung it over her shoulder. She looked at me for a moment and smiled.

"I'm sorry?" she asked, as if talking to a stranger in the street who had had the audacity to stop her and ask for some spare change.

I suppressed a sigh, visibly. I wanted her to know I was frustrated but was making a heroic effort to be reasonable.

"The supporting information for the stationery account. Will it be ready for three o'clock?"

Naomi frowned.

"I'm supposed to be working on that?"

"Yes! It's due in today and I mentioned it several times last week and reminded you first thing this morning that it is due in today."

"I'm quite sure you didn't," she said with a killer smile.

"I most certainly did," I replied firmly.

"Well, I've been working on the catering account this morning. I'm off for lunch and I have my appointment this afternoon, so I won't be back in again until tomorrow now."

Naomi reached in her desk drawer for her keys and nudged it shut with her knee.

"Bye!"

"Just a minute," I said incredulously, as she turned to leave the cubicle. "Are you telling me you haven't done anything at all on it?"

"That's right," she replied, her hands on her hips. "If you'd asked me to do them, I would have done wouldn't I?"

You were probably too busy pinching and eating my snacks, you vicious little...

"See you tomorrow."

She was gone in a puff of perfume. I sat slumped in my seat, my mouth open in shock at the sheer audacity. Had she really not heard me, or was she trying to drop me in it? My heart started to pound again.

There were several hours' worth of work to complete before the supporting information could be added to my main figures. I had nearly managed to finish the main accounts, but even if I worked flat out until four o'clock I would only be able to provide a summary appendix rather than the full report I always insisted upon. My professionalism and standard of work were so important to me as they reassured me that colleagues felt I did a good job and valued my input.

The mean little...

There was nothing for it, other than to get on with it and hope that the report was just good enough. I felt a surge of anger at the calculated betrayal.

"Bloody hell!" I hissed and thumped the desk with my palm.

The desk tidy jumped and clattered. I indulged myself for a moment by dropping my head in my hands and muttering furiously. This would mean no lunch break and no food as the manipulative minion had eaten all my reserves. Wonderful.

I sighed and turned to the computer and pulled up the file.

Four hours later I had managed to put together a passable report for Sarah. My eyes ached, my head throbbed and I was thirsty and starving hungry as I had not even had time to go down to the floor below to the vending machine. In previous years, my desk had been located within sight of this particular box of delights and it had cost me a fortune and been a disaster for my waistline. Being able to see the brightly wrapped treats was like having an askew picture on the wall - I couldn't settle to anything and kept being distracted. Before my department was moved, I had increased my snack intake to two packets of crisps and a chocolate bar a day. Now at least I got some exercise going down a floor to pick up a treat.

I checked the figures for the last time and emailed them to Sarah just before the four o'clock deadline. I sat back in my chair and rubbed my eyes with the heels of my hands, forgetting that I had actually remembered to apply my mascara this morning before leaving for work.

"Mena?"

I looked up blearily, waiting for my vision to re-establish itself after my vigorous rubbing. It was Sarah. I jumped up quickly to make sure that my body blocked Daniel.

"Hi Sarah. I've just sent you the figures through, you should have them by now. About the appendix..."

Sarah glanced around the cubicle.

"Is Naomi not here?"

"No, she has an appointment this afternoon. She'll be back in tomorrow. Can I take a message?"

"Wasn't she supposed to be doing some work on the accounts return today?"

I paused. I would have to speak to Sarah about Naomi's behaviour, but now did not seem like the time or place. The screens partitioning the office space were not at all effective as a sound block and I didn't really want to go into the situation with people within earshot.

"It's all sorted now, but I do need a chat with you at some point," I replied reassuringly. "About the appendix..."

"I'm sure it's fine," Sarah smiled. "I can always rely on you to get the job done."

For a brief moment I felt a small glow inside and I smiled gratefully.

"Just one thing though," Sarah continued in a low voice. "You might want to check your make-up before you do anything else. Thanks for the figures."

As soon as she had disappeared, I rushed to my seat and picked up my bag, rooting around inside for my compact mirror. It opened with a spring-charged click and I was confronted by the disturbing sight of my eyes heavily ringed and smudged with mascara. I looked like I was auditioning for a zombie in Thriller.

"Oh great," I sighed, throwing my compact back in the bag.

There was no way I was walking across the office to the Ladies without covering my eyes up. I looked a complete sight. My fingers brushed against a case in my bag and I breathed in relief and pulled my sunglasses case from under my purse. I slipped the shades on and peered around the cubicle entrance, taking another breath and walking as quickly across the floor as I dared, without wanting to draw too much attention to myself.

I made it to the toilets safely and flung the door open before rushing inside.

"Oooof!" I bounced back, having collided with someone on my way in.

"What's the rush?" asked Kelly, one of our HR team. "Hungover or undercover?"

I smiled. Kelly was a pleasant girl and we had had a few conversations in passing.

"No, worse than that," I said ruefully. "Make-up malfunction."

I removed my glasses and laughed at Kelly's melodramatic intake of breath.

"I see," she laughed. "Good idea with the glasses, even if it does make you look like a pretentious prima donna. I'll leave you to it then!"

I ran water in the basin and began to rinse off the make-up. I had decided to find the humour in the situation. After the day I'd had, I could either haul myself out of the doldrums and draw a line under it or wallow in it. Although I am quite a wallower when I feel the need, today was not one of those days. I would not let that girl bring me down! I had coped with the situation and survived.

I actually felt a little bit proud of myself.

CHAPTER FOUR

I decided to leave for the day at quarter to five. There would be no point in trying to start something new at that time, but I still felt the need to justify my leaving early to everyone in the vicinity on my way out.

"What a day! I'm off now, I had to work through lunch and I haven't stopped. See you tomorrow!"

Andy from the cubicle next door nodded and said goodnight, but the cleaner in the hallway just looked nonplussed.

I caught an earlier train than usual and settled myself into my seat. Usually, I hated the feel of the bristly seat covers through my tights, but today I was just relieved to be on my way home. I closed my eyes for a moment and breathed deeply, trying to ease some of the day's tension from my stressed body.

The train started its journey with a jolt and I looked up to see a man in a suit settling himself down opposite me. We nodded slightly in acknowledgement, before I turned my head to look out of the window. I knew the scenery off by heart, but always found something interesting to look at as the landscape blurred and flashed past.

I started to think to myself about what I needed to do when I returned home. I'd have to open a tin of something if I had indeed forgotten to take the chops out of the freezer. I think we had enough potatoes for me to make some mash and a tin of sweetcorn...

My train of thought was diverted by a repetitive action by the man opposite. I glanced over.

You have got to be joking. That is disgusting!

The middle-aged man opposite me, in the smart business suit and crisp white shirt, was systematically picking his nose – and eating it. My stomach heaved and I couldn't help a revolted expression appearing on my face.

He blithely stared straight ahead as if unaware of my scrutiny and continued excavating his nostrils before popping the contents into his mouth for a vigorous chew. His moist, pursed mouth moved in a circular motion, making the occasional wet sound as his lips parted. I couldn't believe it. I hadn't seen anyone picking their nose and eating it in public since primary school and I certainly hadn't seen an adult doing it before, apart from repulsive men in cars who think they can't be observed through a pane of glass.

My empty stomach started to heave in earnest. I had always been queasy about bodily fluids and extracts and I couldn't begin to imagine why anyone could do such a nauseating thing. I glared balefully at the man, but he seemed entirely unaware. I tried not looking at him, but found that I could still see him out of the corner of my eye. I was feeling distinctly nauseous.

I felt very strongly that I should make it clear that he had been spotted and that I found him revolting. But I can't cope with confrontation, what if he was an axe murderer?

The reptilian creature opposite didn't seem as though he had an axe secreted about his person. However, you never could tell and we were on a train where there were often little axes in glass boxes in every compartment. I didn't want to take the chance. I settled instead for tutting and loudly uncrossing my legs so that my heels clacked sharply on the flooring. I stood up abruptly and stared even more obviously at my fellow passenger, but there was still no response.

"Ugh, sickening!" I said (albeit quietly) and stomped further down the carriage to find another seat. Revolting man.

Thankfully, the rest of the journey was uneventful. I jumped off the train at my usual stop and began to walk purposefully along the platform to the exit, trying to avoid the welded-on circles of chewing gum stuck to the platform. A few speckles of light rain began to fall and I unzipped my handbag and began to fumble around to find my mini-compact umbrella.

"Excuse me!" shouted a voice behind me, which I ignored.

"Excuse me, lady in the black coat!"

I was wearing a black coat. I slowed my pace and glanced behind me.

"You've dropped your pack of tissues."

Unbelievably, it was Mr Nose-picker. He was proffering my cellophane-wrapped pack of tissues with the same fingers he had been picking his nose with moments earlier. I gagged.

You should keep them and try and learn how to use one! said my inner voice.

Ha, yes I should say that, I thought. That would be something that someone with guts would say.

"They fell out of your bag."

He wiggled the tissues and reached out to hand them to me. I couldn't bear the thought of touching the packet after his filthy hands had been on them. I looked at his hand as though he was trying to hand me some diarrhoea. I shouldn't say anything, this man could well live near me and I would probably see him again on the same train. No, best leave it alone and just take the tissues and not say anything.

"Keep them, you should try to learn how to use them, picking your nose like that!" I blurted.

Where had that come from? I immediately flushed and looked down before spinning around and dashing down the ramp as quickly as I could manage. There was no shout of anger behind me and no sound of following footsteps. Perhaps he was as stunned as I was by my outburst.

I raced home in the steady rain, splashing through puddles without a thought, like Gene Kelly on a mission.

My key grated in the Yale lock and I kicked the door open and shook myself off over the doormat, before poking my umbrella outside the door again and removing the droplets in the time-honoured way of opening and closing it several times followed by a final flourish.

"Ooof!" I said loudly, in another time-honoured way to demonstrate that I had just escaped from a downpour.

"Get caught in the rain?" enquired Paddy from the comfort of his armchair, where he sat sipping from another mug of coffee while he scrolled through his phone.

"Just a bit," I replied, avoiding the more sarcastic response that was tap-dancing on my tongue. "You're home a bit early?"

"I was on a visit in Oldham which finished early. No point going back to the office."

"No, I suppose not. I don't suppose you've checked to see if I have taken the chops out for tea, have you?"

Paddy stared at me blankly as if I'd just suggested that he deliver a lecture on quantum physics naked whilst riding a tasselled elephant.

"Chops?"

"Remember when you phoned this morning, I asked if you'd taken the chops out or seen them in the fridge?"

"Um, vaguely."

I paused.

"So have you checked since you got home?"

"No!" he said with a laugh.

"No, of course not, a coffee and your phone is much more important. Silly me."

I started unbuttoning my coat in quite a forceful manner and wrenching the buttons which would have indicated to a more perceptive person that I was not in a good mood.

"Is there a problem? Can't you just have a look now?"

"I suppose so," I grumbled, dumping my coat on the floor by the sofa and heading into the kitchen.

What a surprise, I had forgotten to take the chops out. That would mean a tin of something instead. Very nutritious. I opened the cupboard which flew ajar with an unintentional crash and ferreted around in search of a tin of stewed steak.

"Is something wrong?"

Paddy had followed me into the kitchen and was leaning against the doorjamb, cradling his coffee in his hands. I rocked back on my heels and sighed.

"Rubbish day, that's all. I'm in a bad mood so watch out."

"Leave the tea for a minute, let me make you a drink so you can calm down and warm up a bit," he said, helping me up from the floor and guiding me to a chair.

"The tea won't make itself," I hinted, looking hopefully at my husband to see if he would take the hint.

"An extra half an hour won't hurt," he said kindly, patting my arm and completely missing the point. "I'm not starving hungry."

I sighed again. I wonder if sighing too much is bad for your health, perhaps it causes unnecessary strain on the throat and lungs. Paddy began to busy himself making a cup of tea, opening a new box of teabags (leaving the cellophane wrapper on the counter and a smear of escaped tea dust) and forgetting to put the milk back in the fridge when he'd finished with it.

"So, what happened?"

I filled him in on my day, my vitriol at Naomi's treachery spilling out in a torrent. I left out the part about losing my temper, but included the slog from this afternoon to complete the figures in time. I paused dramatically and waited for a suitably outraged reaction.

"Hmm."

"Hmm? What do you mean, 'hmm'?"

"Are you sure she was being manipulative?"

"Excuse me?"

"Well, is it actually possible that she didn't hear you ask her to do the figures?"

I sat speechless, my mug of tea half-way to my open mouth.

"Of course it isn't possible! I told her about it several times last week and distinctly said this morning that she had to do the figures."

"But you were cross with her when you said that?"

"So?"

"Well, is it possible that you thought you had told her loudly and clearly but in fact you did that thing where you mutter when you try and be assertive?"

"Mutter?"

"Yes, because you don't want it to be too obvious that you're trying to say something you aren't comfortable with but are making yourself do it anyway. So it usually comes out as a growl or mutter. Perhaps she genuinely didn't hear."

"Whose side are you on?" I gasped. I had expected some solidarity and support to make me feel better and was completely blindsided by this approach.

"Yours of course, I'm just playing devil's advocate to check you haven't misread the situation before you stew about it all night and go in all guns blazing tomorrow. You need to think about it and have a word with her to check that you have it right, you don't want to cause a problem if it was a genuine mistake."

Paddy had his reasonable face on which always managed to make me feel like an over-reacting and unreasonable person, and also always makes me want to throw something at him.

"Thanks for the support!" I choked, feeling a well of tears building up.

"Hey," he said, reaching for one of my hands and holding it firmly. "I'm just saying there might be another reason for it. Talk to her tomorrow and see what she has to say for herself. Did you email her about it, so you have something in writing?"

"Well, no, we only sit two feet apart!"

"Perhaps that's something you need to think about doing so you have proof that she hasn't done her job properly. Without proof it's your word against hers."

He was right. I couldn't kick up a fuss as I couldn't prove that she had deliberately dropped me in it. I stared miserably into my tea as if I could dredge up some solace from its murky depths.

"Well, there's no point worrying about it now, just speak to her tomorrow. Now, what are we having for tea?"

I blinked up at him crossly.

"You can have a nice warm bath afterwards to calm you down," he said gently, with a caring smile.

CHAPTER FIVE

I didn't sleep well that evening, with all the adrenaline surging around my system and my brain replaying the incident at work over and over on a loop. As a consequence, I was on an earlier train the next morning, hunched against a window seat trying to compose myself before getting to work.

Catching an earlier train – albeit just twenty minutes – made a big difference to the number of commuters and the quieter atmosphere of the carriage was more soothing to me than the usual chatter and bustle. I resolutely placed my bag on the seat next to me and gave off as many hostile vibes as I possibly could to discourage anyone from asking me if they could sit next to me.

A man in a long grey raincoat and slightly squashed looking briefcase sat down on the first seat over the aisle from me with a loud expulsion of breath and looked over.

"Another day, another dollar, eh?" he said in what he probably thought were jovial tones.

I pretended that I hadn't realised he was addressing me and fixed my eyes on a fascinating pigeon squatting on the train station sign. I always get the odd ones talking to me. There could be a bus full of people and the designated chatter will always perch next to me and introduce themselves. I must give off some 'annoying people tolerant' vibrations, or perhaps I am listed in a 'Soft Touch' directory somewhere.

"Nice and quiet on here this morning," he persevered,

unbuttoning his coat.

Yes, until you got on, I grumbled inwardly.

"At least it stopped raining, I don't mind getting wet on the way home, but I don't like getting wet on the way to work!"

For the love of god!

I turned and stared at him incredulously. He took this as encouragement and smiled at me with unfeigned pleasure.

"Off to work then?" he asked.

Obviously.

"Yes," I muttered, not feeling as though I could be downright rude to such a cheerful person. I was the one in a bad mood, it wasn't his fault.

"In town?" he pressed.

"Yes," I replied, opening my bag and rifling through to see if that would put him off.

"Whereabouts?"

"Just off Piccadilly."

"I'm down on Deansgate. Which is quite handy for the new sandwich shop that's opened, it's really good for..."

"Sandwiches?" I interrupted sarcastically, hoping he would pick up on my tone.

He chortled, there was no other word for it.

"Well yes, but also wraps and ciabattas and all sorts. They do this really good one with chicken and spring onion and they..."

For goodness' sake. Was this man one of those people who you could just point at anyone and they would talk and talk? Today was not my day for humouring him. I pulled out my mobile and considered for a moment. Paddy would be on his way to work but my friend Annie would be up and available. She had two small children and was currently on maternity leave. By all accounts she was up at 5am each day.

I sent her a message.

"HELP! Send me message and will call you back. Stuck on train with talker!"

"...I've never had that combination before and it really works. They also do these breakfast rolls and they grate chocolate on the top and you wouldn't think it would be nice would you, but it really..."

My phone pinged.

"Fine. Am covered in weetabix but avail."

The man over the aisle had paused mid-stream.

"I like your notification tone, not as annoying as some is it? I've set my ringtone as the phone ring from 24, I know it's an old one, but it's a good one, isn't it? It's really distinctive and..."

I held my hand up as if stopping a flow of traffic and smiled blandly.

"Please excuse me, I've got to make a call."

"Oh, yes of course," nodded the man with a smile.

I called Annie and let it ring.

"Saved you again, have I?" she answered with a laugh.

"You have no idea," I replied, fiddling with the hem of my coat.

"The perils of train travel! You need to toughen up a bit and ignore the clingons."

I smiled to myself. Annie refused to suffer fools gladly and would have silenced the chatty man smoothly and efficiently without causing any problems.

"And how are you this morning? Covered in weetabix? Did you miss your mouth?"

"Very funny. I've just been feeding Amy and she decided that a spoon is not the most effective way of eating her breakfast."

"Really?"

"Yes, apparently the best way to eat your breakfast is to grab a fistful of soggy weetabix, shove some into your mouth then smear a bit more into your hair and eyebrows before waving said hand and flicking weetabix globules all over everything in the vicinity."

"Nice!"

"Yes. Lovely."

"And how is Tom this morning?"

Tom is a highly entertaining two year old. He amused Paddy and I no end on a country outing by standing in the middle of a park in his splashsuit and red wellies shouting at the top of his lungs, "I am a FAIRY!"

"Same as usual, all sleepy and tufty. He sends you a cuddle."

"Send one back. You up to much today?"

"Play barn this morning. You should come one time you know, you might enjoy it."

"I don't have a child to bring, I don't think Paddy counts."

"Come with me some time, it would be fun. We can sit and drink coffee while the kids tire themselves out."

"Maybe," I said, refusing to commit to anything which could either be good fun or total hell.

There was a shriek in the background and the sound of

something crashing on the floor.

"Oh shit, better go," said Annie, "Do you want to pop round tonight? You can have a coffee before the kids go up to bed. I haven't seen you for a bit. You can tell me about the christening."

I snorted.

"Fine, I'll come round on my way home. Have fun at the play barn!"

"Will do. You know you could always do the sad single routine on your talker. Assuming it's a man of course. Which it will be. See you later."

I leaned back, sighed and returned the mobile to my bag. I could see the man opposite leaning forward to resume his monologue. I looked over and smiled politely. I had seen Annie do this routine a number of times, but I had never tried it myself.

"That was my friend. She's a lovely girl."

The man nodded eagerly, pleased that I was at last entering into a proper conversation.

"It's such a shame she hasn't met the right person. Anyone would be pleased to go out with her."

The man nodded again, this time a little more warily.

"She's very friendly. I suppose that's partly due to the fact that she's only just been released, she was a bit isolated before. But that was all some silly misunderstanding, she didn't mean to do it. The accident I mean. Well, she *said* it was an accident."

I gave a high laugh and was quite tickled to see the man was looking faintly alarmed.

"And she's on a special programme now to help her with her

anger issues. She's very dedicated."

By now Mr Raincoat was looking rather ill at ease and was fumbling in his briefcase himself.

I gasped and he flinched.

"I don't suppose you would be interested in meeting up with her? Not necessarily for a date, but just to widen her circle a bit? You seem like a very friendly person."

I leaned forward expectantly and smiled in a slightly unhinged manner.

"Um, that's very kind of you but I'm not sure that..." he trailed off and pulled his phone out of his pocket. "I must just make an important call."

He jumped up and clasped his briefcase under his arm before scuttling down the aisle towards the next carriage.

I laughed and texted Annie.

"Thanks, it worked!"

My mood slightly improved.

The office felt like an out of hours airport when I arrived earlier than usual. The pot plants squatted forlornly in reception and the distant hum of a floor buffer caused the fluorescent lights to flicker atmospherically as I approached the lifts.

"Morning my dear, had a row with the husband?"

Oh great. Lucas the Facilities Manager. A man whose personal charisma was matched only by his excellent taste in polyester clothing. I fixed a smile to my weary face and turned around.

"Morning Lucas. How are you today?"

"...because if you have had a row, I'm sure I could comfort you in some way," he leered, actually poking his florid pink tongue out of the corner of his grinning mouth.

I don't think that Lucas understands about sexual harassment, although he was providing a textbook example of it.

"Well, as tempting as that would be, I'm fine thank you," I replied, turning away to jab increasingly desperately at the lift call button.

"You know where I am," he smirked. "You do know that pushing that button more than once doesn't make the lift come any quicker?"

"Is that so?" I muttered, punctuating each word with another push.

"Unlike a woman..." he sniggered.

I fought the urge to be sick on his shoes.

"So, it's a waste of time really..." he continued.

"Maybe so, but it isn't doing any harm is it?" I asked brightly, still with my back to him and punctuating each word with a push.

Lucas chuckled and I felt him brush my lower back with his arm as he swaggered past.

Urgh.

I managed to reach my cube without further incident and threw my handbag into the bottom drawer.

"Morning Daniel," I said with a smile. "How are you today? Mine could be better already."

Daniel did not reply. He was too busy looking thoughtful as he stared off into the distance. Either that or the tight shorts were causing too much of a distraction and restricting his blood flow.

I rooted in my bag and extricated the replacement cereal bars and placed them in my drawer. They have to be laid the same way, front to back and not lengthways across. Otherwise, they offend my sensibilities every time I open the drawer and scoot up and down and I try to avoid any extra sources of stress in my life.

I tried to compose myself and think about how I would deal with Naomi. I took out my favourite pen – a particularly chunky one that I had received from a software representative – and my spiral bound notebook and wrote a heading.

Course of Action.

I thought for a moment and underlined it twice before starting to write.

1) Be prepared and speak calmly and rationally.
2) Express my disappointment.
3) Outline the negative impact of the behaviour.
4) Explain how future dealings will be conducted.

I read it through and felt calmer. I always felt better when I wrote a list, no matter how small. I had every reason to be upset with Naomi and I was going to take the bull by the horns and conduct a calm and measured conversation which would let her know that I knew what she was up to and she would not be allowed to get away with such behaviour in future.

I spent the next ten minutes carefully outlining how I was going to tackle Naomi and firmly but politely get her to realise that I would no longer be a pushover. I thought hard and scribbled down a few phrases which didn't sound too accusatory but would leave her in no doubt of my newfound resolve to manage her shortcomings.

I flipped over a page and replaced the notebook in my drawer. I felt prepared and ready to confront my errant assistant. I sighed and retrieved a strawberry cereal bar and began to peel the wrapper. Today would be the turning point in my managerial career.

My desk phone rang and I summoned up my phone voice.

"Accounts admin, Mena speaking."

There was a pause and someone cleared a throat on the other end.

"It's Naomi," said Naomi breezily. My heart sank. I knew what was coming.

"Hello," I said cautiously.

"Um, yes, just to let you know that I won't be in today."

You could at least say sorry!

"Right..." I said in what I hoped was a non-judgemental tone of voice.

"Yes, I've had a bit of a reaction following on from my appointment yesterday so I can't make it in."

Oh really.

I bit my lower lip. I had my suspicions that her supposed medical appointment had actually been more of the beauty appointment kind but couldn't prove anything.

Fake tan too orange?

There was a pregnant pause.

"OK then. See you tomorrow." She hung up.

I dropped the phone receiver back on the base as loudly as I dared to express my annoyance and tore a chunk out of my cereal bar. She could have said sorry. My phone calls to work to report sickness were always made as an absolute last resort and featured at least a hoarse voice or general feebleness to justify my absence. If I could pause part way through to cough or retch, that was an added bonus.

Great. Another day of working into the ground to make up for an assistant who was supposed to make my job easier. I snorted and sneaked my mobile out of my bag. Yes, it wasn't a designated break, but I was annoyed.

I messaged Paddy.

"Guess what. All geared up to make a stand and she isn't coming in today."

There was no point in waiting for him to respond, he took long enough to reply even when he wasn't at work.

I messaged Annie.

"Was all ready to be firm with Naomi and she's not turned up today. Argh!"

I hadn't even shut my bag back in my drawer when my notification went off.

"Typical. You need to MAKE A STAND!"

That was easier said than done. Annie always says what she likes and other people don't seem to mind at all. "Oh, that's just Annie" they say and take her comments with a pinch of salt.

Still, I would say something to Naomi. As soon as she comes back in.

Piccadilly station was particularly busy that evening, with shoppers clumped together in packs under the large electronic notice board. I was having to slalom between them, skipping past piles of shopping bags dumped on the floor by their feet. Boutique bags, brown paper carriers and canvas bags for life competed for space next to their less popular plastic counterparts.

"Excuse me, sorry, excuse me," I muttered as I hopped and swayed around each obstacle. I was cutting it fine.

I glanced up at the screen by my usual platform entry point and saw that I only had two minutes to make my way up the ramp, across the upper-level concourse and down the other side. There was no alternative, I would have to run.

I grasped my bag more firmly on my shoulder and started a lurching run along the platform to the ramp. I am not one of life's natural runners. I have never been able to run with any sort of panache or conviction. I look on with admiration to anyone who can achieve a springy, effortless gait. When I run, it's like trying to crank up a stiff machine that needs a bit of momentum to get it going. Each stride is an effort and each thud as my feet meet the floor jars every joint from my ankles up to my hips. Paddy has said that I remind him of a creepy puppet with cut strings.

Charming.

However, I was making headway as I ploughed my way up the ramp, weaving past more fortunate passengers who weren't about to miss their train. My breath started to come out in more laboured puffs, which I valiantly tried to hide by opening my mouth a little to provide less audible resistance.

My legs started to feel a little jellyish and I cursed again at the fact that I was so unfit. I really should make the effort to get up to some level of fitness. You never knew when it might come in handy. Relying on the hope that a burst of adrenaline would get you through in the case of a real emergency is not a very good strategy.

I was now on the descent and I could see the train had already arrived and was waiting on the platform. I probably had thirty seconds maximum to reach it before the doors sealed.

"Coming through!" I called out in the manner of a jolly boarding school hockey captain, as I burst my way through a clot of people in business suits who were clogging up the way.

The warning beeps of the train doors closing began to sound as I hurtled to the nearest door, whacked the button and leapt on just in time.

The doors shuddered shut behind me and I took a jagged breath, smoothed down my hair and made my way into the carriage as the train began to move. I gratefully sank down into a seat that was available on a table for four.

An older couple sat at the two window seats. I smiled over at them as I settled myself down next to the husband and placed my bag between my feet. They looked very well-to-do. The husband was the definition of 'natty' in a full three-piece suit, complete with a tufted handkerchief poking out of his breast pocket. His wife wore an elegant shift dress with a matching jacket. I was slightly disappointed that she wasn't wearing a string of pearls, however, she made up for it with a stunning encrusted brooch in the shape of a wreath on her lapel. Her hands were even resting on a fur muff in her lap.

It was a good job Paddy wasn't here to make an obvious joke about that.

The elderly lady, sitting diagonally opposite, smiled back at me.

"Good afternoon," she said, nodding in my direction.

At last! A fellow train passenger who knows how to observe social niceties.

"Good afternoon," I replied, just as formally. "Just made it!"

"Yes, you certainly did, just in time."

How pleasant to have a straightforward conversation.

I decided to carry on rather than pull out my book.

"Have you been shopping today?"

The lady shuffled her hands in her lap and shook her head.

"Not today, we wanted to come into town and give Bertie a change of scene. He does like to get out and about."

I looked over at her husband next to me and smiled. He looked back at me with watery eyes. He had the most amazing red thread veins networking across his cheeks and nose. They were really quite spectacular.

"That sounds fun. Did you enjoy it?" I asked him.

He turned back to the window and studied the buildings flashing past.

"Oh yes, he loved it," answered his wife.

Clearly his wife was the sociable one out of the pairing.

"He specifically wanted to go down Canal Street. It's one of his favourite spots."

I blinked in surprise.

"Really? Yes, it's definitely worth a visit."

"Isn't it?"

It just goes to show that you should never pre-judge a person. I wouldn't have expected that this couple would be particularly keen to go to Manchester's Gay Village, but that clearly shows my prejudice. I took it as a learning point and resolved to be a better person.

"I have to keep him on a tight leash down there, though, goodness knows what he would be up to if I didn't," she continued, confidingly.

"I see."

I risked a sideways look at her husband, but he was still gazing out of the window, seemingly unresponsive.

"He does try his best to get away, but I make sure he's firmly clipped in."

I was beginning to feel perplexed. I openly studied the man seated next to me, looking for any sign of a harness.

"In fact, he's probably ready for something to eat now, after all his excitement."

She tapped her fingernails on the table to get his attention.

"Will you get the food out please and the saucer?"

Mr Dapper sighed and reached beneath the table, his hand emerging shortly afterwards with a tin in one hand and a white china saucer in the other. I did a double take.

Mrs Dapper stretched out her arm and grasped the tin in her hand, before carefully using her other one to pull on the ring pull on the top. With a metallic snap, the tin opened and she began to shake it over the saucer.

"It's no good, I'll need the fork."

A small silver fork was passed across and Mrs Dapper began digging vigorously into the can. The unmistakeable meaty stench of dog food quickly filtered into the atmosphere. At this point, my mouth fell open and I looked on in horror. The contents of the tin were upended onto the saucer.

"Here you go Bertie, dig in."

To my relieved surprise, Mr Dapper remained immobile, staring fixedly at his wife.

She placed the fork, with jellied fragments still glistening on the tines, onto the table top and lifted up her muff. (Honestly, thank goodness Paddy wasn't here.) A pointed nose and small black eyes appeared as a small rat-like creature unfurled itself to stand on her thighs and began to enthusiastically attack the wet dog food.

A couple of small chunks were nosed off the saucer onto the table. My mouth dropped open again.

"Oh don't worry about that, he'll get to those in a minute," smiled Mrs Dapper.

Sure enough, as soon as the saucer was cleared, the dog began to lick the remains off the table.

"There, that's better, isn't it Bertie," she crooned.

I was struggling not to be sick. The dog returned to its seat and curled up with a replete sigh.

"Excuse me," I mumbled as I gathered my bag and moved along the carriage.

Paddy and I would not be having tinned stewed steak for tea tonight, that was for sure.

CHAPTER SIX

Popping round to Annie's on my way home only requires a slight detour. I clicked up the path and rapped hard on the wooden door with my knuckles. I was enough of a regular visitor to know that the doorbell didn't work, along with quite a few other things in Annie's house.

A moment later a smudged outline appeared behind the frosted glass panel and the door slowly creaked open accompanied by "Ouch, let go! No, let go of my hair...just get down a minute!" There was a thud and the door jerked open fully.

"Hello!" said Annie with a big smile, raising one arm for a welcoming hug, whilst balancing on one leg to use her calf as a barrier for Tom who was trying manfully to shoot out the door.

"Evening," I replied, returning the hug and sliding in through the open door past a sticky toddler. "Hello Tom."

I bent down and made slurping kissing noises with my puckered mouth and laughed as Tom flinched in horror and disappeared back up the hallway.

"Works every time."

"You should try it with Paddy sometime," snorted Annie, gesturing towards the kitchen at the back. "Did your day get any better?"

I sighed loudly and sank into one of the kitchen chairs, tucking my handbag underneath the kitchen table. It was usually safer to keep my possessions in close contact with Tom the Klepto-child around. I wiggled my fingers and gave Amy a toothy smile. She was concentrating on chewing on a wooden spoon in her highchair.

"Not really. How about you?"

"Oh, the usual," smiled Annie, turning to reboil the kettle and reach for two mugs from a cupboard above. "We all got excited about the Cbeebies Shakespeare special this morning and the rest of the day kind of failed to live up to those dizzy heights."

"I can imagine!"

Annie and I have been friends since primary school. She's a few rungs ahead of me in the Game of Life path in that she married a few years ago and quickly produced offspring and is on maternity leave from her job as a buyer at the council. Despite having a job, I've never known anyone like Annie for constantly coming up with new ideas for making money.

"So, how's your latest project coming along? What is it again?" I asked.

Two cups of builder's tea plonked onto the wood surface of the table and Annie sat down next to Amy. Her subtly highlighted tawny blonde hair was pinned up in an artistic knot with a few wisps tucked behind her ears. She wore an oversized checked shirt with boyfriend stonewashed jeans and Converse trainers and looked the epitome of casual chic. No matter how tired she is, or no matter how little effort she's made, she always manages to look presentable and as if that is exactly how she meant to look. I've often told her that she could even make a bin bag look like a fashion statement.

"You make it sound like it's a fad," she complained, picking up a pot of fromage frais and pulling the lid off in one practised movement. Amy perked up and started jigging in her seat and kicking her feet.

To be fair, I do the same when faced with a bar of Bournville.

"So, what is it?"

"Well," she said, spooning a mouthful of yoghurt slop into Amy's open gummy mouth. "You know how if you put the word 'Baby' in front of any product you can immediately charge so much more?"

"Right..." I encouraged, taking a sip of boiling hot tea.

"It's like weddings isn't it, you can provide goods and services that you can get anywhere, but the minute you directly aim it at the wedding or baby markets you can pretty much name your price?"

"You mean like your idea to make chocolates with the bride and groom's names on them as favours?" I raised an eyebrow.

"Yes, well, I admit I didn't think that one through too well. The amount of time and effort it took to make the bloody things and then it was almost impossible to fit any name on unless it was Jim or Sue or something equally short. And having to bear in mind the shelf life of the chocolates so they all needed making just before the weekend weddings...and had to be delivered without them getting temperature damaged..."

I smiled.

"A nice idea, but maybe not the most practical for a home business," I consoled, hiding behind my cup again.

"OK, so it wasn't quite the right idea for *me*. But! By calling them wedding favours you could immediately rack the price up and charge a premium. And the same thing goes for baby things. The minute you have one everyone is telling you that you have to have x or y and lots of yummy mummies are trying to outdo each other with their perfect changing bags or cosy toes or sock savers and dribble guards…"

She was losing me. This all sounded too much like baby jargon that I was unfamiliar with. It was a whole new world to me and not one that I felt too compelled to jump into at this moment in time.

"So…" I prompted, watching Annie scrape around Amy's mouth with the feeding spoon with the practised ease of a window cleaner with a squeegee. She shovelled the excess fromage frais back into her mouth.

"So, my next project needs to be something for the baby market. I just need to develop an idea that I've had. You're going to love it," she said, using her other hand to reach for a pile of papers on the edge of the table. "Have a look at this!"

She passed them over to me and I had a quick riffle through. I was confused.

"What is this, some sort of baby grow thing?" I asked, holding a page where a drawing of a baby seemed to show it encased in a full body suit which just left the baby's face peeping out.

"Not just a baby grow," Annie replied, turning to point at the page. "It's the latest innovation in baby sun protection suits. No need to worry about missing a bit with the sun cream or panicking when your baby yanks off its sun hat. If you cover it up almost completely with UV material it's much safer. And, dun der der der dun der der da! Guess what makes mine different?"

"Um, because yours comes with a baby?"

"No, don't be silly. What does the baby look like in one of those suits?" she prompted, making a 'come on, come on' gesture with her hand.

"Like a silly bugger?"

Annie pretended to look affronted.

"How rude. No. It occurred to me that it looks like a... life-sized jelly baby! Don't you think?"

"Oh!" I wasn't quite sure what to say. "I suppose so."

"So, you can order the colour of your favourite jelly baby and you could even have a little belly button like the sweets have and they'd look super-cute."

"I suppose, but what would the jelly baby people think about it?"

"I'd like to think they'd adopt the jelly baby babies into their communities and welcome them with open arms," Annie said with a flourish of the spoon.

"Very funny, you know what I mean. The company that makes jelly babies!"

"Well, I haven't asked them yet. But it could be fantastic don't you think? And the best thing is that you could even make adult-sized ones so you could all dress up as a jelly baby family, what do you reckon?"

I laughed and put the papers to one side.

"Very creative. I think you should speak to the manufacturers before you spend too much time and effort on it, but you never know. I can see you in a weekend supplement spread with photos of you all in chunky knit sweaters in the garden as you publicise your brand. It's a shame you didn't call your kids Casper and Tilly."

"I'll take that as an endorsement then. You've got to admit that it's better than my soft play places for adults idea."

"Yes, I agree with you there."

Annie stood up and fetched another fromage frais from the

fridge. Amy began to jiggle and bounce again.

"Seconds, eh? Lucky Amy."

"This is nothing, she can get through four easily. She's going to have the strongest bones around at this rate."

I spent a pleasant few moments watching Annie feeding her daughter.

"Annie?"

"Yes?"

"Do you know what you do when you're spooning food into Amy's mouth?"

"What?" Annie turned to look at me quizzically. "What do you mean?"

"Have you never noticed it?"

"Noticed what?" she asked, turning back to calm a protesting Amy who resented any slowing down of her fromage frais feeding.

"That when you feed her you open and close your mouth as well?"

"Don't be silly," she said, scraping around the pot.

"No, really."

"I do sometimes, to encourage her to open her mouth…"

"No, you do it every time. Just see."

The spoon made its way towards Amy and Annie's mouth opened and closed in time with her daughter's.

"Oh my god! I do! Let me try again!"

She repeated the experiment.

"Oh, how embarrassing. How many times have I done that when we're out and about? I must look like an idiot!"

"Well, that's fair enough I suppose."

"Shut up, it must be an automatic reflex thing. Just wait until you have one and you'll be doing the same..."

She turned to smile at me, with the spoon poised in mid-air.

"No chance, you know that's not in my long-term plan."

Annie scraped out the last of the pot and put it down on the table, giving Amy the spoon to play with.

"So, you managed to get rid of the guy on the train then?"

"Yes, thanks. It worked a treat. He couldn't get away fast enough."

"Good. What's up then?"

I filled Annie in on my christening excursion and the problems I was having at work.

"Mmm. That's a tricky one," she said thoughtfully. "You've got to be careful when people are off sick, you don't want to be seen as harassing her or being unsupportive."

"I know, it's a minefield. But what do I do about her not doing things I need her to do? She's outright ignoring me and it's getting to be a joke. I was all ready to have a word with her today and then she didn't come in."

"Keep a record for now and see what she's like when she comes back to work. Do what Paddy says as well and put all of your requests in writing. You need evidence or it's your word against hers, particularly if you're covering for her. Could you pass me the wipes please?"

There was a pause while I watched Annie wipe Amy's little

face. She was beaming and crowing.

"I've done some baking today, would you like to try?"

I gave a little start and tried to keep the smile in place without it becoming too fixed.

"I don't know how you find the time..." I began, trying to head her off.

No chance.

"I made some scones, would you like one?"

Now, I love Annie to bits. She is my oldest and dearest friend and she is so talented in so many areas: all things that could raise envy in a person. But there is one thing she cannot do, no matter how hard she tries. She is the world's worst baker. She cooks like an angel, but bakes like an imp from the depths of Hades.

"Thanks for the offer, but I'll be going back for tea in a minute. I don't want to spoil it."

"One little scone? You could call it afternoon tea and then you'd be justified in squeezing one in. Posh people used to do it all the time in the old days."

I laughed and patted my stomach.

"No really, thanks. I've eaten too much today as it is and I'm sure Sam would rather have one."

I thought back queasily to the rock cake that had the hardest ever rock-like surface that could break teeth and a dense floury texture within. I'd had to chip bits off with my molars and I was still chewing it when I left an hour later.

"He says he's on a health kick at the minute. Says I'm feeding him too much cake."

Clever lad, I thought. It gave me an idea though.

"Can't he take some into work? Cakes always go down well in our office."

"I suggested that, but he is always in such a rush in the morning that he never remembers."

I wasn't surprised. I remembered the Victoria sponge cake that had all the texture of a foam pad and was covered with over-whipped cream. The Great British Bake Off has a lot to answer for.

"Oh well, take some for Paddy anyway. I'll put some in a bag."

"Great, thanks."

I could always try him with it. He would eat almost anything.

"I tweaked the recipe a bit," Annie said from the depths of a cupboard. "I've put some olives in it, kind of like an Italian/English fusion thing."

"Marvellous, that'll be a nice surprise for him."

A freezer bag filled with four scones was placed on the table in front of me. They looked like a regular scone, but looks can be very deceiving. Particularly where Annie's baking is involved.

I suddenly realised that I hadn't seen Tom since he'd run off from the front door when I arrived.

"Annie, where's Tom?"

"Oh, I'd forgotten about him! He's been quiet hasn't he? He's probably fine, just posting all of my credit cards down the back of the radiator. Keep an eye on Amy a sec."

She disappeared out of the kitchen and I could hear the lounge door being flung open, followed by a shriek.

"Thomas James Anthony Evans! What on earth do you think you're doing?"

I quickly unclipped Amy from the highchair and hurried after Annie. She was still stood in her lounge doorway with her hands on her hips. I peered over her shoulder to see what the problem was.

Tom was stood by the coffee table looking very pleased with himself. He'd emptied an entire box of man-sized tissues and wet them with his water bottle before covering the leather armchair with the soggy remnants.

"Mashay!" he said proudly, pointing at his work of art.

"What?" asked Annie, clearly confused.

"Mashay model!"

"Oh Lord," she sighed. "He's trying to make a papier mâché model with tissues. We made one yesterday and he's obviously decided to try by himself."

"Ten out of ten for creativity."

I couldn't help smiling. But then again, it wasn't my armchair that had been 'mashayed' to death.

"Do you need me to stay and help you tidy or...?" I asked hopefully.

"No, fine, off you go. It shouldn't take too long to sort out. This sort of thing happens all the time."

Gratefully I deposited Amy on her play mat and made my way out of the room.

"Thanks for the tea," I said, kissing the side of her head as I passed.

"No problem," she sighed. "See you soon. Oh, and don't forget the scones!"

Damn.

I walked home quite jauntily, swinging the bag of scones as I strode along. Annie usually managed to cheer me up. At the very least, it made me realise how grateful I was that I could go home to a relaxing and tidy house. Well, unless Paddy was there. The havoc he could wreak on a tidy environment in a short space of time was legendary.

I crossed the road to our house and skirted the wheelie bin parking barrier before hopping up onto the pavement. My key was stiff and I shoulder-barged the door open and stepped over the post and fliers on the mat, before closing the door behind me.

"Paddy?" I called, even though I was sure he wasn't at home.

I stooped down and gathered up the mail and had a quick flick through. Nothing of any interest. I walked through to the kitchen and tipped it into the recycling caddy by the back door and dropped the scones onto the counter. They made a large thunk noise, which didn't make me feel very excited about eating one.

But aside from that, I was feeling much happier with the world today. I hadn't had to sit next to Naomi all day and had done a good day's work before clocking off on the dot. I would celebrate by making a proper tea.

In our house, we have proper teas and we have quick teas. The quick teas are the cobbled together affairs that often constitute tinned and/or frozen goods and a quick turnaround time. They are usually hearty and filling, but not particularly healthy or gastronomically tantalising. The proper teas are ones that I start from scratch, have some sort of side dish – garlic bread or fancy vegetables – and have actual herbs dusted through them. You can't beat chopping garlic or dicing onion for making you feel like a grade-A chef. Proper teas usually happen on a weekend and maybe once during the week if I feel up to the challenge.

I opened the jar cupboard and rooted around amongst the borlotti beans, passata and the rogue jar of morello cherries that had lurked in its depths for several years. I decided that I would make a chicken and spinach one-pot meal with garlicky passata and mixed beans. I pulled out a part-baked baguette and punted it onto the top of the kitchen worktop. I was just reaching right to the back to grab a tin of green lentils when the phone rang.

"For god's sake!" I exclaimed, pivoting on my heels and cracking my elbow on the edge of the cupboard frame. "Just a minute!"

I shuffled backwards and hauled myself up, before stumbling into the lounge and picking up the phone.

"Hello?"

"It's Evelyn," I heard, before the line went dead.

I sighed. Of course it was. I found my bag and pulled out my mobile, before tapping in the number on the landline and pressing the call button. I really must write her number by the phone.

The phone started to ring. It would be so much easier if I could just return the call on my mobile, but Evelyn has caller ID and will only answer if your name comes up. She won't answer the phone to mobile numbers.

The phone continued to ring.

You've just called me, how can it take so long to pick up?

I was about to hang up when the ringing stopped and I could hear the sound of Pointless in the background.

"Evelyn?" I asked.

"Yes, dear."

"Hello, did you just call?"

"You know I did, you spoke to me dear."

Yes I know, I'm starting off the conversation as per social convention!

I bit back a retort.

"How are you doing, are you ok?"

"Yes thank you, just watching Pointless."

"OK."

There was a long pause. I was fighting my usual instinct to dive in with some small talk. I lost.

"Paddy isn't back from work yet, was there something in particular you needed?"

"Paddy?"

"I mean Patrick."

It's ridiculous really, she refuses to acknowledge Paddy by anything other than his Sunday name. She doesn't just let it go, she always repeats 'Paddy?' as though it's someone she has never met in her life and the minute you say Patrick, she says, oh yes, as in 'oh that's who you mean'.

"Well, I do need some help, I need to leave out my water reading tomorrow on a little card."

"OK."

"Well, I can't get to the meter as it's in the sink cupboard. I don't want to have them coming in my house. I need someone to read it for me and write it on the card."

"OK Evelyn."

"They're coming tomorrow you see."

"Yes, that's fine. I can pop over shortly and do it for you."

"Thank you dear. Are you sure you wouldn't rather leave it for Patrick?"

"No, it's fine. I think I can sort out a meter reading. I'll be around when I've put the tea on."

"Bye dear."

Evelyn hung up. Great, one more thing to squeeze in before tea.

I bustled back into the kitchen and took out some chicken from the fridge. I would just get everything prepped and started and then finish it off when I got back. I was a woman with a purpose, one of life's achievers! I flourished my favourite chopping knife out of the block and got started.

CHAPTER SEVEN

Evelyn lived in a sheltered accommodation bungalow five minutes' walk away from our little terraced house. It sat in the middle of a row of three, with small plain patches of grass outside and a simple concrete path to each of the front doors.

The bungalow to the left of Evelyn had an elegant pair of bay trees flanking the front door, contrasting oddly against the pebble-dash pink and white cladding. The one to the right was the fantasy land that taste forgot, with gnomes, pottery animals, fake garlands and fairy lights strewn haphazardly within a small rectangle which was hemmed in by the kind of barriers you use for crowd control. This was Maud's bungalow and her garden has been the subject of many complaints and also – from some quarters – vocal admiration.

It began quite innocuously shortly after she moved in, with a pair of gnomes placed beneath her front window. They were rapidly followed by a cluster of animals in costumes, such as rats in waistcoats and rabbits in dresses, which were all placed in a circle in the middle of the grass. The local community began to notice and look on with interest and vague concern.

Over the next few months, a new figure would be added every few days, until the whole lawn was a street carnival scene of pottery figures cavorting beneath makeshift bowers and peeping from behind ornamental wheelbarrows. Letters were written to the housing association and the council. The local free newspaper sent a reporter to take a photograph of the scene with Maud standing proudly beside the figures in her floral skirt and pastel blouse with brass buttons, her hair newly washed and set in a typical older lady style I refer to as 'The Queen'.

The climax to the affair came one Valentine's Day when Maud added a new tableau to the ensemble. A pair of blow-up dolls – one man and one woman – dressed in charity shop clothes with red hearts stencilled on, their mouths a round 'o' of astonishment. They were arranged in two deckchairs around a small table, upon which sat two plastic tumblers of wine and a box of chocolates.

Over the next few days as dawn broke, the dolls were found to be in a variety of poses and positions, causing Maud and several other locals great consternation and outrage. The third morning, the dolls had disappeared entirely, leaving behind a note saying they had decided to do the decent thing and had eloped. This was then followed by the appearance of a social media account tracking the two dolls to various local locations in a range of compromising positions.

Maud was upset at the loss of her latest figures, but not as upset as the elderly gentleman who tripped over one of the deckchairs and flattened a gnome and a pottery cat in a basket, sustaining cuts and bruises. Enough was enough and Maud was reigned in by the Housing Association. She was permitted a small space behind barriers, but that was that.

Compared to her two neighbours, Evelyn's house was plain and unadorned. Neat net curtains hang at her front window and a pot plant squatted in the centre of her windowsill.

I stepped up to the front door and rang the bell, following it up with a knock on the frosted glass pane. After a moment, a dark shape appeared and the door opened slightly, hindered by the door chain.

"Yes?"

"Hi Evelyn, it's me, Mena."

"Oh, hello dear."

Evelyn fumbled with the chain and rattled it backwards and forwards within its casing.

"Just a minute, I can't get the thing to come out."

Rattle rattle. I stood patiently, looking up and down the street. More fiddling and muttered words. Eventually the chain released and the door creaked open.

"There we are, dear. Come on in."

I followed Evelyn's retreating back into the hallway and closed the door behind me. The powerful smell of a gas fire assaulted my nostrils as I stepped further in, coming from the lounge to the right, where I could see The One Show on the television.

"Here it is," called Evelyn from the tiny kitchen at the back and a spotted and gnarled hand waved a small pink card through the doorway. "The cupboard is under the sink there."

I pulled my phone out, dropped my bag in the hallway and bent down in front of the sink cupboard. I turned on the flashlight and peered into the dark recess. Old bottles of cream cleaners and Brasso jostled against small tins of paint and rusted tubs of brands I didn't recognise.

"Can you see it dear? It's the round black thing at the back."

"Yes, just about. Have you got a pen to write the numbers down?"

"Oh no, just a minute."

I heard Evelyn's fleece-lined tartan slippers pad back out of the kitchen and waited, half-reclining on the kitchen floor with my head in the cupboard until she returned. I blinked as the smell of chemicals started to make my eyes water.

"Ready now."

I slowly read out the numbers and read them back to make sure.

"Got it, dear, thank you."

I backed out of a cupboard on all fours for the second time that evening and used the edge of the sink to help myself up.

"Right, there you go. Just tuck the card in your door frame in the morning and they won't need to come in."

Evelyn nodded, placing the card and pen on the table. There was an awkward pause.

"Well, I'll be off then and get the tea finished."

"Righto. Tell Patrick I'm sorted out now."

"Yes, I will."

I paused again, wondering whether a thank you might be forthcoming.

"Right then, see you again."

You're welcome!

I picked up my bag and strode the two steps along the hallway, before twisting the catch and swinging open the front door.

Evelyn followed me to the door and stood with her hands clasped.

"He's a good lad, Patrick."

I smiled and stepped outside.

"Bye then."

"Bye dear."

The door closed and the chain rattled. I watched Evelyn's outline recede as she tottered back to her television. Oh well, good deed done. I looped my bag strap over my shoulder and headed down the concrete path. A moment later I flinched, as Maud suddenly blindsided me from the left, brandishing what looked like a pottery weasel holding a parasol.

"Maud! You gave me a shock. How are you doing?"

Maud was not wearing her local newspaper attire today, she was much more comfortably enclosed in what could only be described as beige slacks – complete with ironed creases – and a bobbled cream polyester turtleneck. She put me in mind of an overgrown mushroom. I could never quite understand why some older people liked to dress so blandly, like they were fading away before your eyes.

"Isn't this one a beauty?" she asked, holding up the weasel for me to see. Another one who bypasses typical social niceties without a proper greeting. "I got him for £3 from B and M, what a bargain."

I pretended to admire the monstrosity.

"Mmm, lovely." I was not even convincing the weasel with my enthusiasm.

"And it's multi-purpose," she continued with pride, upending the ornament to show me the base.

"Oh really?"

"Yes, look, you can put your keys or whatever you want in this little hidden bit here at the bottom. Isn't that clever?"

"I suppose so. Fancy that."

"Don't tell anyone though, or they'll all know about it." Maud tapped the side of her nose with her free hand.

"Your secret is safe with me," I replied, before adding a high-pitched laugh.

Shut up, you sound ridiculous.

"Well, must be off. Tea to sort."

I was already speaking to Maud's broad back, as she turned and scurried over to her display. I watched as she began to push the weasel through the barrier into a tiny patch of space next to a gnome listening to a transistor radio.

"Bye then!" I called and headed off down the road.

Thank goodness she didn't live next door to me.

Paddy's van was parked up outside our house when I returned five minutes later. He had reversed right up to the wheely bin to fit in the only available space.

That'll go down well.

I unlocked the front door and wandered through into the kitchen. Paddy was filling up the kettle at the sink.

"Evening! You'll be popular."

Paddy turned to grin at me.

"If you mean where I've had to park, Mr Bins is just going to have to lump it. There wasn't anywhere else and it isn't his personal patch of road."

I leaned up and gave him a kiss.

"I know."

"And his barrier does have a major problem in that it's only two-foot square, so if cars park either side he's only got a wheely bin sized space left over which is no use to anyone."

"I know! You don't need to tell me. But you know what he's like."

"Well, it's tough. He just has to take potluck like the rest of us."

He stood the kettle back in its base and flicked on the switch.

"Brew?"

I put my hands on his hips and squeezed past him in the cramped space and turned the hob back on.

"No thanks, tea won't be long. Can you put the oven on 160 for the baguettes?"

"Ooh, a proper tea is it? On a Tuesday? You must be in a good mood."

I smacked him on the backside with the tea towel.

"I wouldn't go that far after work today, but I've seen Annie for a chat and I've just helped an old lady in distress."

"Nan?"

I nodded and sliced open the packaging on the bread.

"She needed her water meter reading doing. I didn't get a thank you, but you know what she did say as I left?"

Paddy leaned back on the counter and folded his arms, with a smug smile on his face.

"Something about me being wonderful?"

I pulled a face at him.

"She said you're a good lad."

"Well, I am!"

"Hmm."

"I am!"

"Well, she thinks you are, so I suppose that's all that matters. Never mind that you never remember to call her back and it's me that does most of the jobs…"

I flipped open the oven and slid the baguette onto the baking sheet.

"…she will always think the sun shines out of you, *Patrick*."

"Which bit of me?" he asked with a mock leer.

I shook my head and didn't respond, instead reaching for the spatula to give the chicken concoction a stir. Paddy leaned over my shoulder and peered into the pan.

"What are we on tonight?"

"Chicken one-pot with beans and lentils and spinach."

"Sounds great. How long for tea?"

I glanced at the clock.

"About fifteen minutes."

"OK."

Paddy wandered into the lounge and flicked on the television.

"But you should give her a call, she'd love to have a chat with you!" I called.

"Yup," he called back.

I knew he wouldn't.

CHAPTER EIGHT

The train was late. I was waiting for my usual morning train along with a throng of other tired, grumpy and cold commuters. The wind blew along the full length of the platform, biting into any exposed flesh, before screaming off to whip up eddies of litter in the station car park.

I didn't even have the energy to play my favourite game of making up stories about my fellow passengers. Usually, I could speculate about total strangers all day long, the more outlandish and unlikely the story, the better.

I could see some of my previous targets, dotted along the platform. There was Mr Star Trek in his smart suit and briefcase, who dressed as a Klingon at weekends and had studied the language. There was Miss Rainbow, with her multi-coloured ombre hair and unicorn-patterned dungarees. She trades stocks when she isn't at work in the women's shelter and has a penchant for collecting rare Sylvanian Family figurines.

The train finally sidled in, resulting in a scrum to the doors. As always, one person started repeatedly pushing the button, before it had even lit up.

It won't open any faster you know, for goodness' sake.

I sounded like Lucas, I realised with a jolt.

The doors opened with a clank of hydraulics and we all filed in without giving an inch to anyone else. Bags were swung onto racks and slotted between feet and the seats filled. I managed to perch on one of the last free seats next to a particularly large gentleman who occupied a window seat. Unfortunately, he was also spreading into the seat I was attempting to sit on and it wasn't helped by his legs being akimbo.

I twisted ninety degrees, with my knees at an angle in the walkway. The train started off with a lurch.

I opened my bag for my book, just as the man next to me reached into the carrier bag on his lap. I pulled out a thriller, he pulled out a tuna and egg mayonnaise roll.

On the morning commute? Really? And tuna AND egg mayonnaise?

I tried not to pull a face and flipped to where I was up to, ignoring the rustling sound of cling film being unwrapped. The man cleared his throat and crammed a large portion of the roll into his mouth. A small blob of egg mayo squeezed out of the side and plopped onto the seat next to my thigh.

That is disgusting!

I sighed audibly and shifted my body slightly further over, so that only half of my backside was now resting on the edge of the seat. I was, to all intents and purposes, now blocking off the aisle.

Loud smacking noises came from behind me as my fellow passenger masticated his breakfast, followed by another small grunt as he took another large bite. The slightly sulphurous smell of boiled egg drifted across and tickled my nose. I didn't do well with food smells early in the morning before I'd breakfasted and I had to swallow hard to stop my gag reflex kicking in.

I find it impossible not to physically react to two things: gag-inducing reflexes and yawns. I only need to read the word yawn or hear it said and it will actually make me yawn. If I see someone on television yawning, then I have to yawn too. Paddy once told me that serial killers don't catch a yawn as they don't have the empathy to trigger the reaction, which must make me a super-empath. Or highly suggestible. If I'm ever arrested for a murder, I'll just ask them to say the word yawn and I'll prove I don't have the killer instinct. I wonder how that would go down as a defence tactic.

The cling film was scrumpled up into a small plastic ball and there was some movement behind me and more rustling as Mr Breakfast reached back into his carrier bag. A moment later, the metallic sound of a can being opened and a long pull being taken from a fizzy drink. Followed by a stifled belch.

Sometimes, I really hated travelling on trains.

A tap on the screen partition caught my attention from a particularly knotty pivot table issue. I turned around and looked up. It was Kelly from HR.

"Hi Mena," she said, taking a few steps into the cubicle. "How are things?"

I smiled.

"Not so bad thanks, how are you?"

Anyone who knows me, knows that I will always try to say 'fine' to be as positive as possible, and that if I resort to 'ok' or 'not so bad' it usually means I'm feeling particularly frazzled. I should have an infographic I hand out to people with warning signs and handy things to know about me.

"Fine thanks. I just popped by to let you know that Naomi has been in touch to say she won't be in until Monday."

"Oh, OK." I seethed. "She didn't get in touch to let me know."

"She said you weren't picking up?"

"Well, I've been here all afternoon," I replied.

I reached for the phone and picked it up to check the dialling tone.

"It's working ok."

"Perhaps you were engaged," Kelly said in a reassuring tone, her head cocked to one side.

Naomi's just trying to make me look bad.

"Perhaps," I agreed, even though I knew I wasn't.

"She won't need a doctor's note as it's just under the threshold," continued Kelly, "but we might need to have a conversation about her absences. She's had a few recently?"

I nodded and sighed.

"Yes, a few, I was going to have a chat with her about it and a couple of other things when she got back," I explained, trying to sound supportive and firm, like any decent manager should.

"Well, if you need my support or want to talk it through, you know where I am."

"Thanks Kelly."

"No problem."

I watched Kelly retreat out of the cubicle and around the corner and gazed thoughtfully at the wall opposite. I would certainly have to take action now.

I swung around and added an online meeting for Naomi and myself for first thing on Monday morning when she was due to return and emailed the invitation. Enough was enough.

I decided to take the Friday off. I just felt like I needed to potter about for the day and get some jobs done in the house. I could tell that my work situation was getting me down and a day off from the daily commute would be welcome. Plus, Annie had invited me to join her and the kids at the play barn for a coffee. I'd never been to one before and wanted the chance to have a catch up. Jobs first though.

I quite like sorting laundry for the wash. There is something pleasurable in categorising colours and fabrics into different piles and reducing the laundry mountain into something more manageable. I wondered if the Sorting Hat in Harry Potter took a similar enjoyment in its work.

With a practiced flick of my wrist, I assigned socks, underwear and t-shirts into three separate piles. I was in the act of shaking out one of Paddy's comedy slogan tops when a knock at the bedroom window startled me.

I quickly turned to see the top ends of a ladder rhythmically shaking against the windowsill outside as someone made their way up the rungs. A melodic whistle floated up.

Oh no, the window cleaner.

In a swift, reflex motion, I dropped the t-shirt onto the bed and hurled myself face-first onto the floor under the window. My cheek pressed to the carpet and I slowly slithered my way over until I was pressed up against the wall.

My heart was pattering rapidly in my chest and I felt a genuine thrill of panic. I clearly had no option now, but to wait it out until he went back down the ladder. There was no way I could style out emerging from underneath the window like a demented jack-in-the-box. This was ridiculous, I always panicked when the window cleaner appeared at the window.

There was a thump and a wet, squelching sound and I could hear the soap being lathered onto the glass pane. The light flickered on the carpet as he moved backwards and forwards and an occasional grunt of effort escaped him as he reached and swiped.

My phone started to vibrate in the back pocket of my jeans. Marvellous. Soon Elvis would be blaring out about wanting more action and that might tip off my absurd behaviour to the window cleaner.

I slid my hand into the back pocket and quickly pressed the answer button. Paddy.

"Hello?" I whispered as quietly as I could.

"All right, Happy Harriet? Why are you whispering?"

"I can't really talk right now," I mouthed.

"Why not? What are you up to?"

Outside the window, the cleaner began to use his squeegee, whistling away.

"Is that whistling?"

"Look, I'll call you back in five minutes, OK?"

A loud clank of the bucket as the cleaner rinsed and squeezed.

"It's not the window cleaner again, is it?" he asked shrewdly.

"No," I said, clearly lying.

"Where are you this time? Hiding behind the door again?"

Paddy thought it was hilarious that I couldn't brazenly go about my own business when the window cleaner arrived. Several times he'd found me hiding: behind doors, in corridors between rooms and once, notably, in the bath with the shower curtain pulled across.

"Look, I can't talk now, I'll call you back in a minute. Bugger off!"

I ended the call – but not before I could hear Paddy's shout of laughter. It's all right for him, he couldn't care less about the window cleaner peering in. He clearly didn't have my cringe factor levels. I sighed and resumed my patient waiting.

Less than two minutes later I heard the window cleaner treading heavily down the rungs as he disappeared from view. My phone buzzed again. Paddy had sent me a meme of a person hiding in a washing basket. Very funny.

I slowly raised myself up onto my hands and feet and peeked out of the window. The ladder wavered and disappeared from sight. I waited another moment before standing up.

The doorbell rang, followed by the letter box rattling. I brushed my hands on my jeans and hurried down the stairs.

"Hello sweetheart! I wasn't sure if you were in or not," said the window cleaner with a wink.

"Oh yes, yes I am, just busy pottering around," I twittered, wondering if the wink meant he had caught sight of me and knew what I'd been up to.

"That's just £5 please," he said, unzipping his bum bag and looking at me expectantly.

"Just a sec," I turned back into the lounge and grabbed my handbag. I fumbled for my purse.

"I bet you must see all sorts, when you're doing the windows," I said for something to say as I flipped open the notes section.

Mr Window Cleaner chuckled.

"I certainly do, I should write a book! You wouldn't believe some of the things I've seen. There's nowt so queer as folk," he said, shaking his head at the goings-on of his fellow human beings.

"I can imagine." I handed over a five-pound note. "Here you go."

"Thank you kindly," he said, doffing an imaginary cap with his index finger.

I felt as though I was in a Dickens novel, sharing my largesse with the chimney sweep. I wondered what his character name should be, probably something like Jeremiah Squeegee.

"Bye!" I called out, before closing the door with a shove.

Next time I would be rational and pretend he wasn't there. It couldn't be too hard to do, surely.

I headed back towards the stairs to continue with my laundry duties. As I passed through the doorway, the landline began to ring. Suppressing a sigh, I turned back and picked up the phone.

"Hello?"

"It's Evelyn!"

The line went dead.

I pulled out my mobile and tapped the number into the landline handset, thinking again that I really *must* write down the number by the phone.

The phone rang twice and was picked up. There was a pause of several seconds.

"Morning Evelyn?" I prompted.

"Morning dear," came the reply, starting off in the distance and growing louder as she adjusted the phone to her ear.

"How are you today?" I asked, tracing my finger around the light switch on the wall while I waited for Evelyn to get going and tell me what she was calling for.

"Not bad dear. I'm in a bit of a pickle though."

My heart sank. I had so much I wanted to get through today and I couldn't be late to the play barn.

"Oh?"

"Yes, I could do with a bit of help with a couple of things that seem to have broken. Could you come and have a look?"

I wrestled with my conscience for a moment. I could pop over straight away and have a look before starting anything else, but then I didn't want Evelyn to get used to me being at her immediate beck and call for anything that wasn't urgent.

She's never that grateful when you do help anyway.

I immediately chided myself for being uncharitable. I was sure she did appreciate my help, she just never specifically said so.

Or I could make a point and do some jobs first before heading over to the play barn.

I had a vision of Evelyn sitting mournfully in her lounge, waiting for assistance with nothing to distract her but Homes under the Hammer. I decided to polish my halo.

"OK, I've got a minute now, I'll be over shortly."

"Right dear," replied Evelyn, before the audible click signalled that she had put her phone down.

I grabbed my keys, shoved my arms into my coat and pushed my feet into my patent pumps. With my mobile in hand, I released the catch on the front door and slammed it behind me.

I tried to think of the positives of the interruption to my morning as I strode along the pavement in the direction of Evelyn's bungalow.

I was doing a good deed for an elderly person who needed my help. The benefits of helping those in need to your sense of wellbeing are well-documented. It also meant that I got a walk out in the fresh air and got my heart rate up, contributing in a small way to my goal of increasing my appalling fitness levels.

I still felt irritated though and had a firm word with myself to get over it. Hopefully, it should only take half an hour out of my day.

I hurried up the path to Evelyn's bungalow, casting a glance to the left as the net curtains at Mrs Bay Tree's bungalow twitched. I was tempted to wave a cheery greeting but thought Evelyn's neighbour might not like to have been caught out snooping.

I rapped on the frosted window of the front door and stepped back. A moment later, Evelyn's outline appeared and the familiar rattling sound of the chain began. I tried to wait patiently as Evelyn clearly struggled to release the chain mechanism, punctuating her attempts with muttered exclamations and exhalations of breath.

Finally, the door jerked open.

"Morning Evelyn," I said, moving forward to step inside.

"Morning dear," she replied, stepping aside to let me through.

The familiar thick soupy atmosphere of gas fire heat and odour of boiled vegetables enveloped me in a cloud as I entered the hallway.

I shrugged off my coat and hung it on the hook by the door, next to the dog lead that had hung there for as long as I'd been visiting. Evelyn's little dog Dotty had died at least fifteen years ago, but her lead remained as a sad memento.

"Can you take your shoes off please dear, I had to sweep up last time after you came round."

I tried to fight off my immediate reaction of being offended and swallowed down my annoyance.

"OK then," I said in a brittle, cheery tone and slipped my feet out of my pumps.

"Bits of dirt and mud up the hallway..." she continued, as she turned and headed to the kitchen.

I pressed my lips together and followed.

"What's broken?" I asked, slightly more sharply than I would otherwise have done.

"It's this hoover," she said, reaching for her hand-held vacuum with a long pole attachment that was clipped to a charger on the wall. Paddy had installed it for her last year and of course that led to several months' worth of hero-worship from Evelyn about how talented he was.

She detached the vacuum and handed it over.

"I can't empty it and it won't suck."

I checked for the release mechanism and pushed the two red buttons together simultaneously. The lid came off with a slight click and a couple of dust bunnies made a bid for freedom and floated down to the kitchen floor lino.

"Careful!" barked Evelyn, "You're making a mess!"

I counted to three.

"Sorry, I should have opened it over your bin. If you can just move out the way, I'll empty it for you."

Evelyn shuffled to one side and I removed the swing lid from the top of the bin with one hand and then emptied the vacuum's contents in with the other. I swiftly clipped the lid back on and pointed to the two red buttons.

"You see Evelyn, you need to press these two red buttons at the same time and they pop it open." I did it again. "If you don't do it simultaneously, it won't do it."

Evelyn set her mouth in a line.

"It didn't work a minute ago."

"Here, have a go."

I guided her hands to the buttons and pushed them. The lid sprang open. Evelyn pulled her hands away.

"I know how it works, it just wouldn't do it."

"OK," I conceded and went to clip the vacuum back on the wall.

"It still won't suck though."

"Let me have a try. It might work better now that it's been emptied."

"You can try it on that dust you dropped on the floor," she continued.

I forced my voice to remain neutral.

"Good idea," I agreed and switched on the unit.

Evelyn stood back and watched with folded arms as I passed the cleaner over the floor.

"See, it's not picking up."

I kept the unit running and ran my hand by the motor where there was a rushing of air.

"Here look," I said, pointing to a circular hole. "There should be a bit in here to plug this gap."

I placed my palm flat against the hole and the vacuum changed sound and began to work.

"Have you dropped a bit somewhere? It will be a plastic circle?"

I cast my eyes around on the floor to see if I could see if a piece had dropped off and rolled away into a corner.

"I don't think that's it," said Evelyn. "I would have noticed."

"Look, feel for yourself that when you cover it up then it starts to suck."

Evelyn kept her arms folded.

"It's always been like that."

I sighed.

"Do you want me to take a look for it?"

"I think I'll wait for Patrick to take a look at it."

I frowned.

"I don't mind having a look."

"I'm sure he'll know what's up with it," she continued.

I wasn't in the mood for this.

"OK fine, I'll let him know when he's back from work, but he might not be able to come around until tomorrow."

"He knows best with things like this," said Evelyn, smiling to herself.

"Right, well I'll be off then."

I clipped the vacuum back on the wall and spun on my heel to head back up the hallway.

"Before you rush off," Evelyn called in a raised voice. "I've two bags of things to go to the charity shop."

Oh no. For such a small bungalow, Evelyn can manage to rustle up an impressive amount of stuff for her regular charity shop clear-outs. She can't bring herself to throw anything away, believing that even broken things or items with missing bits would be welcomed into any charity shop with open arms. Despite my frequent explanations that things like clothes with holes, recipe cards from the 1980s or biscuit tins with buttons and zips aren't really suitable, the tide of bits and bobs continues to flow. I've had to rotate which charity shops I visit so that I don't earn a lifetime ban.

"Why don't we leave them for today and Paddy can collect them tomorrow when he comes round to look at your vacuum, he can bring his van."

I moved off purposely towards the door. Look at me, with my assertive attitude.

"I want them out of the way today, they're in my way," countered Evelyn, trumping my poor effort easily.

"I'm sure you can manage one more day with them," I rallied feebly, knowing that we both knew I'd already lost.

Evelyn shuffled into the lounge and her back emerged a moment later as she dragged two bin bags with her.

"Here you go dear," she said, releasing the tied ends of the bags and stepping back. "Just a few bits, I'm sure they'll be useful to someone."

I was just as sure that they wouldn't be. I stepped forward dubiously and took the knots in both hands. A clanking noise issued from one of the bags and the sound of something like beads cascading followed. Goodness only knew what was in there.

"Right you are, I'll see Patrick tomorrow then. Tell him I'll have those biscuits he likes."

I had been dismissed. Evelyn nimbly stepped past me and opened the front door, pulling it wide to allow me past with my cargo.

I lifted the bags and shuffled out through the door. Something sharp and angular shifted in the bag and a pointed corner connected with my calf, causing me to exclaim. The bags were surprisingly heavy and cumbersome.

"Right, I'll be off then Evelyn," I said in a louder voice than usual. "I'll take all your stuff with me."

"Bye dear," was the response and the door closed with a click.

Bloody unbelievable. Thank you Mena, I appreciate it Mena, thanks for making the effort on one of your precious days off Mena.

I growled and set off down the path, bags swinging and shifting with every step. A hole emerged in the plastic and an acorn and a washer popped out and bounced down onto the path, before disappearing into the long grass.

Marvellous.

CHAPTER NINE

The Play Barn was hard to find, tucked away as it was on the back end of an industrial estate. "Cheeky Chimpz" looked like a storage unit from the outside, of the kind where bodies were found wedged into freezers by jaded detectives.

"Chimpz". I rolled my eyes. Why would they do that? It sets my teeth on edge and just smacks of trying too hard to be playful. There is a hairdresser in town called Kidz Cutz and I surreptitiously make a rude gesture at it every time I pass. Not that I have a child to take, but still, they've lost my business.

The tiny car park was rammed with people carriers and SUV's of all sizes and descriptions. Several had stick art cartoons on the back depicting their families, including pets. I pulled up and drummed my fingers on the steering wheel. I was already cutting it fine on time and I had no idea where else to park.

I looked up as a harried looking woman forcefully pushed open the tinted entrance door with her backside and backed out into the car park. She held a heavy looking car seat with both hands and a small toddler was hanging onto the seat handle, red in the face and wailing. A very bulky bag swung from her shoulder.

"Enough, Sebastian!" his mother bellowed.

The boy roared anew and screwed up his face and his mum jerked the car seat as she towed her cargo to the car. The baby seemed to be enjoying the ride, peering out calmly, in stark contrast to her enraged older brother. The mum glanced over to where I was waiting. I gave her a small wave and a small sympathetic smile and she nodded to acknowledge that she was leaving.

She deposited the hefty bag and the car seat on the ground by the rear wheel of the car. The toddler was hauled by the hand to the opposite rear passenger door and lifted bodily into the back, into his own car seat. A scuffle ensued as the toddler bucked and arched his back, kicking and screaming in his mother's face. I watched in awe as she demonstrated a well-practiced manoeuvre of pushing his hips back and flipping the straps over his flailing arms and into the release mechanism. Now that he was secured, his mum returned to the other side and hauled up the car seat. The baby's head bobbed and swayed as the mum opened the rear door and squeezed the seat through the gap, at a very strange angle. She ignored the thud of the door against the neighbouring SUV and her top half disappeared into the depths of the car for several minutes. She was doing something, but I wasn't sure what. There seemed to be a lot of adjustment going on and handing out and redistributing of items between the two tiny passengers.

After what seemed like an age, the mum's head re-emerged, slightly pinker than it was when it went in and she slammed the door with gusto. She picked up the bag and opened the boot, before laying the bag on top of the pram already nestled there and opened the zip.

What now? This is a military operation!

My patient and sympathetic waiting face was starting to slip. This was taking forever.

A brightly coloured plastic toy flew out through the open boot door and bounced with a crack onto the concrete.

"Sebastian!" barked the mum, picking it up and throwing it into the boot. "If you think you're getting that back, you've another thing coming. There are consequences!"

The mum then returned to the bag and disappeared elbow-deep into its innards, like a frazzled Mary Poppins. It seemed to contain a treasure trove of items that looked too big to fit in one bag. Nappies, wipes and a changing mat were all pulled out and deposited on the pram, before a small carton of juice and a pack of raisins were excavated. The mum took them round to the toddler's door.

"Here, have these and do NOT make a mess. If I see you squirting that at your sister again there will be no Cbeebies this afternoon."

Thankfully, there was no attempt to neatly repack the bag, everything was shoved in and the boot door slammed down.

Head down and without making eye contact, Sebastian's mum headed to the driver's door, before doing an abrupt about turn and re-opening the boot again. After another rummage, she pulled out her car keys and shut the door again and scurried back to get in and start the car. The reverse lights came on and the car backed quickly out of the space. It braked suddenly, before moving off with a squeal. I just had time to catch a glimpse of Sebastian peering out of the window, engaged in pushing raisins up his nose with great concentration.

Wow. I thought I had trouble getting Paddy organised.

I pulled into the space and turned off the engine, before reaching for my car lock. I'm never going to complain about the faff of taking it on and off again. It was a walk in the park compared to what I'd just witnessed.

I was momentarily stunned by the wall of sound that hit me when I pulled open the entrance door of Cheeky Chimpz. I took an involuntary step back and looked about in surprise at the size and space of the interior, nearly stepping into a mum coming through with her daughter.

"Oh sorry," I apologised, before stepping inside again.

The façade was most definitely deceiving. The interior was huge, with soaring ceilings and multi-level climbing frame areas the size of a sports hall. Over to one side was a baby and toddler section with a ball pool and slides and padded floors and blocks. Near the entrance was a packed coffee area, filled with mums and the occasional dad and grandparent.

I was dazed by the hive of activity and the assault on my senses and stood at a bit of a loss of where to go.

"Hello? Can I help you?"

I looked to my left to see a counter and a girl with henna red hair waiting and realised that everything else was behind a barrier that stretched the length of the entrance.

"Oh hi, sorry, I've never been here before."

The girl smiled and her nose stud flashed. I've always fancied a little jewelled nose stud.

"Have you got children?" she asked.

That felt like a bit of a personal question, considering we'd only just met. I paused for a moment, thinking about how to answer.

"Are you bringing a child in today?" she clarified, clearly wondering what she was dealing with.

"Oh sorry, I didn't..." I laughed. "No, I don't. I'm meeting a friend and her children. I'm not planning on using the facilities myself."

I laughed again at the thought.

"OK, that's fine. That'll be £4 please."

"Sorry?"

"That'll be £4 please. Adults and older children are £4 each."

I felt a bit thrown. I hadn't realised that adults had to pay for the privilege of taking their children to play.

"Oh right. I hadn't realised I'd have to pay. Just a minute, sorry."

I reached into my bag and felt about for my purse. My phone started to ring and I looked up apologetically, mindful of the mum waiting behind me.

"I'll just be a minute," I told the girl and then scooted myself and my bag further along the counter and pulled out my phone. It was Annie.

"Hi Annie, I'm just here."

"I know, I can see you! Look, I'm over by the baby bit."

I looked up and could see her frantically waving, Amy in her arms and Tom nowhere in sight.

"Hi! I'm about to pay, I'll be in in a minute."

"Yes, sorry about that, I'd forgotten that extra adults have to pay. I'll get you a coffee to make up for it."

"Don't be daft, it looks like you've had to pay a fortune to get in as it is. I'll be with you in a sec."

I hung up the call and waved over at her again and went back into my bag for my purse. I turned back to the girl at the counter, who was now dealing with the mum and her toddler.

"I'm telling you, she's two years old," said the mum, gesturing at her child.

"Have you got anything with you to say how old she is?" asked Miss Henna.

"Obviously not, I don't carry her birth certificate around with me," retorted the mum.

"Do you have her health visitor baby book, some parents bring those in?"

"No. She's two now, I don't need to carry that about."

"OK. It's just that she is very tall for her age and so we usually do need to see some form of proof of age."

"Look at me!" gestured the mum. "I'm 5 foot ten and her dad is nearly 6 foot 7. I can show you a photo if you are really going to push the matter."

She started to pull out her phone and scroll through photographs.

I had no idea that children could be carded going to soft play areas. Were they worried they were going to illicitly partake in illegal over-age activities?

"That's us together, you can see how tall he is," said the mum, leaning over the counter with her phone. "It's genetic."

"Right ok. If you can just put her shoes in this basket, I'll get you your ticket."

The girl had clearly given up on the challenge. The mum picked up her daughter's shoes and slapped them on the worktop.

Miss Henna eyed them up and couldn't resist commenting, "Big shoes for a two-year-old!"

The mum pursed her lips and narrowed her eyes.

"Well obviously, if she didn't have big feet she'd keep falling over! If you're going to make such a big deal out of this, you should charge by height and not age."

The entrance door opened and a manicured mum with

caramel and blonde highlights and a camel coloured long-length cardigan entered with two small children trailing along behind her. She made me think of a whipped cream frostino.

"Jo! Thank goodness," said the mum at the counter. "Tell this person how old Charlotte is."

"Oh, um, she's three isn't she?"

The tall mum almost exploded with frustration.

"You're her godmother! You should know her age! *Your* Olivia has turned three, you know Charlotte isn't having her birthday until next month, you're coming to the party."

There was an air of vagueness around the other mum, as though her languid air came at the expense of thinking about anything else much in particular.

"Oh yes," said Jo. "She's two then."

"And tell her how tall Michael is."

"Your Michael?" clarified Jo, looking puzzled. "I have no idea."

Tall mum was en route to a coronary.

"He's tall though isn't he," she prompted with some desperation.

"Well yes, taller than you."

Tall mum gave up.

"She's two," she re-affirmed to Miss Henna, who had clearly decided it was in the best interests of everyone to let the matter drop.

"OK then, off you go."

She clicked a release button and Charlotte and her mum went through the barrier.

"I'll get a seat in the café Jo, see you in a minute."

Miss Henna looked back over to me waiting with my purse.

"Are you ready to pay now?"

"Yes, here you go, £4. Does it matter how old I am, do I need ID?"

The answering smile didn't quite reach Miss Henna's eyes.

"Not today," she replied, through slightly gritted teeth.

The gate clicked as she pressed the release button.

"You can go through now."

"Thanks," I responded and headed through into the main area, towards Annie.

Annie met me halfway and we leaned forward to kiss on the cheek, slightly squashing Amy, who didn't seem to mind.

"Well hello! Welcome to your first soft play experience," smiled Annie, swinging the arm that wasn't holding Amy around in an expansive gesture.

"Why thank you," I replied. "But...Chimpz?"

I raised an eyebrow and emphasised the 'z' in the name.

"Yes I know, I knew if you knew that you wouldn't want to come, I know how weird you are about things like that. All these places have silly names, usually referencing animals, scamps and rascals. It's like nurseries. I quite fancy opening one called "Little Buggers" and seeing how that goes down."

I laughed.

"Has it made it into your book of business ideas?" I teased.

"Not yet, I'm still mulling it over. It would take a lot of outlay.

Come on."

Annie led the way over towards the café area.

"Where's Tom?" I asked, looking around to see if I could spot him amongst the darting children weaving in and out.

"He's made a friend with a boy called Riley. They're currently in the ball pool. We won't see him for a bit. He'll come back when he's thirsty."

We pulled up at a table with Annie's changing bag on the seat and a jug of weak-looking juice on the tabletop.

"This is ours, you have to get in early to get a table in the café in the mornings. The baby brigade come in early and head off soon after 12 to get home for naps before the toddler brigades come in again later in the afternoon. A £2 jug of juice is a great marker for saving a space."

I looked at Annie in awe.

"You know all the tricks, don't you."

Annie smiled and shook her head, her tawny waves bobbing. 'Artfully tousled' I would say, although I know that it's completely natural and takes ten minutes to achieve. Not that I'm at all envious.

"You pick it up. You soon learn that you don't order your hot drink until you've had a little play first, so that you're more likely to be able to sit down and enjoy it. And you order your lunch early at about 11 so you're not stuck waiting ages for it to come in the lunchtime rush hour from 11.30 onwards. Did you get parked ok?"

"More or less. I was lucky that a lady was just coming out when I arrived."

"It can be a bit of a scrum in the mornings if you aren't here first thing. I'll get the coffees, if you sit with Amy for a minute."

Little Amy was deposited in my lap and Annie grabbed her purse and headed off to the café counter.

"Usual?" she called back.

"Yes please!"

This was the second time in recent weeks that a small child had been entrusted to my care. Fortunately, Amy was quite used to me and didn't seem to mind.

"Well hello Amy, how are you doing today?" I asked conversationally.

Amy peered up at me. She had the most amazing eyelashes, very dark and very long. She smelt like a mixture of baby shampoo, banana and a slightly sour smell that I hoped was milk. She popped an index finger in her mouth, sucked it and reached up to touch my face.

"No thanks," I said, leaning slightly backwards. "I've already had a wash this morning."

Amy frowned and returned her index finger to her mouth. I glanced over to see Annie loading the cups onto a tray and balancing her purse alongside. She made her way back over and banged down the tray on the table and shuffled the jug to one side.

"Here you go, one latte to make up for you having to pay to meet up with us."

"Thanks sweetheart, you didn't have to though."

"Let me pop Amy in a baby seat."

Annie dragged a seat from the side, gave it a quick wipe down with a baby wipe and shoehorned her daughter into the seat. Despite the wipe, it still looked as though it had been host to a large number of small children. Annie noticed me looking.

"I know, it all helps build up immunity though," she smiled, taking out a small pot of something and opening it in front of Amy. "You soon get used to it at these places."

"I didn't realise they would be so hot on checking ages here," I said, picking up my drink and a teaspoon. "There's a mum over there was very insistent upon explaining that her daughter is tall for her age."

I used the teaspoon to scoop off some latte foam and sucked the spoon.

"Oh, it's to do with the age brackets."

I scooped another spoonful of foam.

"Age brackets?"

"Yes," replied Annie, ripping the end off a paper bag of brown sugar. "Babies up to two are one price and then it goes up after the age of two as they can do more."

"Oh right, I see." I laughed. "She was showing the girl photos of her husband and all sorts to explain her daughter has tall genes."

"These places can work out really expensive, particularly if you are coming along a few times a week. There's the entrance fee, the food and snacks, sometimes there are extra activities like go karts… Then again, if her daughter is really tall for her age then she must be fed up of having to justify it all the time. These places can be a nightmare."

Annie vigorously stirred her coffee.

"So. How did you get on with that girl at work yesterday?"

Now that I was here, I wasn't really in the mood to think too much about Naomi on my day off. I quickly gave Annie an overview, trying to make light of my annoyance that I was finally trying to take charge of the situation and had been thwarted in my efforts.

Annie, always a good listener, nodded at the right moments and looked interested as I talked.

Tom barrelled over and squeezed between the baby seat and the table to lay a sweaty little hand on his mum's thigh.

"Mum, mum!"

He grabbed her hand and gave it a tug.

"Come on, mum!"

"What's up Tom, do you want to show me something?"

"Yes!" he said, pulling her hand again.

Annie glanced over at me and raised an eyebrow.

"You know Tom," she said leaning down and speaking directly into his ear. "Auntie Mena hasn't been here before, why don't you show her instead? I'm sure she'd love to see."

Tom swung around and forced his way back past his sister and took hold of my hand.

"Mena, come," he commanded.

I looked over at Annie and mock scowled.

"If you don't mind," she said. "It'll give me a chance to feed Amy before we have something to eat, it's really hard lugging a baby around up there."

"OK, if you're sure you trust me with him. I'm not promising vigorous activity though."

"That's fine," she smiled. "You'll just need to take your boots off – stick them under the table here and I'll keep an eye on them."

I sighed and unzipped my ankle boots. Fortunately, I had put on a pair of presentable socks that morning that didn't have holes. I tucked the boots under the table and allowed Tom to take my hand again and pull me across the floor to the multi-level section.

Five minutes later, I was kneeling on a padded block, trying to manoeuvre myself up through a small hole to the level above. Tom's face appeared in the gap and he was beckoning encouragement.

"Come on Auntie Mena!"

The longline cardigan had clearly been a mistake. It kept tangling up and restricting my movements as I hopped, climbed and squeezed my way up through the levels. I was currently on the penultimate level and had just crossed a cargo net obstacle that was very painful on my sock-clad feet. I could tell I was flushed in the face and my hair was dishevelled.

"Just a minute Tom. Auntie Mena is a lot bigger than you, this is hard work."

I placed both hands on the lip of the hole and dragged myself up at an angle, skidding onto the floor like a crocodile sliding into a river.

"Oof!" I said and lay there for a moment to catch my breath.

Tom giggled and clapped his hands, before pulling at my cardigan to get me to keep moving.

"All right, all right."

I righted myself onto all fours and began to crawl in Tom's wake beneath what looked like swinging punchbags that were suspended from the ceiling.

"I'm going to shoot you dead!" shouted a high voice with startling emphasis.

I looked up to see a young boy sitting in a Perspex porthole, holding his fingers up at me like a gun.

"That's nice of you, thanks very much," I replied, shuffling forwards.

"Don't move! I'll shoot you!"

"That's not very nice is it," I said in my most reasonable grown-up voice, as I passed him.

"I'm going to splatter your brains and rip out your stomach," he continued.

Not if I get you first, you little psycho.

"Charming. But good luck with that," I muttered as I continued on my way.

"You stink and you're ugly!" he called.

What a delightful child.

I caught up with Tom at the end of the punch bag section, squatting next to a startled looking two-metre-tall inflatable penguin. How bizarre. There didn't seem to be an Antarctic theme anywhere else in the building.

"All right mate, you're hard to keep up with!"

He pointed past the penguin and my heart stopped.

We were at the top of a wavy slide, of the kinds you find on piers at the seaside. It dropped through all four levels of the activity zone, vomiting its passengers out into a padded space at the very bottom, near the entrance to the climbing area.

"Auntie Mena, slide!"

Good god.

"Um, I'm not sure that we're supposed to go down there, aren't you too small for this?"

Tom frowned and pointed back down again.

"Slide!"

"I'm not sure your mum would want you to go down here."

"Slide with me!" he insisted.

I hesitated. It was a long way down. I looked back the way we had come, past the assassin child, the hole in the floor and the numerous obstacles and challenges. I wasn't sure that I would be able to coax Tom back that way if he was set on going down the slide. I didn't have the negotiation skills or experience to deal with this situation.

I jerked sideways as a tiny girl, about the same size as Tom, came barging through, knocking me on her way past. Her Elsa from Frozen dress shed turquoise sparkles as she crawled to the top of the slide and plonked herself down at the top.

"Do you have anyone with you?" I asked hopefully, looking around but seeing no-one.

I might have been invisible. Utterly ignoring me, the girl pushed herself forwards with both hands and shot down the slide, her snowflake cape fluttering behind her as she flew. I watched as she skidded to a halt at the bottom, scrambled to her feet and ran back to the entrance again.

Well, if she can do it.

"OK then buster, let's do it together. You're not going on your own."

Tom seemed happy with this and trustingly climbed into my lap.

"Go, go!" he said, bouncing slightly.

"Ow, just a minute. We'll do it after three. Hang on a sec."

I pulled out my cardigan from under me and shuffled to the edge. It did look a very long way down.

"One, two, three..."

I held Tom tightly around his stomach with one hand and pushed off with the other. We jerked down a couple of feet and then stopped.

"Go, go!" Tom repeated, smacking his hands on my legs.

I shoved again and suddenly we took off, gathering pace as we hurtled down the slide.

"Ow!" I exclaimed as I was zapped with multiple static shocks.

I tried bracing my feet against the sides of the slide to slow us down a bit, but to no avail. Tom was shrieking with laughter as we sped faster and faster.

We reached the end of the slide and were propelled into the air, before I landed awkwardly on the padded mat with our full weight on my coccyx, through trying to keep Tom safe on my lap.

I carefully placed him on the floor and then rolled onto my face and groaned into the mat.

"Again, again!" Tom clapped.

"No chance, sorry Tom. Auntie Mena is feeling a little damaged at the minute."

I breathed in and out for a moment, trying to let the pain subside.

"Wheee!" I heard and a moment later, two small feet ploughed into my side where I lay prone, knocking any remaining stuffing out of me.

A child giggled and then jumped to her feet, calling, "It's

dangerous to hang around the bottom of slides!" before dashing away again.

Tom pulled on my arm.

"All right bud, I'm getting up now," I muttered and pulled myself up onto my hands and knees. Tentatively, I managed to stand up. "That's it for me for a few minutes though, let's go and find your mum."

Tom took my hand and escorted me out of the activity area.

I returned to the seating area and gingerly lowered myself down in a chair opposite Annie. Tom dated away like a minnow.

"Have fun?" asked Annie, with a definite smirk.

"No," I replied shortly. "It'll be fun, you said. You can play with the kids, you said. You didn't tell me I'd be risking life and limb."

"Oh, it's not that bad," laughed Annie. "It's good exercise."

"Not my kind of exercise," I grumbled.

"It's good practice for next weekend anyway."

I glanced at her, puzzled.

"Next weekend?"

"Tom's third birthday."

"Well obviously I know it's his birthday party. Aren't you having it at home?"

"No, it's going to be here. Much easier. Didn't I tell you?"

"I don't think so, I just assumed you'd be having it at home."

"You're bringing Paddy too, aren't you? Once the kids party is over we thought you could both come to ours for drinks.

The kids should be shattered so we might get some quality drinking time in."

I thought for a moment. Paddy would be horrified about the Play Barn but the thought of a boozy session with his pal Sam would probably outweigh the mortification.

"Sounds good, I'll let him know."

"We can even have a kitchen *supper*," she glanced slyly at me through narrowed eyes as I stiffened.

"That's not funny," I replied.

"Why do you hate the word supper anyway?" she asked, not for the first time.

"I don't hate the word supper. I hate the way it is used. Supper is a piece of toast or a crumpet and some hot chocolate before bed. It's a snack. "Supper" in that context," I said, using my fingers to encase the word in quotation marks, "is just a silly posh word for tea and it sounds really pretentious."

I shuddered to prove my aversion.

"Let's sit around the Aga, Clementine, and have a kitchen supper," I said in a silly, faux posh voice. "Ridiculous."

"Yes you are," giggled Annie. "You're such an inverse snob."

"Yes I am and proud of it too," I said, with a firm nod of my head. "Do you want me to bring anything?"

"We'll just order pizza," said Annie. "You can bring some booze if you like."

"Great, it'll be fun."

"Speaking of food, let's get these lunches ordered or the kids will be grumpy."

CHAPTER TEN

My weekend passed swiftly, with only one visit to Evelyn (to reprogramme her heating) and a pub lunch with Paddy. Monday morning soon came around. The day of the proposed big confrontation with Naomi.

I'm always less tolerant of the quirks and foibles of my fellow train passengers on the morning train into work, but today I was even more on edge than usual. Perhaps that was unsurprising. But I always say, show me a morning person and I'll show you someone with serial killer tendencies.

The train this morning was busy as usual. I joined several fellow commuters in standing in the aisle of the carriage, leaning my hand on the top of a seat to keep my balance.

"Not long now," I heard a woman say in the sing-song voice that is always used to address children. "Let me just find it on my phone and then I'll put it on for you."

I let my gaze drift along the ceiling of the carriage as I tried to marshal my thoughts and wake up fully. I didn't want to make accidental eye contact with anyone and risk having to interact with them.

"Here you go," continued the woman's voice. "Your favourite Moana song!"

I glanced down to the table at the side of me. A middle-aged mother was sat next to her toddler son and she pressed her mobile phone into his hands. Sat opposite them was a smartly dressed man in a suit and a young student tapping away on her laptop, frowning in concentration.

The phone startled into life, broadcasting a jaunty tune throughout the carriage. The toddler squirmed in delight and the mum smiled.

I waited for the earphones to be produced. Mr Suit was looking very irritated. The song continued to play, something about being welcome for something as far as I could tell.

The mum sighed, rummaged in her capacious bag and pulled out some earphones.

Thank goodness.

And proceeded to twist them into her own ears and sit back with a look of relief as she turned to look out of the window.

Mr Suit visibly balked, before looking accusingly at the small child, who was now singing along loudly and kicking his feet in time to the annoyingly catchy song. Thud, thud, thud went his tiny trainers against the supporting pole for the table.

Miss Student began to frown. A line of tension appeared along her jaw.

"You're welcome!" crowed the boy, now slapping his hands on the table in time with the kicks of his feet.

The vibrations finally caught the attention of his mother, who turned slightly and said in a raised voice – due to not taking out her own headphones – "Don't do that Oscar."

Naturally, little Oscar totally ignored her and carried on battering the table. If looks could kill, Mr Suit would soon be doing twenty to ten in the pen.

There was a brief moment of silence as the song suddenly stopped. The passengers in the immediate vicinity held their breath.

"Again!" chuckled the boy, quickly pressing his fingers to the touch screen.

The same song started up again.

You have got to be kidding me.

Over the next fifteen minutes, we were all treated to the same song on repeat with accompanying percussion. My head started to throb.

Miss Student abruptly shut down the lid of her laptop and glared at the mother, who was totally oblivious. No doubt listening to a podcast about being a wonderful parent or some such.

I jumped as Mr Suit suddenly slapped his own hands palm-down on the tabletop.

"That's enough!" he bellowed.

Oscar jumped, knocking the phone which – mercifully – stopped warbling. He blinked up at the man opposite, his eyes suddenly tearing. His mother frowned and turned to look at Mr Suit, who immediately began to bluster.

"How can you possibly think it's an acceptable thing to do, inflicting that noise on everyone? You've clearly heard of earphones, so kindly use them for your child!"

Oscar's mother reached up and removed her earbuds.

"Excuse me?" she said, her brows knitting together.

"I said, put those earphones in that phone or turn it off. How arrogant – or ignorant – do you have to be to think it's acceptable to subject everyone else to that racket?"

Good point well made.

I realised that I had stiffened and was holding my body rigidly.

I tried to breathe in deeply and relax a bit. It was very obvious that everyone else in the immediate vicinity was straining every sinew to look as though they weren't fascinated by the altercation playing out in front of them.

"It's only a children's song. I can't believe you're making such a fuss."

"What's that got to do with it? It's still noise pollution and not something I want to listen to. How would you feel if I decided to play my choice of music through my phone and just broadcast it to the carriage? Heavy metal?"

Mr Suit was working himself up into quite a temper and was beginning to gesture with his hands, not unlike a lawyer protesting his case.

"I quite like heavy metal," said the mother, narrowing her eyes and smiling thinly.

"But you won't have chosen to listen to it. It's about courtesy. Look at this young girl here…" he suddenly turned and waved at Miss Student, who flinched. "She's trying to work hard and concentrate and she has to put up with a fatuous song on loop!"

Oscar's mum's eyes flicked to the student. The student flushed and looked out of the window.

"So kindly turn it off or give him headphones. It's not difficult to realise you're inconveniencing everyone else just to keep your kid quiet."

The woman continued to stare at Mr Suit and we all waited to see what would happen next. After a momentary, tense stand-off, she reached out her hand and scooped up the phone.

"I'm sorry Oscar," she crooned in honeyed tones, "but apparently not everyone appreciates the Moana song. *Apparently*, it's too annoying to hear your favourite song, even though no-one else seems to be complaining."

I wouldn't make that assumption.

"I know," she continued brightly, "why don't we practice your counting?"

Oscar shuffled in his seat and turned to fully face his mum.

"Why don't you start counting up to one hundred? Nice and clearly now, I need to hear you're getting it right."

Oscar's mum smirked at Mr Suit, the smugness coming off her in waves.

"One, two, three, four, five…" began Oscar with gusto, nodding his head with each number.

Mr Suit scowled. He knew that he had been outmanoeuvred. He could hardly complain about a small child furthering his education.

"…seventeen, eighteen, nineteen…"

I sighed. The next twenty minutes were going to feel interminable.

I walked into the cubicle, pulled out my chair and sighed. My shoulders slumped. I was really not in the mood for a confrontation this morning, but never mind. I opened my drawer, dropped in my bag and shut it with my foot. This could be the first day of the rest of my managerial life, on a new footing and with increased purpose.

I sank down into my chair and pushed the power button on my PC. It began its torturous process of warming up and switching on. I pulled down the cuffs of my favourite shirt and straightened the collar. I had dressed carefully this morning, wearing my lucky work shirt and tailored trousers, rather than my usual everyday black jersey trousers or skirt. I wanted to feel professional and felt that by dressing like a manager I might feel more like one.

A faint noise emitted from my drawer and the desk began to tremble. Elvis again.

I retrieved my bag and managed to pull out my phone just before it cut off onto voicemail.

"Hi Annie," I said softly. I knew it was early and I was the only one on the floor so far, but old habits die hard.

"Morning lovely, how are you feeling today? All geared up to take charge?"

I could hear Amy crowing in the background and the sound of objects being dropped from a height.

"I suppose so," I said, trying to channel my inner positivity, although to be honest, I wasn't entirely sure I had any. It must be very well hidden.

"Come on, that won't do," cajoled Annie. "You need to believe in what you're going to say if you've got any chance of her listening to you."

"I know, it's just…"

"Just what?"

"What if I totally mess it up and she makes a complaint about me?"

"Well, why would she do that?" asked Annie, sounding genuinely puzzled.

"You know how tricky HR can be, what if I inadvertently get something wrong and she says I'm being unsupportive or discriminating against her or something."

Annie sighed.

"You need to get past this worry about getting things wrong. We're not at school anymore, the teacher won't put you in detention."

"I never had a detention at school," I said proudly. "Only a class one and that didn't count as it wasn't my fault."

"You see? That proves my point. Getting things wrong sometimes is just the way of the world, it won't bring about Armageddon. Don't be shackled because you're worrying about getting into trouble. Just stick to the facts – what she did, the impact and what needs to change. She can't really argue with that."

"I suppose," I muttered unconvincingly.

"What's the worst that can happen if you do get it wrong?" asked Annie with barely suppressed exasperation. "Tell me."

"OK. I handle it really badly, she goes off to HR and makes a complaint about me, they uphold it and I get fired. I can't pay my half of the mortgage, Paddy kicks me out and I end up on the street."

"Wow. OK, you really didn't need to think about that did you? Right Mrs Catastrophe, what is the best outcome that you can have?"

"The best?"

"Yes, what would happen if it goes perfectly?"

"I don't know," I frowned.

"Because you're not used to thinking of the glass half full, you're used to thinking of the glass being catastrophically smashed and empty with people bleeding to death from the shards…"

"Hey, steady on!"

I had to laugh though. She had a point.

"Well?"

"I suppose that she takes on board everything I say, she agrees that she is totally in the wrong, apologises and from now on has a personality transplant and is a pleasant and helpful colleague."

"OK! Not quite as extreme an outcome as the catastrophic scenario, but I'll make allowances for the fact that you haven't had as much practice at thinking of positive outcomes."

"Why thank you," I said, sarcastically.

"You're welcome. Now the reason for doing that, is to point out that both of those situations are pretty much implausible. You'll probably end up with something somewhere in the middle. But if you imagine both the best and worst, it helps you realise that both are unlikely and help you to be a bit more..."

Annie paused.

"A bit more...?" I prompted.

"A bit more rational," she finished.

Silence.

"Because let's face it, you can be a bit over the top sometimes."

More silence.

"I'm just trying to help," she said. "You just need a little bit of a reality check every now and then."

"Thank you?" I offered, once again the sarcasm was clear to hear. I think Annie operates on a different frequency sometimes though as she didn't seem to register it.

"You're welcome," she said, and I could hear the smile in her voice. "I hope it goes well. Just remember, you're in the right, you just need to stick to your guns. Don't let her push you around."

"OK, thanks. Well, believe it or not, I do actually feel a bit better for your pep talk, but I wouldn't give up the day job just yet if I was you."

Annie gave a throaty chuckle.

"Anyway, I have to go, got to get Tom to nursery. Good luck!"

She disconnected the call and I stared thoughtfully at my mobile, before muting it and returning it to my bag.

Preparation was the key. I pulled out the notepad with my plan of action and began to run through it again. If I stuck to that, the meeting was less likely to go wrong.

The floor began to fill up with staff. Some slouched in under sufferance, whereas others breezed through the doors with their heads held high and a smile on their faces. Needless to say, I had marked those people down as probable sociopaths. I would have to try yawning in their vicinity.

Although most people tended to get in earlier, our expected start time was 9am. I kept myself busy answering emails with one eye on the clock in the corner of my screen. 8.58am. Naomi should be in shortly.

My eyes flicked over my list again. Be prepared. Tick. Speak calmly and rationally. I would do my best. Express my disappointment. That shouldn't be too difficult. Outline the negative impact of her actions. State how things will be in the future.

I took a deep breath and smoothed down the front of my shirt. I could do this.

Fifteen minutes later, I was fighting against a rising tide of resentment and was gulping down my third cup of horrible instant coffee from the vending machine. I just wanted to get this conversation over with and the wait was making everything feel worse. I had felt relatively calm and in control at 9 o'clock. If Naomi took much longer, she might well end up talking to a jittery and deranged harridan who shrieked at her the minute she showed her face.

I slotted the empty cardboard cup into the rising tower that I was collecting for the recycling bin by the lifts. This was ridiculous, fancy getting so nervous about one difficult conversation. People have them all the time. Just because I had made it my life's work to avoid conflict at all costs, didn't mean that I couldn't change the habits of a lifetime. Conflicts are a natural part of life...

Naomi swept into the cubicle in a cloud of scent and swishy, newly highlighted hair.

I took a deep breath.

"Good mor..." I began.

Naomi dropped into her chair and swung around to face me.

"Mena," she stated firmly.

I was somewhat startled.

"Er, yes?" I managed. This was not how this was supposed to go.

"Can we have a meeting together? Now?"

She stared at me appraisingly and I noticed that she had new false eyelashes. I wrestled to regain control of the situation.

"Actually, funny you should say that, I have put in a meeting for..."

"Great, now?" she interjected, cutting me off. "Which room

have you booked?"

"Room 2?" I somehow managed to make it sound like a question, rather than a statement.

"OK, I'll see you in there," she said, standing up and swinging her bag over her shoulder.

As she disappeared out of the cubicle, I sat back in my chair and exhaled loudly. I felt like Dorothy after she emerged from the cyclone.

I couldn't help but admire Naomi's direct approach. In many ways she was much more suited to being a manager than I was.

I gathered up my notepad and favourite pen and headed off to meeting room 2 in her wake.

Naomi sat behind the desk with her hands folded on top, looking the very picture of someone who was about to put me through a job interview. She gazed at me steadily as I shuffled in, closed the door and pulled out a chair facing her.

"I hope you're feeling better," I began, as I sank down onto the seat. I was aiming for supportive and interested rather than feeble and toadying. I wanted to start this encounter off on a positive footing.

"Better? Oh, yes," responded Naomi.

"Good. I need to speak with you about…"

"So anyway Mena," Naomi interrupted me again, sweeping some lint off the table top with her hand as she leaned forward. "I think we can both agree that this relationship isn't really working."

I sat back in my chair and clasped both hands in my lap. If I hadn't been so surprised, I'm fairly sure my mouth would have fallen open.

"That's exactly why I…"

"I don't respond well to being micro-managed, I find it hinders my productivity."

"I don't micro-manage you," I squeaked, before clearing my throat and starting again in a lower register. "I give you a list of things that we need to get through and expect you to do them, that's hardly…"

"It's just not working out for me," she continued, as if I hadn't spoken.

I was beginning to wonder if she could actually hear me. Perhaps my voice is on the wrong frequency for her ears to pick up, like older people and high-pitched noises.

"Well, it's not really working out for me either," I responded, sitting forward again and starting to raise my voice. "You left me in a difficult position with those stationery accounts last week and I don't intend…"

"Anyway, it doesn't really matter now."

I trailed off, like a steam train running out of puff.

"Why not?" I asked in surprise.

"I've been offered a job as an Accounts Supervisor," she said as she rummaged in her bag and pulled out an envelope. "Big promotion, actually. This is my resignation letter."

She pushed it across the desk towards me.

"Oh right." This really wasn't how I was expecting the meeting to go. "Who with?"

"Bradleys on Deansgate."

They were a big firm with a much larger accounts department.

Although technically her job title would be the same as mine, she'd be managing a larger team and on more money. I felt kicked in the teeth, punched in the gut (or whatever other fight-based analogy you might want to use). I also felt a bit silly, sitting in my power outfit and totally outmanoeuvred. I could feel all of the nervous energy I had built up fizzing around me and curdling into resentment in my stomach.

"Well," I said briskly, twitching the letter off the table and standing. "I'll pass this on to HR then."

Don't say it, don't say it...

"All the best in your new role," I muttered, turning to open the meeting room door.

"Why thank you," replied Naomi, scooting to her feet and managing to get to the door before I could go through it.

I stood back as she swept through triumphantly and I once again followed in her wake.

The HR department is housed on the floor above. Their open-plan space at the end of the floor is beautifully laid out with most of the desks lining up with large windows that look out onto the bustling street below. They can actually see trees and sky from their windows, no fluorescent-bathed cubicles for them.

I approached Kelly's desk. She was absorbed in what was on the screen, typing furiously.

I paused for a moment.

"Knock-knock," I said, tapping the envelope onto the desk in time with my words.

Kelly's eyes flickered over to me and the frown switched to a smile.

"Good morning, Mena," she said, in tones that paid homage to Robin Williams. "Everything ok?"

She glanced at the envelope.

"An interesting development," I began, with a wry chuckle. "Naomi has just handed in her notice."

"Oh! OK... Has she got a new job?"

I pushed the letter over to Kelly.

"Apparently so. She's going to Bradleys, she's going to be an Accounts Supervisor."

Kelly eyed me shrewdly, before using her thumb to rip open the envelope and pull out the sheet of paper inside.

"That's a bit of a step up for her, isn't it?" she asked, scanning the contents.

"It is, yes," I said noncommittally.

"Funny that this happens just after she was off ill for a few days last week," she continued, looking up to give me a wink.

"Isn't it just."

"But maybe it might be a good thing for you and your section?" Kelly raised her eyebrow and looked at me appraisingly.

Good grief, everyone knows that I can't control Naomi and she doesn't do her job properly.

"How do you mean?" I asked hesitantly, hedging my bets.

Kelly shrugged.

"Just that a bit of a change might be good."

I didn't reply, I could feel a faint flush colouring my cheeks. I felt that this whole situation was not reflecting on me particularly well. There was an awkward pause.

"OK, no problem. I'll process this and let her know her notice period and copy you in on it."

"Great, thanks Kelly."

I turned and made my way to the nearest stairwell. I wasn't entirely sure how I felt about this latest development. I felt a bit cheated. I had spent so much thought and nervous energy preparing to challenge Naomi and now it had nowhere to go.

I shoved the stairwell door open savagely and gritted my teeth. I also felt as though Naomi had had the last laugh as well. I could just imagine her smug smile as she planned her exit.

I clattered down the stairs and instead of emerging on my level beneath, I carried on down the stairwell for another floor. The vending machine was calling to me, this called for desperate measures. An extra-large Fruit and Nut at least.

I settled back into my seat on the train with yet another sigh. Closing my eyes for a moment, I tried to relax my shoulders and took in a deep breath. Releasing it slowly, I re-opened my eyes and looked out of the window. The carriage gave a lurch and we started to move.

I reached into my bag and pulled out my phone and checked for messages. I jumped as a young woman with startling lilac hair swung into the chair next to me with a thump. She shoved her bulky holdall between her feet and unzipped the bag with a flourish.

I tried to sneakily watch out of the corner of my eye as she bent double and rummaged in the contents. She emerged a moment later and slapped an A4 sized notebook on her knee, before placing a small plastic pot with a lid on top of it. Inside was a lilac-coloured liquid that almost matched her hair colour.

Out came some cotton wool discs and a small box that seemed to contain some kind of kitchen foil.

I felt a sense of foreboding, this could not be good. Was it something to do with drugs?

The woman cleared her throat loudly and then began to rapidly pull-out pieces of foil from the box, lining them up on the edge of the notebook.

Next, the lid to the pot was removed and the sharp tang of pear drops filled the air, a horrible chemical smell that brought tears to my eyes. Deftly, the woman dipped a cotton disc into the liquid and then wrapped it around one of her fingernails, before topping it off with the foil in a twist. She repeated the process for all of the nails on one hand.

The stench was overpowering.

Why on earth would you do that on a train?

Little Miss Lilac cleared her throat again and started on her other hand. Dip, wrap, twist. Dip, wrap, twist. When she had finished, she manoeuvred the lid back on the top of the pot and clicked it shut with the heel of her hand.

"Tickets please!"

The conductor made his way up the train, swaying with the motion of the carriage.

Good, he'll have something to say about whatever she's doing.

He approached our seats, one hand resting protectively on the ticket machine that hung on a strap around his neck and nestled on his hip.

"Ticket please?" he asked the woman next to me, not seeming to register any kind of surprise about her Freddie Krueger nails.

The woman beamed up at him coquettishly.

"I'm sorry, I can't get into my pockets at the moment," she said, wiggling her fingers in the air to prove her point.

"Oh." The conductor looked slightly discomfited.

"It's in my top pocket though, you can reach in and take it out?" she suggested, not breaking eye contact for a second. She slightly moved her shoulder to indicate the pocket in her blazer that was situated over her left breast.

The conductor cleared his throat. Perhaps it was catching. Either that or the fumes.

"You're ok."

He looked up at me. I tried to communicate my disapproval of the nail bar set-up next to me through the power of extra-sensory perception. Surely he could smell the chemicals?

"Ticket please?" he asked instead.

I sighed and pulled my ticket out of my bag.

"Thank you," he said and nodded, before moving on to the next row.

Miss Lilac smiled a secret smile and sat back in her seat.

I scowled. Unbelievable.

CHAPTER ELEVEN

The door slammed just as I was tipping the dried pasta into the boiling water on the hob.

"Home is the hunter!" shouted Paddy from the lounge.

A moment later, his head popped through the kitchen doorway.

"Hello, hello," he said. "How's my little currant bun?"

"Evening," I replied, poking the spaghetti ends into the pan and swirling the water to stop the strands from clumping together. "Not so bad, how are you?"

"Fine, good day," he said, stretching his arms up over his head with a groan. "So how did the meeting with Naomi go?"

I hadn't bothered to message Paddy earlier in the day about what had happened. He rarely responds to messages and when he does it's usually a couple of words, which is not helpful at all. I wanted to talk it through with him properly in person. I was actually very impressed that he'd remembered about my Naomi confrontation without prompting.

"Well."

"Oh dear," he said. "That bad?"

I perched my backside on the edge of the countertop and folded my arms.

"You know how I'd planned out everything I was going to say and geared myself up to sort her out?"

"Ye-e-s-s…"

"Well, I didn't get to say any of it. She totally took over the meeting, told me our working relationship 'wasn't working out'," I used my fingers to visually illustrate the punctuation marks, "…and then handed her notice in!"

I could feel my indignation rising up, the frustrations of the day bubbling over at the re-telling of the story.

"So that's it! She's off to Bradleys to a better job than mine and she doesn't deserve it!"

I could feel self-righteous tears threatening and my voice had a decided wobble.

"Hey, come on," said Paddy, coming forward to give me a hug. "Look on the bright side, at least she won't be your problem for much longer."

I pulled back and swiped my hair out of my face.

"I don't want to look on the bright side, I want to be annoyed that she's got one over on me again, after being an utter nightmare to work with for the past year!"

Paddy shrugged.

"OK, so be annoyed."

"Sometimes you just have to let yourself feel angry or sad, not just focus on any positives and move along before you're ready."

Paddy raised both hands in a surrender motion.

"Fine, be annoyed then if it helps." He smiled. "And *then* be pleased that she won't be your problem anymore."

I swatted him on the arm.

"So, what's for tea?" he asked, peering over at the pasta.

"Is that it on the discussion?"

He looked puzzled for a moment.

"Is there more?"

I wish I lived in a world where everything was so cut and dried. I swear that Paddy walks around and the only sound going round and round his brain is a happy voice singing "la la la la la".

"No, it's fine," I said in a voice which made it clear it was very much *not* fine. "I'll thrash it out with Annie later. At least *she's* a good sounding board."

"Oh great, I'm out with Tony again later," said Paddy. "I'm going to get changed, shout me when tea's ready."

He leaned down, pecked me on the cheek and smacked me resoundingly on the bum before sauntering out of the kitchen. I stared after him and shook my head.

The bubbling of the pasta sauce distracted me and I hurried over to stir it with a wooden spoon.

A moment later, the landline started to ring.

"Paddy!"

No response.

"PADDY!" I yelled.

Still nothing.

"For God's sake!" I muttered, viciously banging the spoon on the side of the pan to remove residue and slamming it down on the counter. "Do I have to do every bloody thing around here."

I flounced into the lounge and pulled the phone off its base.

"Hello?"

"Patrick?"

"No Evelyn, it's Mena!"

There was a pause. I struggled heroically with the urge to exclaim in frustration and satisfied myself with rolling my eyes instead.

"Are you ok?"

"Can Patrick come round?"

"Not tonight Evelyn, he's about to have his tea and then he's off out with Tony."

"Oh I see. I'm glad he's going out and enjoying himself."

There was another pause.

"Was there something you needed?" I prompted, conscious of the pasta sauce simmering away in the kitchen.

"If you could come round. I've got something I'm not sure about."

"OK, it will be after tea though, in about an hour or so?"

"It's a shame Patrick can't come."

"Yes, isn't it, but he's going out tonight. So it's me or nothing I'm afraid."

I could hear the sigh down the line and swear I could feel the puff of air escaping the phone receiver.

"I'll see you in a bit then, shall I?" I said, as if to someone who was hard of hearing rather than simply awkward.

There was no reply and I realised that she had already gone.

I huffed and shuffled as I waited for the usual unlocking ceremony of Evelyn's front door. I often found Evelyn's attempts to open the front door amusing, but I was not in the mood today.

Eventually, the door swung open and Evelyn stood on the threshold like a budget Beefeater in a navy blue velour tracksuit, attractively accessorised with a red tabard with gold thread trim. She was just missing a bonnet.

I waited to see if she would greet me first. I pulled my cardigan together at the front to cut out the breeze and looked up expectantly.

Nothing. Evelyn stood staring back, as if I was a double-glazing salesperson about to start my patter. Surely she would break first.

I smiled uncertainly. Still nothing.

Maud emerged from her front door and called across.

"Coo-ee! Hello, love!"

I don't think I've ever heard anyone say 'Coo-ee' in real life before. I looked over, almost expecting her to be enthusiastically waving a handkerchief.

Disappointingly, she wasn't.

"Hi Maud!" I called back, smiling and nodding.

I looked back at Evelyn. I wondered if Maud could sense the Mexican stand-off taking place next door through the dusky gloom.

See, that's how you do it Evelyn, it's not that hard!

I cracked. Life is too short.

"Evelyn," I said, nodding again, but this time without the smile. If she was going to be rude, then so was I. I felt like a petty child, but part of me enjoyed it.

As if voice-activated, Evelyn nodded and opened the door wide. I took a breath and stepped inside.

That was weird.

"Hello dear. It's in the lounge," she said, closing the door forcefully behind me.

I headed into the first room on the right with Evelyn close on my heels. I hadn't been in this room very often, usually my duties were in the kitchen. I had certainly never been invited to sit down for a cup of tea on one of the floral swirled armchairs, or perch my feet on the tasselled foot-stool.

Unlike Paddy of course. He was regularly invited to sit down and put his feet up on his visits, before being plied with chocolate biscuits. And not just any old chocolate biscuits, the special ones that come covered in foil. Paddy found it all hilarious. Not that I'm at all resentful about that, you understand.

I had been so excited to join Paddy's family and inherit a

grandparent. I'd never had one of my own and had had rosy images of home-baked cakes and cosy chats over tea as we gossiped about the past and family history. I had fantasised that Evelyn would open up to me and reveal an exciting past in the swinging sixties, or a secret career as a novelist or code-breaker and she would see me as the granddaughter she never had. Unfortunately, nothing could have been further from the truth.

I looked around the small room. Despite the large picture window at the front which let in a fair amount of light, the room felt dark and gloomy. A traditional sideboard spanned the whole length of the room and was covered with a selection of fancy china and teapots, each piece resting on some kind of crocheted doily.

There was only one photograph on the wall and that was a framed photo from a couple of years ago of a bashful Evelyn enveloped in a bear hug by her beloved Patrick. The photo had been taken at our wedding and Paddy looked very handsome in his suit and was grinning from ear to ear. If you peered closely, you could see the flare of my dress and part of my arm. Not totally cropped out, but near enough.

By all accounts, Evelyn's marriage to her husband Derek had been an unhappy one. She never mentioned him and there were no clues that he had ever existed aside from the thin wedding band she still wore. Paddy's family weren't really into talking about themselves and their history. I love family lore and stories, but they just don't seem interested. Whenever I ask Paddy for details of their past, he just shrugs and looks as though he can't even begin to imagine why I'd be interested.

For once, the television had been turned off and it was a relief not to have the sensory assault of light entertainment television blasting at me.

Evelyn reached down to the octagonal occasional table placed precisely between the two-seater sofa and the armchair and snatched up a letter between thumb and forefinger. She held it out to me like an unpleasant piece of rubbish and wrinkled her nose.

"I can't make head nor tail of it," she said. "I wasn't sure if it might be important or not. Patrick is always saying you're good at letters and things so I thought you might know."

I momentarily basked in the glory of one of the only compliments I had ever received from Evelyn, even though it was a second-hand one and she didn't sound as though she quite believed it. I'd take whatever I could get.

I sighed quietly and shook out the letter. It was quite clear at first sight that it was a scam phishing letter.

"It's a scam phishing letter," I said out loud, skimming the text.

"A what?" she asked, brusquely.

"It's a letter where they try and get you to give them some money for something that doesn't exist or that…"

"I know *that*," she interrupted rudely. "I know what a scam is for goodness' sake. What's this about fishing? I didn't read anything in there about fishing."

She peered at me suspiciously. She was clearly doubting Paddy's assertion that I could read.

"It's PHISHING, with a ph not an f. That's what it's called when people try to hook you and reel you in and get you to part with your cash," I explained, as neutrally as I could manage.

Good luck with that by the way scammers, Evelyn is more careful than pre-redemption Scrooge.

"The best thing you can do with it is rip it up," I said, making a move to tear it in two.

"Don't do that! I'll use the back for a shopping list," said Evelyn quickly, plucking the paper from my hands.

"OK then. If that's it...?" I suggested hopefully, making a move towards the doorway.

"If you could just get me these bits from the shop..." Evelyn stated matter-of-factly, leaving no room for doubt that I would.

I frowned.

"Have you run out of things already?" I asked. "Paddy brought your shopping round at the weekend, didn't he?"

I knew he had, I was the one who had packed Evelyn's supermarket shopping into separate bags for him to bring around. Every week when we did our big shop, we always bought for Evelyn according to her instructions and dropped them off for her.

"There are a few extra bits I need," she said firmly.

"It would be handy if you thought about the whole week and then we can just get it for you when we do our shop," I said, more patronisingly than I would have liked, but honestly.

I didn't mind shopping for Evelyn at the same time as we did, but then having to go on additional – and in my view unnecessary – sorties was irritating to say the least.

"There are a few extra bits," she repeated, reaching into the pocket of her tabard and pulling out a list.

At first glance, I could see that there were at least fifteen things on there.

"Right, fine, I'll go now," I said through gritted teeth. "Are you sure that you have everything on there you want until we do another shop this weekend?"

"Oh yes," replied Evelyn, like butter wouldn't melt.

"Fine. But just bear in mind these will be more expensive from the Express, you'd save lots more if you put them on your big shop list."

I couldn't resist the parting shot and had the satisfaction of watching her blanch slightly.

"See you in a bit!" I called, spirits boosted and I set off down the path to the shop.

CHAPTER TWELVE

The rest of the week flew by and before I knew it, it was Saturday. The weekend of Tom's third birthday party at Cheeky Chimpz, no less. I had managed to persuade Paddy to come with me too, with the lure of drinks with Sam afterwards.

I stepped out of the car and slammed the door.

"Can you get the present off the back seat please?" I called through the closed window to Paddy, before swinging my bag over my shoulder.

Paddy fumbled about locking the steering wheel column and took his time opening the door. I ground my teeth.

"Come on, I've seen arthritic snails move more quickly than you!" I chided, trying to look as though I was making a joke, although we both knew that I wasn't.

"Steady on, it's a three-year-old's birthday party, I'm sure it won't be a problem if we're ten minutes late."

"More like fifteen by the time we walk there from here," I grumbled, watching him open the rear door and retrieve the present. "I knew we wouldn't get parked in that tiny car park, we should have left earlier."

"But we didn't, so what's the point in going on about it?" asked Paddy in his most reasonable of tones.

I wondered again what the grounds for extreme provocation were in manslaughter charges.

"Besides," he continued, "that's not a thing."

"What's not a thing?" I asked, completely bewildered and not in the mood.

"Arthritic snails, you can't get those. They're too gelatinous and don't have joints."

"Normally I would be suitably impressed by your use of the word gelatinous, but now is not the time. Get a move on."

I set off at a determined pace along the weed-tufted pavements. We had parked three blocks away from the play barn in the first available stretch of road without double-yellow lines. Paddy trailed behind me, doing a very good impression of casual sauntering.

"You did say Sam was going to be there, didn't you?" he called to my bristling back.

"Of course he is," I tossed over my shoulder. "It's his son's third birthday, of course he'll be there."

"Will there be beer?"

I ignored him and continued thumping along, skipping over a patch of broken glass fragments outside a scrap metal merchant unit.

"Mena? I said, will there be beer?"

His footsteps sped up and he scurried alongside me.

"Don't be ridiculous, can you imagine it's a good idea to sell beer at a children's play barn? Lots of boozed up parents wrestling in the ball pool and competitively racing down the slides? You'll have to order an Americano and live dangerously."

I took pity on his crestfallen expression.

"But we're going back to theirs after, remember, so we'll have a few drinks there. This is for the little ones."

He visibly cheered up.

"Here we are."

We turned into the Cheeky Chimpz car park and skirted around several illegally parked cars, one of which was mostly blocking off the entrance door.

"Now just be prepared, it's a bit noisy in here."

I swung open the door and we headed inside.

"Oh, shit!" exclaimed Paddy, looking slightly terrified as the wall of sound hit him.

I had thought the noise was impressive last time, but on a weekend it was even more amplified. Throngs of older children had joined the baby and toddler clientele and swarmed in packs, hanging off equipment and shrieking at each other.

"It's ok, just follow me," I said reassuringly, taking him by the arm.

Miss Henna stood behind the till. I wondered if she ever went home.

"Morning, do you have kids?" she asked, without fully making eye contact.

"Bit personal, isn't it?" Paddy whispered in my ear.

"Honestly, she means have we brought any to play!" I said in the patronising tones of someone who knew how the process worked.

"Just this one," I replied, gesturing at Paddy. "I haven't brought his baby book though, will we have to pay the adult's rate?"

Miss Henna fixed me with a look that filled me with shame.

"I'm so sorry," I muttered. "Just two adults please."

Clearing her throat, Miss Henna tapped into the till.

"That will be £10 please."

"£10? But it was only £4 an adult the other week!" I exclaimed.

"Prices change on a weekend," replied Miss Henna, curtly.

Paddy placed the blue gift bag on the counter and I slapped the birthday card next to it as I went to open my bag.

"Oh, are you here for the party?" she asked.

"Yes, Tom's party," I replied.

"Oh well, there's free entry for adults going to the party," she said. "Just go on in."

The door-release mechanism clicked and Paddy and I collected the birthday paraphernalia and hurried through.

"Thank god for that," whispered Paddy. "Ten quid just to come in here!"

"Shush," I muttered. "Look, they're over there."

I waved at Annie and headed over, Paddy in tow.

"Hello lovely," I said.

"Hi!" she responded, reaching around me for a quick hug and a pat on the shoulder for Paddy.

She was fussing around a table that was loaded with brightly coloured gift bags and presents, trying to add a couple more to the pile without starting a landslide.

"Here's ours," said Paddy, leaning forward and dropping the bag underneath the table.

"Thanks Paddy," smiled Annie.

"Like he even has a clue what it is," I muttered in Annie's ear.

"Where's Sam?" asked Paddy, looking around slightly anxiously.

"Don't worry, he's in the party room checking everything is ready. Go and join him if you like, it's over there."

Annie pointed to a door set in a wall which was festooned with birthday banners and balloons.

"Just take your shoes off first, you can leave them under the table."

Paddy needed no further invitation and whipped his shoes off and disappeared, not even pretending to look out for the birthday boy.

"How's it going, is there anything I can do?" I asked.

"Not really, that's one of the good things about having a party somewhere like this, they do the food and all the mess, you technically just have to schmooze a bit and that's it. I think everyone is already here, we've got these two tables for the parents."

"I'm so sorry we're late, I just can't get Paddy moving sometimes and then we had to park miles away and walk."

"Oh, it's fine," replied Annie, waving her hand dismissively. "You haven't missed anything, only fifteen minutes less time in the ball pool."

"Paddy will be gutted," I grimaced. "That's his favourite bit."

"Hi Annie," said a voice behind me. I turned to see a small, pinched looking lady holding a large and florid baby. They looked as though they might actually weigh the same.

"Hi Ingrid," replied Annie with a smile. "Mena, this is Ingrid, her son is in Tom's nursery class. Ingrid, this is my old schoolfriend Mena."

We exchanged nods.

"I'm just checking that you've got Toby's vegan option for the party food. I know I texted it in the RSVP but…"

"Absolutely, no problem. He has his own platter ready to go, I've checked."

"Great, thank you. I always think it's best to make sure."

"Of course! I hope he enjoys the party," said Annie. "Sugar-free juice jugs on the table, help yourselves."

Ingrid nodded and wandered away, swinging the baby on her hip.

"Nice lady," muttered Annie, "but that Toby is a bloody nightmare. He's always taking chunks out of the other kids, Sam has a theory that he's rebelling against his vegan lifestyle. It can be so difficult being nice to other kids' parents when they've been utter shits to your own. Toby left visible teeth marks on Tom's arm the other week."

I was horrified.

"Bloody hell, it's like Lord of the Flies! I didn't think they started like that so soon?"

"Oh, don't kid yourself, they can be utterly vicious. That mum over there with the red hair?"

I took a peek.

"I saw her little girl hold another child's hand in a cupboard and slam the door on it the other week."

I gasped.

"And that dad there in the checked shirt and baseball cap?"

I casually swung around and scanned the tables

surreptitiously. Daniel Craig would have been proud at my espionage skills.

"Yes?"

"His little darling raked his fingernails down the face of another kid a few months ago, left big scratches that didn't go for weeks. Caused a huge fuss and a memo to all parents about keeping nails short. It was even worse because the victim was having his passport photo taken that afternoon. It did NOT go down well."

I felt shaken.

"Don't worry, I believe it's quite natural and not necessarily a sign of psychopathy."

"Oh."

"Am I putting you off yet?" she laughed.

"I've never been 'on' the idea as you well know and you're not helping! I'm going to get a hot drink, do you want anything?"

"Ooh, a strawberry and blueberry smoothie would be lovely thank you, I've got more chance of drinking that than something hot."

"No probs."

I levered my shoes off and headed over to the coffee bar. As I passed a small child in a grimy highchair I felt rather than heard a crunching sound underfoot. I lifted my foot and checked the underside of my sock to see the ground up remains of a cheesy Wotsit. I wrinkled my nose and tried to wipe my sock backwards and forwards on the floor to dislodge the bulk of it. The toddler peered up at me and offered me another one from its encrusted fingers.

Not today, thank you.

I shuddered and joined the back of the queue behind two mums, one of whom was carrying a tiny child. The little girl was dressed in a red romper suit with white polka dots and had a matching hair band complete with bow. I was impressed. I had reached my thirties and I still couldn't manage to accessorise. This child had it down already.

"And have your stitches healed yet?" asked the mum's friend, in a concerned voice and with her head tilted on one side.

It never ceased to amaze me how new mums could discuss the most personal of business quite openly in public. Perhaps once you've squeezed an object out of your vagina in front of an audience, you lose any inhibitions you may have had.

"Yes, not too bad thanks," replied the child's mum. "Still a bit sore but getting there. How are you getting on?"

"Oh fine, still no sleep, but what can you do?"

The friend laughed, slightly too manically and with a definite lip wobble. I turned and studied the chalked menu board on the wall.

"Oh look, here's Laura. I haven't seen her in months, have you?"

"No, not since before Isla was born," said the mum, patting her little daughter's back.

"Hello! I haven't seen you two in ages, how are you?" breezed Laura (I presume), giving a hug to the friend's mum and a squeeze on the shoulders to the other one. She then manoeuvred herself next to them, firmly in the queue.

Cheeky cow!

"I see you've had the baby, last time I saw you you were ready to drop! Let me have a look, oh what a beautiful little face."

Laura was not only a sneaky queue-jumper, she was also one of the least sincere people I've ever seen. She set my teeth on edge.

"Yes, that's right," smiled the mum proudly, turning so that Laura could get a better look.

"And what's his name?" continued Laura.

There was a terrible pause.

I turned to look on with blatant interest.

"I'm sorry?" said the mum.

"Your baby," gestured Laura to the sleeper on her shoulder. "What did you call him?"

The new mum took a breath.

"It's a girl."

"It's a... Oh I am sorry! She just looks..." blustered Laura.

It was fantastic.

"She has a bloody bow on her head," hissed the mum. "What more do you want?"

"Oh, she's... beautiful." Even Laura couldn't style this out. "Just beautiful. Anyway, lovely to see you."

Laura lifted her head and walked past the rest of the queue to the back. The mum's friend was valiantly striving to keep her face straight and look sympathetic at the same time.

"She always was a bitch," she muttered consolingly.

"Here you go, one smoothie," I said, plonking the plastic cup with a straw on the table next to Annie.

"Thank you," sighed Annie, grabbing it and taking a big suck.

Amy had appeared and was ensconced on Annie's hip,

gumming on tendrils of hair.

"Hello gorgeous!" I said, leaning forward and blowing a raspberry at her. Amy giggled.

"Not so gorgeous at 3am this morning," said Annie, wryly.

"Oh dear," I sympathised, feeling smug in the knowledge that the only thing that bothered me in the night was Paddy's snoring and that could be swiftly remedied with a well-placed elbow.

I reached for my coffee and took an appreciative sip.

"At least they do good coffee here," I murmured. "None of your instant rubbish, a proper coffee machine and everything."

"They have to keep the mums happy somehow," replied Annie. "Quality coffee, smoothies, herbal teas. They want to feel they're treating themselves in some way, even while they are covered in dribble and bits of food."

"Speaking of which," I said, showing the sole of my sock to Annie.

"Wotsits?" she asked.

I nodded.

"You soon learn to keep your eyes open in these places. I've trodden in all sorts. And you really don't want to know what's in the bottom of the ball pool. The lost treasure of Atlantis could be hidden in there, although in my experience it tends to be treasure of a totally different kind."

I made a mental note not to go into the ball pit. If required, I would send Paddy in instead.

"Sam once lost his wedding ring in there. Before he found it, he turned up several dummies, a sock and a used nappy."

"A what?"

Annie nodded.

"Yup, a used nappy. And I once knelt in some baby sick at the top of the toddler slide. Occupational hazard."

I felt a bit ill. Paddy might be a messy house companion but at least he kept most of his bodily effluence in the right places.

Sam and Paddy appeared, looking pleased with themselves.

"The party room is all set up. They're going to do the announcement in a minute."

"Great," said Annie, handing Amy over to her dad. "We'll just finish our drinks and be right over."

The speaker system came to life and invited all guests at Tom's party to head to the Party Room.

A number of mums and dads began to collect their belongings and head towards the decorated door.

"Drink up," said Annie. "We're not allowed to take hot drinks across the play area. Health and safety."

"Fair enough." I drained my cup and manoeuvred my way out from the table.

"It'll be over before you know it. An hour in the party room for food and a mini disco and then another half hour of free play before everyone goes. Then back to ours for some actual fun."

Annie rubbed her hands together and looked decidedly impish.

"Paddy can't wait for that. He was very disappointed there wouldn't be a bar in a play barn!"

Annie laughed.

"Poor wee soul. Can you imagine the carnage?"

"That's what I said," I snorted.

A young toddler skittered past us, wearing just a t-shirt, his mini tackle flapping as he ran.

"What the...?" I managed, looking aghast as he ran over to a group of women and sat – on his bare bottom – on the coffee table.

"My advice is not to look," whispered Annie. "You see all sorts here. Come on, or we'll miss the free for all. If you can just help me take the presents across..."

I followed Annie across the floor into the Party Room. The party guests were lined up either side of a long table, perched on benches. At the head of the table a very proud looking Tom sat on a carved throne, wearing some sort of crown. Parents leant against the walls behind their children, ready to assist at a moment's notice like casual silver-service waiting staff on a day off.

I helped Annie stack the gift bags and boxes in a corner of the room.

A slightly harassed-looking young girl in a play barn t-shirt ran backwards and forwards through a side door, bringing platters of finger food and bowls of crisps. Each child had a paper plate, a napkin and a small cup of red juice. The tension was intense. It felt like the start of an important sporting event.

"OK everyone, dive in!" called the girl, plonking the last bowl of mini sausages down on the table.

Immediately, a number of little hands shot out and began to grab. The parents stepped forward and began to slip sandwiches and cucumber onto plates to go with the more appetising treats selected by their children.

"Not you Toby!" came Ingrid's shrill voice over the sound of the hubbub. She leaned forward and wrestled a mini picnic egg from his grasp. It took a lot of effort. "Look, here's yours!"

The girl emerged from the door again with a paper plate covered in clingfilm.

"Sorry, here's the vegan plate," she said, swiftly unwrapping the plastic and placing the plate in front of a less-than-impressed Toby, who was giving his neighbour's plate the side-eye.

After a few moments, the chaos subsided and the dads leaned back against the walls with folded arms, whilst the mums hovered over their children, encouraging and chiding. I sidled over to Paddy and Sam, who were having a giggle over something. Amy's head lolled on her dad's shoulder as she fought off sleep.

"All right boys?" I asked.

"Not so bad," replied Sam. "How are you enjoying your first play barn party?"

"It's different," I smiled. "It's not every day you see someone sitting on a coffee table on their bare bum, but hey, I'm open minded."

"Yeah, sorry about that, I should restrain myself," said Sam.

Paddy barked with laughter.

"Seriously though, it all goes on in these places," Sam said.

"So I believe." I pulled a face.

"Not tempted you to change your mind?" Sam asked Paddy.

Paddy pulled a horrified face.

"Not in the least mate. You can do it for the both of us."

The frantic sound of collective chewing abated and the girl came back to clear away the plates into a bulging bin bag. As if they had been given a secret signal, several parents leaned forwards and began gathering handfuls of crisps and picnic food for themselves from the platters and bowls.

"Help yourselves," said Sam. "I would say it's a shame to let the untouched food go to waste… Well, it might have been touched a bit and put back again but that's a risk you have to take."

"You're ok, thanks," I muttered. My love of a buffet didn't extend to ones that might have been fingered by unwashed little hands.

"Don't mind if I do," said Paddy, moving over to the table and returning a moment later with sausage rolls, crisps and mini pizza slices in his mitts.

The table cleared, a teenage boy appeared from the side door and clapped his hands with enthusiasm.

"Okay guys! Time to get your best singing voices out for the birthday boy!"

Tom perked up and straightened his crown.

The teenager moved towards the sound system and pushed a button. A very tinny and cheesy version of Happy Birthday burst out of the speakers. The boy wagged his hands like a conductor.

"Haaaaaaaappppppppppyyyyyyyy…" he began to get the kids started and the buffet server appeared once more with a tray carrying a huge birthday cake.

Annie sidled up next to me.

"What do you think?" she asked. "I think it's turned out quite well."

"Is that…?" I trailed off.

It was an impressive cake, with a long, lit candle sticking out of the top of a poo swirl.

"Tom wanted an emoji poo cake. Looks cool, doesn't it?"

"Erm..."

Paddy was in hysterics next to me.

"I thought it was actually a good idea," continued Annie, "it's an excuse for lots of chocolate frosting. And who doesn't love chocolate cake?"

"Quite right," spluttered Paddy, cramming more crisps into his mouth.

The recorded song finished with a fanfare and the children finished a few seconds later, woefully out of time with the music.

"Three cheers for Tom!" called the teenager. "Hip hip!"

Three cheers were dutifully called and Tom pursed his lips and enthusiastically blew out the candle, spattering one edge of the cake in candle wax.

"Hurray!" shouted the compere, before signalling for the cake to be taken away. "Now, who's up for a bit of dancing?"

Twenty tiny people scrambled off the benches and moved to a patch of floor beneath a glitter ball, well-versed in what comes next. The play barn pair quickly moved the benches and trestle table against one wall.

"OK, I'm Gavin and I'm going to be your DJ for the next forty-five minutes. So let's get dancing!"

I admired his enthusiasm. He reminded me of a young Stephen Mulhern.

Gavin headed back over to the sound system and pushed a few buttons. Music blared out again and the majority of the party guests began jigging up and down.

I looked at Annie in dismay.

"Isn't that song…"

"The 'I'm Horny' song? Unfortunately, yes."

The toddlers were all determinedly wiggling and stamping.

"Isn't it a bit…inappropriate?" I muttered out the side of my mouth.

"Probably, but the kids seem to like it and they play it at every party, along with 'So Sexy in the Club' and 'Don't you wish your girlfriend was hot like me'. The kids don't have a clue about what it means and the dads usually think it's hilarious."

I glanced around the room and saw that several dads were indeed smirking. One or two mums looked disapproving, but the majority were just chatting amongst themselves.

One three-year-old girl in a very prim party dress and satin bow in her hair was twerking against a visibly terrified boy in a Minecraft t-shirt.

"OK, if you're sure."

"It's fine, you soon get used to it," smiled Annie.

Sam deposited a sleepy Amy on his wife and turned back to Paddy to continue an animated conversation that involved lots of arm-waving.

"I can't believe you've got a three-year-old now," I mused, watching Tom powering around the dance floor like an aeroplane. "How the hell did that happen?"

"I know!" exclaimed Annie. "I don't feel like a responsible mother of two."

"That's because you're not one, to be fair," I countered.

"Very funny," she laughed, nudging me with her elbow. "I try my best."

"Well, they're both still alive and your house is still standing so you must be doing something right."

"Too bloody right, there's a lot to be said for that."

Paddy sidled back over to us and I knew what he was going to ask before he even opened his mouth. So, apparently, did Annie.

"The disco is nearly finished, then it's half an hour of free play. For the *kids*," she clarified. "Then it's time to go back to ours."

He grinned and headed over to Sam, where they both started to do silly dancing to the Baby Shark song.

"He's such a child," I said, shaking my head apologetically.

"And Sam isn't?"

I looked over to see Sam trying, and failing, to do the worm. Rather him than me on that floor, with all the crumbs and rubbish from the party food.

"That's why they get on so well," I agreed.

"As soon as the disco is over, we'll get them ferrying the presents to the cars, that'll keep them busy until it's time to go."

"Sounds like a plan."

A sudden vibration in the back pocket of my jeans distracted me.

"Oops, just a sec."

I fished out my phone to see Evelyn's name displayed. I sighed.

"Paddy's nan?"

"Yes, Evelyn. She doesn't normally like calling mobiles as it's expensive."

I tapped to answer and moved away towards the doorway.

"Evelyn? Are you ok?"

"Is Patrick there?"

I looked behind me to see Paddy doing a very bad impression of a robot dance.

"We're out with friends at the moment, he can't come to the phone," I said loudly, as if talking to a child. "Are you ok?"

"Oh. Just tell him I called."

"OK, we won't be back until late tonight though, can he come round tomorrow?"

If he's in a fit state, I thought to myself.

"Right dear."

And she was gone.

I sighed and headed back to Annie.

"Problem?"

"I don't think so, she just said to tell Paddy she called. She won't speak to me unless she can help it."

Annie shrugged.

"Can't be that important then. Send him round in the morning."

Gavin interrupted by clapping his hands loudly.

"Did you enjoy the disco everyone?"

Twenty small children and two husbands cheered enthusiastically. I frowned over at Paddy who gave me a wink.

"Great! Well, half an hour free play and then it's time for your goodie bags."

The little guests were well-versed in the schedule of play barn party activities. As one, they stampeded out of the room and back into the main play area, followed swiftly by their parents, the majority of whom headed straight to the café area. Within a few moments, the detritus from the party and a slightly over-heated atmosphere were the only indicators that the session had taken place.

"Right! Boys, I've got a job for you," commanded Annie.

Paddy was in a cheerful mood as we headed back towards the car.

"That was a bit of a laugh," he said.

"Glad you enjoyed Tom's third birthday party," I replied sarcastically.

"What?"

"About yours and Sam's level," I continued, flashing him a smile to take out any sting.

"That's about right," he agreed.

"Evelyn rang by the way, she wouldn't leave a message. Just said to tell you she'd called and I said you'd go round tomorrow."

"OK."

"I would say that I don't know why she phones me instead of you, but of course it's because I always answer my phone and you never do."

"I'll go round tomorrow, I need to take her shopping anyway."

We reached the car and I swung into the passenger seat as

Paddy climbed in the driver's seat.

"You put the drinks in the boot, didn't you?" I asked, realising that I had forgotten to remind Paddy in the rush to get out.

Paddy looked across at me from the driver's seat with an 'are you crazy?' look.

"Of course, I never need reminding when it comes to the drinks," he answered, earnestly.

Of course not.

Twenty minutes later, we pulled up outside Annie and Sam's house.

"It's just us, isn't it?" asked Paddy, engaging the handbrake.

"Yes, thank goodness," I responded, reaching into the footwell to grab my handbag.

I wasn't in the mood to small talk with people I didn't really know. I was already exhausted from the number of people at the Play Barn. The older I got, the less inclined I felt to make chit chat with people I probably wouldn't be seeing again.

I started off up the path. Tom's bright little face popped up at the bay window and he waved enthusiastically, before disappearing again.

"Hey, come and help!" called Paddy.

I stopped, turned and headed back to the car, where Paddy had the boot open and was reaching into its depths.

"Why, how much did you bring?" I asked.

"Just the essentials," he said, his voice muffled as his head was out of view.

I peered inside.

"Good grief, Paddy. It's a drinks night, not a weekend away," I exclaimed.

"You never know with these things, it's best to be prepared," said Paddy, emerging triumphantly. "You take the wine and I'll bring in the beer."

I pulled out a carrier bag containing four bottles of wine and watched as Paddy manoeuvred what looked like a shrink-wrapped pack of twenty cans of beer.

"Oh, just a sec. You can fit the whisky in there as well," he said, dropping a bottle of Laphroaig in with the reds.

I shook my head and made my way back up the path. Sam was stood at the door, eagerly looking past me to see where Paddy was.

"He's just bringing half the brewery," I said, tossing my head towards the car. "If you'll excuse me..."

I squeezed past him and headed into the house.

"In the kitchen!" called Annie.

I made my way down the hallway and emerged into the sunlit room at the back of the house. I plonked the carrier bag down onto the table, the action accompanied by a melodic clinking noise.

"Ooh great," she said, reaching in and pulling out one of the red wines. "Shall we start with this one?"

She waggled a bottle of Rioja at me.

"Yes please," I replied, pulling out one of the bar stools and perching on the edge. "Paddy is on his way in with his supplies."

In no time at all, Annie had pulled the cork, taken down two glasses from a high cupboard and produced a bowl of fancy crisps.

"Here you go. I can have one glass before the kids go to bed and then I'll have some more when they're upstairs and settled."

Paddy staggered into the kitchen and dropped the beers onto a side counter. Sam followed and ripped the wrapping, extricating several cans and shoving them into the fridge.

"Here, these ones are chilled," he said, taking two bottles from the fridge door. "Follow me, my friend!"

Sam marched off to the front room, waving the bottles over his head, closely followed by my husband.

"Yes, let's go into the lounge," said Annie. "Tom's in the process of opening his presents and he won't be happy if we don't watch him."

Annie swiftly poured two generous glasses and set off after Sam and Paddy.

"Bring the crisps!" she called back over her shoulder.

Following on behind, I stopped on the threshold of the lounge doorway and took in the chaos.

"Good grief!" I exclaimed.

Annie placed the wine out of reach on the mantelpiece and threw herself down onto one of the squashy armchairs, which thankfully bore no traces of the papier mache excitement of the other week.

"I know, right? How can so much mess be made in such a short space of time?" she asked wryly.

"You only got back a few minutes before us!"

"That's the power of a toddler typhoon," she shrugged, reaching forward to grab some crisps.

Amy was ensconced in some kind of inflatable, covered doughnut in the corner, crowing and waving her pudgy fists around like an excitable mini cheerleader. Our boys sat like matching mirrored bookends on either side of the leather Chesterfield sofa in typical bloke relaxed pose of arm extended along the sofa arm, beer bottle clasped loosely, legs slightly akimbo with feet together and heads resting on the back.

It was the remainder of the room that had given me a bit of a shock. Brightly coloured wrapping paper littered the floor and every other available surface, in shreds and scrunched balls. Tom whirled about between the furniture, causing eddies of paper wherever he spun and leapt, a blue satin ribbon fluttering in his hand like some kind of demented rhythmic gymnast.

"Look at me, Auntie Mena! Look at my things!"

"Yes, Tom, I can see!"

Annie polished off her crisps and leant towards Sam, reaching out her hand.

"Throw us the bin bag, will you?"

Sam reached down and tossed a roll of bin liners over to Annie, who looked over to me with a smirk.

"The trick is to make the tidying up a game," she said in a low voice.

She peeled off a bag and shook it to open the mouth.

"Right," she said, "Can you get the wrappers in the bag?"

I looked over at Tom, who was still twirling about, flapping his ribbon, totally ignoring his mum. To my surprise, Sam and Paddy both put their beers down, reached for some wrapping paper and started scrunching it into aerodynamic balls. Within a moment, balls were firing over into the bag from the direction of the sofa, accompanied by shouts of laughter and mocking comments.

I leaned down myself and lobbed a couple of pieces in too.

"I see what you mean," I murmured. "I thought the game was to get Tom involved, I didn't realise it worked on Sam and Paddy too."

"It's a total game changer," laughed Annie, shaking the bag. "If I put the Mission Impossible theme tune on my phone I can get Sam to clear his rubbish away in no time."

"I'll have to try it!"

With the stuffed binbag stowed next to Annie's armchair, we all picked up our drinks and sank into our seats. Annie's home might be chaotic at times, but the furniture was the comfiest around, you couldn't help but start to relax.

Tom scurried backwards and forwards to his pile of presents to select the next gift, clearly fuelled by adrenaline and cake. Paddy and Sam were having an earnest discussion about the new Indian takeaway on the high street.

I took a sip of my wine and relished the full-bodied flavour as it filtered across my tongue and down my throat.

"Mmm, I do love red wine," I sighed happily, swirling the glass gently so that the red liquid winked in the light.

"Lush," snorted Annie, taking a large mouthful herself.

Tom ran over and waved some kind of flashing bubble gun in my face.

"Cool, Tom, why don't you show Paddy?" I suggested.

Tom zoomed over to the sofa making aeroplane noises and shoved the bubble gun into Paddy's face.

"I hate kid's parties," muttered Annie, reaching for some more crisps.

"Really? But you did it so well, you were calm and friendly and made sure everything was right for everyone."

"Well, you have to step up when it's your turn, but there are just so many of them," she sighed. "Some weekends you have two or even three to go to and it's always the same people and the same activities and it can just take over your life and get so boring," she complained. "You sometimes feel like you're just passing presents around and ticking a box."

I studied my old friend's face a bit more carefully and noticed small signs of tiredness etched around her eyes and in the corners of her mouth. It wasn't often that her cheerful, can-do attitude slipped.

"And if you don't go along with it all, you feel like you might be disadvantaging your child and you don't want them to get left out."

Not for the first time, I felt thankful that it was just Paddy and I in our little family. He was big enough and ugly enough to fight his own battles.

"Still," she said, brightening. "Like I said, that's that for this year at least, definitely something to celebrate."

"Absolutely," I agreed, raising my glass in her direction.

I smiled fondly at my old friend. Always matter of fact, always determined to just get on with things. Annie stood up and carefully replaced her wine on the mantelpiece and clapped her hands towards Tom, who was studiously ignoring her.

"OK troops, time to go up. You can have your milk upstairs, no need for baths tonight, you can have an extra-long one tomorrow instead. Say goodnight!"

There was a pause when nothing noticeable happened.

"Come on birthday boy, up you go. You can take two of your new toys with you."

Sam handed Paddy his bottle and reached forward to grab his small son, who shrieked and kicked in delight.

"Come on mate, time to go. Oof, you weigh a ton, must be all that birthday cake," he scoffed, standing up and throwing Tom over his shoulder in one swift movement.

"Daddy!" shrieked Tom in delight.

Annie strolled across to Amy's doughnut and scooped her up onto her hip.

"We'll be down in a few minutes. You can amuse yourselves? You know where the drinks are," she said, reaching down to pick up Amy's fleece blanket from a footstool.

"Yes, we're fine. Just let me know if we can help," I offered, enjoying the look of naked panic that flashed across Paddy's face.

The Evans family disappeared out of the room and tramped up the stairs. The room seemed to breathe a sigh of relief once they'd gone. I would also bet any money that Paddy did.

"Pretty full on," said Paddy ruefully, taking a swig from his beer.

"Yup," I agreed, taking a sip from my wine.

"I don't know how they cope with the chaos," my husband

continued, shaking his head.

"I suppose you must get used to it," I shrugged, taking the crisp bowl and offering it over to Paddy.

There was a crackle from the bookshelf by the window and the sound of Sam thundering around after Tom pretending to be a dinosaur blared out.

"Can you get the milk?" asked a remote Annie, in a faint voice.

Paddy and I looked at each other and raised our eyebrows.

"Baby monitor!" I whispered.

"Why are you whispering?" he asked, looking puzzled. "They can't hear us, we can only hear them."

"I know," I replied indignantly, still more quietly than usual.

He rolled his eyes.

Sam headed down the stairs to the kitchen and rooted around in the fridge. A moment later, the sound of a microwave as he heated the milk, followed by various cupboard doors opening and closing.

Paddy and I sat quietly, sipping our drinks. My thoughts turned to the takeaway pizza we would shortly be ordering.

"What pizza are you having tonight?" I asked.

Without even an apparent moment's thought, Paddy parroted his order.

"Volcano pepperoni with extra green peppers, mushrooms and ground beef."

"Blimey, you didn't even need to think about that!" I said in awe.

"Oh, but I have," he said, raising his index finger like he was about to expound a new theory to a class full of students. "I've been thinking about it most of today."

I could well believe it.

"It must be nice to have just that as the main demand on your thoughts," I said, with more than a little trace of envy and annoyance.

Paddy shrugged.

"Why not? Why give head space to anything else if I don't need to?"

"I wish I could do that."

"If you can't do anything about whatever is stuck in your head, then you're wasting your energy. Put something else in there in its place."

"If only it was that easy," I said bitterly, taking another gulp of wine, preferring to put wine in my mouth instead.

Sam thumped back up the stairs and from the accompanying noises it sounded as though he was carrying a laden tray of drinks and paraphernalia.

"Don't let that work stuff spoil your weekend. It'll still be there on Monday, deal with it then."

"Thanks guru, I feel so much better! I'll just shelve it all and not give it another thought. Cheers!" I waved my empty glass in his direction.

The annoying thing was that of course he was right. But it is impossible to change the anxious habits of a lifetime in one fell swoop. I stood up abruptly.

"I'm going to top up our wine. Do you want anything while I'm in the kitchen?"

"Another beer please," he said, happy to divert the conversation.

I collected Annie's glass and wandered back into the kitchen. I spent a couple of moments carefully measuring out the remaining wine into our two glasses.

I opened the fridge and pulled out one of the cans we had brought, tucked it under my arm and carefully carried a glass of wine in each hand back into the lounge.

"Cheers," said Paddy, reaching to pull the can out from under my elbow.

Storytime was clearly in full swing upstairs. Patchy sentences filtered down through the monitor. I returned Annie's glass to the mantelpiece and settled myself back in my chair.

"Is it a good story?" I asked, trying to lighten the mood.

"Something about a snail and a turtle. There's been some disaster with a storm. I'm sure it'll really get going in a minute," he said.

"Do you think we should turn it off?" I asked, furrowing my brow.

"Why? Too exciting for you? It's only a bedtime story."

"I know, but still."

"You are daft sometimes," he said affectionately.

"...the end."

"Maybe it won't get going," said Paddy, tutting and rolling his eyes.

"I'll start the pizza order," I decided, pulling my phone out of my bag and opening the App. "We already know what you're having."

"Yup," said Paddy, with a pleased smile.

I tapped in the options.

"But we also know what you're going to have," he said.

"Well, that's amazing, because I haven't actually decided yet," I protested indignantly.

"You might think you haven't, but I know exactly what you'll have."

He paused for effect, looking at me with an indulgent look on his face.

"You do the same every time. You're going to spend ten minutes narrowing it down to three different options. Then you'll decide to be a bit maverick and start building your own. And finally, you'll decide it's too expensive and too much hassle to do it that way and you'll order your usual American hot with extra jalapenos."

I blanched.

"I might not this time," I managed, weakly.

"Yes, you will, because we both know that you "fear change","" he said, putting on a silly high-pitched voice and using his fingers to do the speech marks.

"Arse," I muttered, sticking my tongue out at him.

The annoying thing was, that I knew that he was right. How can someone who seemed to go through life without seeming to take too much notice of anything know you so well?

I began to jab in my order for an American hot with extra jalapenos.

You see? You can't even take control of your own pizza order without being utterly predictable.

"...Tom, have you washed your hands after your wee? OK, good boy."

The thumping sound of Tom stomping across the room upstairs slightly shook the light fitting in the ceiling rose. There was the noise of a small body launching into a bed, with the accompanying protesting squeak of the bed frame.

"Now young lady, let's sort this mess out."

The harsh rip of Velcro tabs being torn open filtered through the monitor speaker.

"Oh, my lord!" exclaimed Sam. "Right, you're going to have to do this one Annie, I don't even know where to start."

"Don't be so feeble," protested Annie. "Just get on with it."

"It's all up her back and on her clothes!"

Paddy pulled a disgusted face. More thumping sounds from upstairs.

"How did it even get in there?" Sam continued. "No, no, no, don't roll over!"

"For god's sake! Move over. Go and fetch the wipes and a new set of clothes."

There was the sound of drawers opening and closing and the crackle of a wipes packet.

"Shouldn't we hose her down?" asked Sam.

"Don't be so dramatic, she'll be fine with the wipes. I don't know why you're making such a fuss, you dealt with worse on that stag do in Amsterdam."

"Yes, but I was hammered then and that definitely helped," said Sam.

Paddy snorted and hid his grin behind another swig of his beer. I looked over at him with my eyebrows raised.

"Didn't you go on that stag do to Amsterdam?"

He nodded, laughing.

"What the hell happened?" I asked.

Paddy shook his head.

"What goes on tour, stays on tour," he said annoyingly, tapping the side of his nose with the hand that held the can.

"Annie clearly knows!"

Paddy shrugged and took another a swig.

"Here," said Annie. "Take these down and put them into soak and I'll finish up. Tell Mena I'll have a thin crust vegetarian special and garlic bread."

I immediately started tapping my phone and began adding Annie's pizza to the order.

"Ooh, garlic bread is a good shout, add another one on there for me," said Paddy from across the room.

I was just finishing up when Sam came back into the room, with a can in his hand.

"Have you washed your hands after your wee?" mimicked Paddy.

"I've just had to bleach them after that disaster, mate!" Sam grinned. "You wouldn't believe the mess. For such a little thing, she can produce some right…"

"All right, that's enough," interjected Paddy hastily. "You don't want to put us off our pizza."

Sam laughed.

"I suppose so. Mena, can you put me down for a meat feast with jalapenos? And Annie would like…"

"I know, a thin crust vegetarian special with garlic bread. Baby monitor," I said, pointing over to the bookcase.

"Ah, of course," said Sam. "Thank goodness we didn't say anything embarrassing."

"Oh no," said Paddy, sarcastically. "Just too much info about poo."

"I'm sure you can handle that, remember Amsterdam?" countered Sam, dropping onto the sofa. "Right, let's get it ordered, I'm starving."

Several cans and a couple of bottles of wine later, we had our feet propped up on the coffee table in the middle of the room and were putting the world to rights. I had forgotten how much I enjoyed our get-togethers. They didn't happen anywhere near as often now that Annie and Sam had the kids, but they were still fun when they did.

"Why is pizza such a comforting food to eat?" I mused, eyeing up the stack of empty boxes on the floor.

There was a moment as everyone gave the question due consideration.

"Because it's the sort of food that clags you up inside and makes you feel satisfyingly full and replete?" suggested Annie.

"Replete, that's a good word," I said, nodding approvingly.

"Clags is an even better word. Pizza is great because it stimulates so many of your senses," added Sam. "It looks great, tastes amazing, smells unbelievable, you have to use your hands..."

He ground to a halt and screwed up his forehead.

"What's the other one?"

"Sound, mate. I'm not sure how you can add that one in," said Paddy, whacking Sam on the upper arm.

Sam was not a man to be put off easily.

"You have to listen out for the doorbell when the delivery comes?" he tried.

"Good effort, well done dear," said Annie, deep from within her chair.

She was looking adorably drowsy, half-curled and covered with a fleecy throw.

"Are you ok over there?" I asked, not wanting to outstay our welcome.

"Yes, fine," she said, wriggling slightly. "I just get a bit knackered these days with being up so much with the kids and the early starts. But it is nice to be a grown up and be silly again for a change."

It had certainly done me good to have a night with comfortable friends. I felt a bit more positive about my worries.

"How about you?" returned Annie. "You look a bit more relaxed than you were earlier?"

Not for the first time, I wondered whether Annie could read my mind. Between her and Paddy, I had nowhere really to hide, I must be so easy to read.

"Yes thanks, I was just thinking it was nice to switch my brain off for a bit."

Sam snorted.

"You should know the benefits, Paddy does it all the time!"

Annie shouted with laughter and made us all jump.

"What the hell was that?" I asked incredulously.

"Sorry," giggled Annie. "I wasn't expecting that. It woke you all up though. But seriously, you can start to move on from all that work stuff now. Naomi is on her way out, you won't have to worry about her any more. Just make sure you get a good one next that suits your..."

I waited.

"My what?"

"Your..." Annie was clearly casting around for the right words.

"Come on, spit it out!"

"Your unique brand of personality and has the same ethos as you," she finished, looking around triumphantly.

Sam and Paddy were studies in nonchalance, one starting up at the ceiling and one inspecting the ring pull on his can.

"My unique brand of personality?" I repeated slowly.

"Yes," nodded Annie.

"I'm not so unique, am I?" I asked, genuinely bewildered.

"In a wonderful way," smiled Annie, wagging her finger. "What some people might see as uptight and slightly obsessive, we see as a person who always wants to do her best and get things right, because we know you."

"Oh," I said, faintly, not sure what to make of that.

Did people think I was uptight and obsessive? Surely everyone wants to do their best and not mess things up? Instantly, the rosy glow of the evening disappeared and I felt tired and ready for bed.

"Come on you," said Paddy, draining his can and setting it on the table. "Time to go."

"Yes, no doubt you'll be up early. Thanks for having us," I said, pulling myself out of the chair, which was suddenly as difficult to climb out of as quicksand.

"You're welcome," said Annie, sitting up with some effort. "Thanks for coming to the party and for Tom's present."

We all managed to get ourselves upright and shuffled around giving unsteady hugs goodbye.

"See you next week!" I called as I grabbed my bag and headed out to the hallway. "Thanks again!"

Paddy and I lurched companionably arm-in-arm down the pavement away from Annie's house.

"Have fun?" I asked Paddy, pulling my coat across my chest against the night chill.

"Yes, it was a laugh," said Paddy, with a spring in his step. "The Play Barn thing was a bit of an experience, but I've had fun tonight."

"Still happy that we made the right decision?"

"What about? About kids?"

I nodded.

"Absolutely, if anything today has made me even more sure. Aren't you?"

I thought for a moment. Very occasionally, I did experience a pang at the thought of what my own child would be like. But it quickly passed and I loved our life the way it was. I enjoyed Annie's kids, but didn't feel strongly enough that I wanted that for us.

"Yes," I said with conviction. "I'm still sure."

"Great," said Paddy and I could hear the relief in his voice.

We walked along in silence for a couple of streets.

"Uptight and slightly obsessive?"

Paddy sighed.

"I knew you were going to fixate on that."

"Well, wouldn't you!"

"I mean, I knew you were going to fixate on those words and not what she said after about it being because you want to do a good job and you hate getting things wrong. That's the positive side to what she was saying."

"But am I though?"

"Well, yes. But it comes from a good place."

"Hmm."

I wasn't sure what to do with that. I would have to have a think.

CHAPTER THIRTEEN

I love Sunday afternoons when I have nothing in particular to do. It's always prime old film time for me, an indulgent couple of hours where I can settle into my fleece hoodie and go back in time. Unless Paddy is watching some sport, in which case I substitute the old film for a good book and retire upstairs to snuggle in bed. But if it's a particularly important sporting event, he'll take himself off to the pub to roar along with his mate Tony and leave me in peace.

The question for today: did I want to watch an old favourite DVD or stream something new instead? I wandered over to the bookshelves and ran my finger along my classic film library, looking for inspiration.

There was a crash as Paddy made his way in from the kitchen, laden down with multiple supermarket carrier bags.

"Watch the lamp," I said, rather redundantly, as the lamp rocked on its side.

"I'm off to nan's," he grunted, dumping the bags by the front door. "I've got her shopping, is there anything else I need to take?"

I turned and considered, my hand resting on my hip.

"I don't think so. Just find out what she was ringing about yesterday, see if she needs some help with something while you're there."

"OK, will do. I'll probably stay for a cup of coffee while I'm there and I might go for a quick pint with Tony on the way back."

"Great, that gives me time to get my film finished before you come back and try and spoil the ending," I said, raising an eyebrow.

"How can I spoil the ending?" he asked incredulously. "You've watched all those ones hundreds of times!"

"Yes, but I like to pretend that I haven't," I said, as if explaining to someone who is slow on the uptake. "It ruins the atmos when you start chipping in."

"Fine, I'll be back for tea anyway."

Paddy reached to open the door.

"Er, hello?"

"Oh yes," he smiled, before making his way over to me.

He gave me a big bear hug and kissed me firmly on the lips.

"See you later, monkey trousers."

"See you later. I would say to say hi to Evelyn for me, but she wouldn't really care if you did or not."

Paddy gathered up the bag handles and pulled open the door. He didn't deny it.

"Bye!"

The door slammed shut and the knocker rattled a couple of times before settling. Peace at last.

I resumed my search of the shelves. Now, what mood was I looking for today? My eyes caught on The Wicked Lady and I paused for a moment. A thrilling tale of a nobly born woman who goes rogue, gets mixed up with a dastardly highwayman, unleashes her inner vixen and causes all kinds of havoc.

I pulled out the DVD and stared at the blurb. Lady Barbara Skelton. Feisty, unwilling to compromise and prepared to do things differently. I bet no-one ever referred to her as uptight and obsessive.

I felt a flare of anger. Just because I liked to do things properly and be organised, that wasn't such a crime was it? Surely other people liked to keep their anxieties at bay by keeping control of things as much as they could? Maybe a bit of an alternative perspective might be helpful, perhaps Lady Barbara could help me channel any hidden extrovert qualities.

I flicked open the case and inserted the disc into the player. The swirl of dramatic Gainsborough studio music filled the room as the menu appeared on the screen.

I just needed to finish my preparations. I headed back into the kitchen and flicked the switch on the kettle, before turning to rummage in the cupboard above. My chocolate stash. I pulled down a family-sized bar of Bournville and tucked it in my back pocket. I grabbed my film watching mug from the mug tree and popped in a tea bag. It was the perfect shape for a comforting film session, chunky, with a satisfyingly looped and substantial handle and with a pretty botanical pattern. Heaven help Paddy if he ever used this mug, he'd only made that mistake twice.

I quickly made the tea, then made my way back into the lounge and prepared the sofa. Sheepskin rug beneath me, just so, two cushions under my head and one at my feet. I pulled the little coffee table forward so I wouldn't have to reach too far for my tea and placed my mug and chocolate neatly on top.

Perfect. I settled down and started the film.

Paddy came back about six o'clock, shouldering open the door with a bang that gave me a start.

"Having a snooze?" he asked as he made his way in.

I sat up and gave my face a rub.

"Just a little one. I didn't sleep great last night."

I had spent too much of it worrying about work and dwelling on my apparent 'unique' personality failings.

Paddy kicked the door shut behind him and came over to kiss me on the head.

"Have you had a good afternoon?" I asked, stifling a yawn.

"Yes, great," he replied. "Dropped the stuff off at nan's, ate several chocolate biscuits, had a catch up with Tony..."

A tantalising smell tickled my nostrils and I glanced at the white plastic bags Paddy was carrying.

"Oh, I thought we could try that new Indian takeaway that Sam was talking about last night. Saves you having to cook. I know you're feeling a bit, you know, at the minute."

"Why thank you," I said wryly.

"I got your usual," he said, moving away to the kitchen.

My usual. How predictable. Lady Skelton would not approve. She would probably have asked for several off-menu dishes to be made just for her, before robbing the till and leaving with a flourish.

Crashes and bangs emanated from the kitchen as Paddy flung open cupboards and pulled out trays, plates and bowls. The sound of a spoon ringing against the bowl as he shook off the excess sauce.

"How was Evelyn?" I asked dutifully.

"What?" he called back.

"Evelyn? How was she?"

"Oh fine," he bellowed.

He emerged with a tray a moment later and deposited it on my lap.

"What did she want yesterday? It's not like her to call my mobile?"

He shrugged and licked his thumb.

"Not really sure," he said. "I asked her and she just said everything was fine. She said she didn't need anything doing."

Paddy disappeared again, before returning with his own tray and a can of beer under each armpit.

"Here you go," he said, squatting slightly so I could reach up and pull mine out.

"Silver service here, nothing like a beer from under an armpit," I said with a smile.

"Nothing but the best in this house! Are we ok to watch the football?" he asked, flicking the TV on and navigating to the channel.

Looks like it!

"Yes, fine," I replied. "Thanks for the curry."

I picked up my fork and began to eat my usual.

Monday morning. I sighed and stretched my back, twisting

my neck from side to side to ease out the kinks. I was struggling with my tasks today, somehow adding formulae to a spreadsheet and calculating stationery spend wasn't lighting my fire like it usually did. Perhaps the Wicked Lady had unsettled me yesterday after all.

It didn't help that Naomi was sat to the side of me with an almost permanent smug smile on her carefully contoured face. She looked like Mrs Bennet from the TV adaptation of Pride and Prejudice, sat in her parlour waiting for Jane to finish her audience with Bingley and announce her engagement. The 'cat that got the cream' look was definitely there, oozing out of her in waves.

She had worked out her notice period with Kelly and would only be in the office for another week and a half. Whilst it was a relief to me that her end was in sight, I was also aggrieved that she was able to use her remaining leave to finish early after all of the casual absences in the last few weeks that I was sure were not genuine. But I had no proof. So, the resentment swirled and curdled in my stomach, leaving an acidic taste in my mouth.

I had reacted in the only way I had left – I had given her a list of tasks that I wanted her to do before she finished. And this time I emailed them. I had learnt my lesson, even though it was too late to be of much use. Each task was clearly outlined in the email and the deadline for the work to be done before she finished.

We both knew that she probably wasn't going to do them all, because really, what sanctions could I use if she didn't? But it made me feel slightly better that I had managed to implement my proposed changes just before she finished for good.

My email notification sounded with a ping and I clicked on the preview to open it up. It was an invitation to a meeting with Sarah this afternoon and Kelly was also listed as an attendee. The meeting title was "Accounts department catch up" and in the details section there was just one sentence: Discussion re future direction of Accounts.

I clicked on the Accept button and absent-mindedly twirled from side to side in my chair. It must be the catch-up meeting to discuss Naomi's replacement. We would need to get the advert out soon. As it was, I would be having to do all the work of the team by myself for a minimum of six weeks after Naomi left. Not that she was much use, but some help was better than none.

I reached for my notepad and pen. I would need to do some prep for the meeting and come up with some thoughts about working patterns, hours and qualifications. I would have to make sure that I stressed that it was more important to get the right personality for the team this time. The right person can be trained, but the wrong person in a small unit was disastrous, as I had already discovered to my cost.

"All right ladies?"

I didn't need to look up to know that Lucas had smarmed his way over to our section.

"Lucas." I acknowledged, without turning around.

"Hi Lucas," said Naomi and I could tell by her voice that she was treating him to a smile.

"I understand you're leaving me, Naomi. I'm not sure I can

allow that!"

With my back still to him, I pulled a face.

Naomi laughed.

"Well, you know, onwards and upwards. I can't turn down a big promotion, even for you!"

I rolled my eyes. She was so full of it.

"Besides, I'm sure you'll get over it soon enough. You'll still have Mena."

This last comment was dropped with an audible side-order of sneer.

Lucas scoffed.

"Not the same though is it, love?" he said, chuckling.

Charming.

I reached for my bag and phone and stood up to leave the cubicle.

He was leaning against the partition (which was a feat in itself as it was a very wobbly screen) with his arms folded. I couldn't get past him without edging much closer to him than I wanted to be.

"Excuse me, Lucas."

"Pardon me," he said with fake civility and made a bow as he moved aside.

I wondered, not for the first time, whether he kept up this act the entire time. Was he the same outside of work, with his creepy little comments and unctuous smile? Or was it a persona that he donned like an outfit each time he came into the building and shed when he left for the day? And if this was the case, why on earth did he choose this one?

I scooted past and left them to it. I knew that Naomi would only play up to him all the more if I was there to hear. She'd soon send him packing if she no longer had an audience.

I shoved open the door to the stairwell and clattered down a level. Today was going to be annoying, I could tell that I would require a minimum of a packet of crisps and a chocolate bar to get me through it.

I opened my purse and scooped up my spare change, feeding it in without needing to check the amount. I punched in the codes and stood tapping my foot as the vending machine disgorged my bounty.

My bag vibrated briefly against my side and I reached in and pulled out my phone. It was a message from Paddy.

"Can you go and check on nan after work? Had a weird message from her and won't be back until after 7."

Fine, I tapped back, before throwing my phone back in my bag and reaching into the dispenser tray to get my treats.

One more thing to add to the list.

I approached the door to Meeting Room 1 at 2.59pm exactly. I could see Sarah and Kelly through the glass, seated on the far side of the table. They were having an earnest discussion and I hovered in view, clutching my notepad and pen to my chest like a 1950's secretary. I just needed a cardigan draped over my shoulders and a pair of cats-eye glasses on a chain to complete the look.

Sarah looked up and smiled, waving for me to come in. I opened the door and sat myself in the single chair facing them both. The door clicked behind me.

"I feel like I'm interviewing," I laughed, carefully placing my pad and pen down in front of me.

Why do you always say such daft things? Does it add anything to the situation? No, shut up!

Sarah and Kelly smiled politely.

"How are you doing at the moment, Mena?" asked Sarah.

I cleared my throat.

"Obviously it's a blow that I'll be losing my assistant," I began tentatively, gauging their faces for a reaction. "But I don't think it's any surprise to you both that we weren't necessarily the best fit and there were some issues…"

I paused. I felt it was no secret that I had been having some problems with Naomi doing her work. Kelly nodded and Sarah looked thoughtful. I felt encouraged to carry on.

"Despite my efforts to address some of those issues, I feel it's actually going to work out quite well if Naomi does leave so that we can get the team right."

Sarah sat slightly forward in her seat.

"Yes, I did get the impression that Naomi wasn't fitting well into the team."

I released a puff of air that I must have been holding in.

"I did work around the issues as much as possible but before we could make progress she handed in her notice."

It was Sarah's turn to nod.

"I was at the point where I was going to sit down with Kelly," I gestured to Kelly with my hand, "to talk through some of those issues but we didn't get that far before Naomi decided to leave."

"OK," said Sarah, sitting back again. "It's a shame that this didn't work out. Kelly has told me that Naomi will be gone by the middle of next week? What's our situation with the reference for her new job?"

I looked to Kelly to answer as this was something that we had discussed.

"We will be providing Naomi with a basic reference which clearly outlines her absence record. It will also reference that her qualifications are sufficient for her new role and how long she has worked here. It will be up to her new employers if they accept that adequate. I believe Naomi has outlined to them that one of the reasons for her leaving us is due to a personality issue so they might not be put off by a less than glowing reference if she has convinced them that she is right for the job."

I flushed pinkly and shifted in my seat. This sounded bad, as if I had been a horrible manager who had been part of the problem.

It was Naomi who was the problem, not me! I tried hard with her and just wanted to do a good job.

I felt a bit sick. Perhaps all the snacks before I came in hadn't been a good idea.

"OK," repeated Sarah. "I think we need to have a chat now about where we're at with Accounts and future directions."

I sat a bit straighter and nodded eagerly. I felt that I needed to make a better impression and show that I had already made some notes about what the team needed to move forward.

"Yes," I agreed, flipping open my notepad. "I've been making some notes about that. I've learnt a lot from this experience with Naomi and I think we really need to make sure that we get the right person this time. It's very important in a small team..."

Sarah cut me off efficiently and carried on as though I hadn't spoken.

"I've been having a chat with other management and Kelly about this situation. It hasn't been ideal, in that despite Naomi's appointment last year, your team does seem to lack capacity."

I swallowed.

"I always do my best to make sure that the work is done," I began.

"And I've always appreciated the work you put in," said Sarah with a fleeting smile. "But we are very heavily reliant upon you as an individual to produce the Accounts for us and I feel that maybe your skills lie in the technical work, rather than in managing other members of staff."

Ouch. Perhaps it's clear to everyone just how much you hate managing people and can't control anyone other than yourself.

I glanced at Kelly, who was looking at me sympathetically across the table.

"Naomi handing in her notice has given us the opportunity

of looking at the Accounts function as a whole and its place within our organisational structure. I feel it's only fair to let you know that we are exploring the possibility of outsourcing our accounts function to an external service provider."

I could feel the colour disappearing from my cheeks.

"Depending on the outcome of that exploration, we may be looking at redundancy for you. I appreciate that this will come as a bit of a shock, but we will keep you updated as soon as we have any further developments."

I clasped my hands together in my lap and could feel clamminess blooming on my palms.

"Oh," I managed.

"If you have any questions in the meantime, once you've had time to digest this situation, then please don't hesitate to talk to Kelly," Sarah finished, in a slightly more gentle and less official tone.

"I... I will. Thank you."

Why are you thanking her? For goodness' sake.

I started to gather up my pad and pen and pulled myself to my feet.

"I'll wait to hear then," I said, turning to the door and fumbling with the handle.

"Thanks Mena," they both chorused as I left the room.

Well, you made it nice and easy for them. You could have made them feel a bit more awkward about crapping all over you from a great height. After all the work you've done!

I walked slowly in a bit of a daze towards the ladies toilet and leaned shakily against the sink. I looked up at my reflection and was not at all surprised to see my chalky complexion and shocked eyes staring back at me. This was not what I had expected in a million years.

I turned on the cold tap with trembling fingers and splashed my face, drawing in a shuddering breath.

I didn't know what to do. I shuffled into a cubicle, locked the door and sat on the toilet lid, for once not thinking at all about germs. I dropped my head in my hands and the tears started to fall.

After managing to compose myself, I headed back to my cubicle, which was thankfully Lucas-free. Unfortunately, it was not free of Naomi, who was very much in evidence at her desk. This was all her fault.

I swept in, making sure not to give her a view of my blotchy face and logged back on in what I hoped was an efficient and no-nonsense manner. The facilities accounts appeared on my screen and I started to methodically check the entries. It was soothing to have something mundane and straightforward to latch my scattered thoughts onto.

My clock crept sluggishly towards 5pm. By 4.40pm I had had enough. I logged off, grabbed my phone and bag and hurried towards the lift. I didn't even bother to say goodnight to Naomi, there was no point in trying to keep up appearances with her anymore.

I exited the building and dashed through the drizzle towards the station. I just wanted to get home.

For once, the train journey home was thankfully uneventful. I didn't think I could cope with any anti-social or discourteous behaviour at the moment. It might just be the last straw in my current state.

I expended as much nervous energy as I could in the brisk walk home from the station, skirting the puddles and keeping my head down. I wasn't in the mood to speak with anyone or go through the usual rigmarole of deciding whether to nod at another passer-by or not.

Well, there you go. They couldn't wait to get rid of you. All that time you thought they valued you and your work and they must have been chuckling to themselves about your smug attitude and how rubbish you are.

I jammed my key in the door and rushed inside as quickly as was humanly possible. I leant back against the inside of the closed door and tried to breathe in deeply through my nose and out through my mouth. I always struggled with this exercise, I feel as though I have a permanently blocked nasal passage. It always actually panics me more as I think that I can't get enough oxygen into my lungs, so it's a bit of a waste of time.

I glanced over at my beloved classic films shelf on the other side of the room.

Of course. What would Joan Crawford or Bette Davis do?

I dropped my handbag on the floor and headed into the kitchen and the drinks cupboard. I rummaged amongst the bottles until I found what I was looking for. Paddy and Sam had demolished our whisky, so I would have to make do. Evelyn had given Paddy a bottle of sherry a couple of years ago and it would do the job at a pinch. We always laughed about it and it was a staple comedy routine of ours about whether we should break it open. Well, now was the time.

I pulled out our only crystal drinks tumbler (I broke the other one washing it up) and poured in a generous slug. The amber liquid swirled satisfyingly in the heavy-based glass and I took a large swig and felt it tickle its way down my throat and into my unsettled stomach. I could see why they did it in the old films. It felt satisfying.

I took another gulp and then headed back into the lounge and sank into my chair.

"Well, this is rubbish," I said inadequately to the room at large. "I wasn't expecting this."

I allowed myself to stare morosely at the wall, sipping my sherry as the light outside the window began to dim.

My bag began to vibrate and I sighed. I had purposely not looked at my phone since leaving the office. My initial instinct had been to message Paddy and Annie straight away and pour out my woes, but I managed to restrain myself. I wanted to calm myself first and take a breath. I also felt that by keeping it to myself for a little bit longer, it was less real.

I set the tumbler down with a clunk on a coaster and retrieved my bag from the floor. My fingers found my phone and pulled it out and I squinted at the screen.

It was an unrecognised number. Well then, they could sit and whistle. It was probably spam and I wasn't in the mood. I waited for the call to cut off and then scrolled through my messages.

I suddenly realised that I had forgotten about visiting Evelyn with all the excitement.

What can she possibly want now? Some nonsense or other. Why can't Paddy do it on his way home?

I scowled to myself. Maybe I should leave it and tell Paddy to go round later. She probably wanted to complain about something that was working perfectly well not working. Or another flyer for something she didn't want and was offended by.

After the day I'd had, no-one would think it was out of order if I didn't go around. It wasn't like I wasn't round all the time. Surely for once I was well within my rights to say stuff it.

I sat back in my chair again and picked up the sherry, feeling very sorry for myself.

She could manage for a bit, she needed to realise I wasn't at her beck and call all the time.

But what if she actually needs help this time? What if she's needed help all day and she's struggling?

I sighed and set the tumbler back down.

I picked up the phone. Perhaps I could ask her over the phone and triage the situation. I dialled her number and let it ring. I tried again. Sometimes, when she was watching The Chase or Pointless at this time of night, she had the volume up high. Still no response.

I hung up and switched the phone for the tumbler. Sometimes you just have to put yourself first.

Two and a half hours later, the front door crashed open and woke me with a start from my doze on the sofa. The empty crystal tumbler rested on the mini coffee table to the side and I hazily remembered that I had made my way through half of the bottle of sherry.

Paddy walked in and snapped the main light on, causing me to blink and shield my eyes as I adjusted to the sudden glare.

"How was nan?" he asked in a purposely neutral tone.

I shook my head slightly and blinked again. Oh yes, Evelyn.

"Only I had a call from her on my way home, she said you hadn't been round and she was panicking. I told you I wouldn't be back until after seven, why didn't you go and see her?"

"I tried calling her when I got in, I tried twice and she didn't answer. I was planning on going round in a bit," I said, remembering suddenly that that wasn't the case. "But then I fell asleep."

"So I see," he said, tight-lipped.

Paddy doesn't often do angry, but when he does it always upsets me. He starts off like this, all clipped and clenched, before snapping and losing his temper. I felt my own anger flicker and flare.

"I've had a totally shit day actually and for once I thought I would put myself first and come home, have a drink to relax and then think about going round!"

"I *told* you that I was worried about her," he said, raising his voice a notch.

"No you didn't," I countered. "You said you'd had a weird message, that's a different thing. That could have been anything! She could have pressed the wrong buttons and written gibberish, I didn't know what you meant!"

"But I told you that I wanted you to go round!" he said, up another notch.

My cheeks flushed and the potent combination of half a bottle of sherry and chronic injustice erupted.

"I'm always bloody going around!" I shouted. "On my days off, when you're not here, when you're out with Tony, it's me that always has to go! And what thanks do I get? None! She barely speaks to me, she treats me like a skivvy and I'm sick of it!"

Paddy scowled.

"She's an old lady and she needs our help. I didn't realise it was so hard for you to give my nan a bit of support when she needs it."

"And I've always done it, so don't make it about me not helping out. I always help out, even when I don't feel like it, but I told you that today I just couldn't face it when I got home. I didn't mean to fall asleep, but I did. Not much I can do about it now is there?"

"There's no need to be like that about it," Paddy retorted.

"Actually, I think there is," I said, standing up and wagging a finger in his direction. "I'm fed up of always trying to do my best and still getting grief for it. I'm round at your nan's most days of the week sorting her out. You go two or three times and get treated like her knight in shining armour. So don't tell me I don't pull my weight!"

There was a short silence. After a couple of angry breaths, my usual guilt reflex began to kick in.

"Why, what was the matter, what did she want?"

Paddy folded his arms, his mouth twisting.

"Do you care?"

"Of course I bloody care!"

"If you must know, I'm not really sure. She seemed upset about something, but couldn't seem to tell me what it was, she looked a bit confused. So, I checked everything out, calmed her down and came home. It would have taken you ten minutes out of your day, if you'd bothered to go round."

Screw this.

I reached down and picked up the crystal tumbler. I launched it at the closed front door and heard the satisfying sound of the glass shattering and cascading onto the door mat.

Paddy took an over-exaggerated comedy step back and raised

his hands.

"What the hell did you do that for?" he asked in shocked tones.

Because I'm sick of always trying to do the right thing and not let people down and I'm fed up of it!

"Because I'm sick of always trying to do the right thing and not let people down and I'm fed up of it!" I shrieked.

Paddy stared at me, his mouth open.

Wow, did you actually just say that out loud? You never say what I say out loud!

"Well maybe it's time I did!" I said loudly.

"Did what?" asked Paddy, suddenly looking confused.

"I said I'd had a totally shit day and you didn't pick up on it, you were too busy having a go at me. I don't deserve what you're saying and you don't know the half of it, so I'm going upstairs to calm down before I say something I'll regret!"

Great job, assertive but reasonable and expressing your disappointment. I'm impressed!

I swung around and hurried towards the stairs, catching the banister and hauling myself up, all the while angry tears leaked from the corners of my eyes.

So unfair, all the things I do for him and his bloody nan, the one time I would like some support and he doesn't even listen...

I rushed into our bedroom.

Slam the door. Go on, slam the door.

I turned and slammed the door with a flourish. BANG! I flinched at the noise but then felt strangely proud of myself. I never slammed doors.

I flung myself onto the bed and began to wail.

I wiped my eyes and examined myself in the mirror. Smudged mascara, bird's nest hair and a blotchy complexion. Sexy.

I reached for the face wash and squeezed a generous amount in my open palm, before rubbing my hands together and lathering the bubbles over my face. The coolness of the gel felt soothing and I rinsed it off with cool water, before gently patting my face dry with the hand towel.

I felt a bit silly now. I'm not a person who is prone to outbursts and fits of passion. I pride myself on keeping everything in check as much as I can and spending an inordinate amount of effort keeping my simmering resentments under control as I go about my daily life.

Don't feel silly! You were justified in making a point. It's about time that people stopped taking you for granted. You're a doormat.

I'm not a doormat! I chided myself. I make my own choices.

Yes, but people take advantage of you. You just don't like it when you don't get appreciation for it.

I sighed. I couldn't hide away upstairs all night.

I tentatively made my way down the stairs and stood in the doorway of the lounge. Paddy studiously stared at the television, watching an old episode of Top Gear.

I padded over to my usual spot and sank down. I joined him in staring at the screen.

Don't you dare be the first to say anything.

Paddy cleared his throat.

I mean it. Let him make the first move.

I picked at my fingers and miserably stared at Jeremy Clarkson interviewing a celebrity I didn't recognise.

"I've cleared up the glass," he said, in tones that could be taken as aggrieved. "I've done the best I can with the dustpan and brush and the hoover."

"Thank you," I said, quietly.

What does he want, a medal? Well done on finding the household implements? Don't apologise!

"I'm sorry about throwing it, it was a bit over the top."

For god's sake.

There was a creak as Paddy shuffled in his seat. Our faces glowed in the light from the screen.

"That was our last nice tumbler," he muttered. "You'd already broken the other one, but in a slightly less *dramatic* way."

"Well let's face it, I would have broken it by accident sooner or later," I growled through clenched teeth.

Another silence.

"So what went on today then?" he asked.

I turned my head and managed to raise a rueful smile.

"It turns out that with Naomi leaving, they're talking about outsourcing accounts. Not replacing Naomi and getting someone else to do it. They're going through the process but redundancy was mentioned. I get the feeling that they've already decided."

"What? But you work so hard for them!" said Paddy, sounding pleasingly outraged on my behalf.

Tears sprang to my eyes again.

"I know, I've really done my best. It seems so unfair," I sniffed, wiping my nose on the back of my hand.

"But why would they do that? You always get great appraisal feedback."

"They said that they don't think my skills lie in managing a team, that I'm more suited to the technical aspects of the job. They obviously don't want to employ someone else that I can't manage properly," I hiccuped. "Clearly it's too much hassle for them to deal with my personality defects."

"Hey now, come on," said Paddy reassuringly, moving over to the sofa to sit next to me. "You're not that bad!"

Oh thanks!

"Oh thanks," I muttered, wiping my nose again.

"I mean, they're not *defects*," he battled on, "they're more traits. And they benefit from those too, the attention to detail, the perfectionism…"

"In other words, uptight and obsessive."

"Two sides of the same coin," said Paddy kindly, rubbing my arm with his hand.

"I can't lose my job!" I gasped. "What will I do?"

"You'll get another one," responded Paddy matter-of-factly. "You just need to find the right place for you."

"But what about the mortgage?" I continued, determined to wring as much bleakness from the situation as possible.

"Well, we'll be ok for a couple of payments, so don't start panicking just yet. They haven't given you formal notice, but you can start looking at what's out there. If push comes to shove, you could always temp."

I ground the heel of my hand into my eye and rubbed thoughtfully. I felt a crushing sadness. My work goes a long way to validating my sense of self and how much I'm valued.

I felt miserable.

Paddy patted me on the back.

"You know what you need?" he said gently.

"What?" I asked, raising my bleary eyes to look at him.

"Chippy tea. I'll go and fetch one. That's one less thing for you to have to think about."

He stood up and patted my shoulder, before heading to the front door.

See, he doesn't even need to ask you what you want. You're so predictable and pitiful.

My head sank forward into my hands.

CHAPTER FOURTEEN

It was a quiet weekend. I kept my mind off things at work with the housework and various black and white films, which I watched from my huddled cosy nest on the sofa. I was determined to wallow in my own pit of misery and lack of self-esteem.

Paddy did the food shopping and tended to Evelyn and although it was a little awkward at first with Paddy making a point of tiptoeing around me, we settled back into our usual patterns.

I couldn't get rid of this sense of sadness. I felt like a failure. I obviously wasn't good enough and clearly wasn't valued for my contributions. The vision of how I thought I'd been seen by my colleagues, as a hard-working and reliable employee, had disintegrated. Now I could only imagine how pleased Kelly and Sarah had been at the opportunity of getting rid of me. How I saw my place in the world had been rocked.

If my view of how I was seen as an employee was wrong, what if it was also true of how my friends, family and wider circle saw me? What if they also felt I was a waste of space and just put up with me?

You're being self indulgent.

Yes, I was. But I couldn't seem to haul myself out of it.

Monday morning rolled around, as it always does, whether we want it to or not. I dragged myself out of bed and went about my usual routine, albeit with sluggish feet and a sense of dread.

Paddy murmured something as I quietly left our bedroom and I took it as a gesture of encouragement. To be honest, it could have been sleep talk but I was determined to grab onto any hints of positivity.

The front door closed with a click behind me. I closed my eyes, took a deep breath of the chilly morning air and blew it out again through pursed lips. My chest felt tight, the air only reaching the top portion of my lungs, the ribs refusing to expand. My jaw was rigidly clenched and I realised that my shoulders were tight and shrugged them up to my ears and rotated them slightly.

Suddenly, I was startled by a mountain bike rushing through the small gap on the pavement between me and the row of parked cars along the kerb.

"Oh!" I exclaimed and jumped backwards in a reflex move, banging the back of my head on my own front door knocker.

I whipped around to seee the retreating figure on the bike, a man of indeterminate age dressed all in black.

"Sorry love!" he shouted, the sound floating back to me over his shoulder.

You're an arsehole!

"Arsehole!" I shrieked, surprising both myself and a woman down the road who had emerged from her front door at just the wrong moment.

I cringed and raised my hand in salutation.

"Morning!" I chirped in a totally different tone of voice and was unsurprised when she quickly turned and rushed to her car.

I felt two small spots of pink embarrassment bloom on my

cheeks.

Well, that was embarrassing.

I shook my head and tilted my chin, then turned and set off on the short walk to the train station.

Crossing the road, I did my best to walk with purpose. Today was just a day like any other, I muttered to myself under my breath as I strode along.

"Today is just a normal day. I'll go to work as usual, put in my usual amount of effort and make them realise what a mistake it would be if they decide to let me go. Just do your best and see what happens."

I'd heard about this positive affirmation business and decided to give it a try. I cleared my throat and began to chant, trying to channel any inner cheerleader I might have inside me.

"I am strong! I am capable! I am…"

I paused for a moment. I couldn't think of any other positives straight away, which I suppose was an indication that my self-esteem had clearly packed up and taken itself away on an extended holiday.

This is pathetic.

I pulled myself up taller and decided to try again. I turned into Station Road and wove my way through the wheelie bins awaiting collection on the pavement.

"I am strong! I am capable! I am valued!"

My voice wobbled slightly on this last one. I felt anything but, to be honest, but I was trying to give it a go. Fake it until you make it. I headed up the ramp by the ticket office and entered the doors.

"I am efficient! I am powerful! I am…"

"About to miss the train?" smirked the uniformed employee behind the glass screen at the ticket office desk.

I glanced across the barrier to see my train already waiting. It was later than I had thought. I clutched my handbag and raced through the turnstile, banging my hip painfully in my rush.

That will bruise.

A familiar beeping sound started as I shot across the platform and scrambled onto the train as the doors began to close. Thank goodness for that, missing my train would hardly have helped me to bolster my positive mindset attempts.

I rested my hand on the wall and was surprised to see it slightly trembling. Clearly, bursts of exertion on an empty stomach were not a good idea. My eyes felt damp and I sniffed loudly.

Come on, get a grip.

The train juddered as it began to pull away from the station and I pushed the button to enter the carriage. The fusty atmosphere of weariness and resignation enveloped me as I made my way up the aisle. Those who had braved the early morning train obviously felt as motivated as me today. Heads bowed, earphones resolutely in place, eyes skittering away from other human beings. Good. I was not in the mood for any interactions beyond the minimum.

I spied a set of two vacant seats up ahead and gratefully sank into the one against the wall, firmly placing my bag on the seat next to me. Keeping my hands around the strap, I closed my eyes and rolled my head back onto the rest.

Bring it on.

I marched into the lobby at work and jabbed the lift button with feeling. A strong feeling of resentment began to build in my chest. I had given years of hard work to this place and look at my reward. I had worked over my hours and gone above and beyond to do a good job and they couldn't care less. Well, they wouldn't take it away from me without a fight.

I jabbed the button again and clenched my jaw.

"That won't help," came a voice from behind me. "Pushing the button more than once doesn't make a difference."

Lucas.

"I know, you've said so before," I muttered, without turning around. "But I don't care."

"Well, that isn't the attitude, is it," he sniggered nasally. "You're in early, have you had a…"

I spun around.

"A what? A row with the husband? Are you going to offer to comfort me again? Make some more totally inappropriate suggestions?"

Lucas frowned and his eyes slithered to one side.

"I was only just…"

"Only just what?" I interrupted. "Being friendly and making small talk? You know what, don't bother."

I turned back to face the lift. He snickered weirdly and cleared his throat.

"Well, looks like you're living up to your name today, you couldn't be *Meaner* if you wanted to!"

He expelled some kind of dry laugh, clearly very proud of himself.

Oh, just sod off.

The lift doors opened and I stepped inside, before turning around in the doorway to block his way in.

"Just sod off, you cretin!"

I wasn't sure who was more shocked, me or Lucas. He blinked rapidly a couple of times and the doors began to close. The last thing I saw as he disappeared from view was Sarah's surprised face over his shoulder as she came up behind him in the lobby.

Oh good grief. Just what I needed, Sarah thinking I was an abusive employee with a short fuse. Well done, Mena, great start to the day.

Unsurprisingly, Naomi wasn't at her desk when I arrived at our cube. Only a couple of the tasks I'd given her had been completed and she was finishing on Wednesday. There was no way she would complete the rest in time.

I dropped my bag on my desk and sank down in my chair, without taking my coat off. What was I doing? I had planned on coming in today with a positive can-do attitude and wowing everyone with the amount of work I was going to power through. And what had I done? Insulted the office creep and disappointed my manager. Great job.

With my head lowered, I swung the chair left and right in a soothing movement, using my heels. I felt in danger of sinking into a black fog of despair.

"Knock-knock?"

I looked up to see Kelly standing by the wobbly divider, a smile on her face. I summoned up an answering one, albeit a distinctly watery one. I didn't have the energy to jump up and block her view of Daniel.

"I know you'll have been thinking a lot about what we talked about on Friday," she said calmly, maintaining eye contact.

I nodded.

"And as Sarah said, we'll be exploring the other options this week so we should have more of an idea which way we will be going by this Thursday. Are you free for a meeting then? Say 10?"

I was trying to gather as much information as I could from her body language. She wasn't giving much away. She was being polite and approachable, but I still felt that she already knew what was going to happen.

"That's fine," I said. "I don't need to check my calendar, I already know that I'll be finalising reports on Thursday, I don't put meetings in on that day if I can help it otherwise."

Kelly smiled again.

"That's great, 10am in the same meeting room as last time."

"OK, thanks."

She disappeared out of view. I sighed. I had a horrible feeling that they were just going through the motions. There was a distinct reserve in her manner that I hadn't been aware of before. Or was I just being paranoid?

They just want to get rid of you. Face facts, you're expendable.

I spun around in my chair and switched my PC on, my tired eyes burning. I waited for the familiar clicks and whirs as it shuddered into life.

The stale air in the cubicle shifted behind me and I could tell without turning around that Naomi had entered the space. A moment later, a waft of strong perfume enveloped me and caused me to gag. I wasn't sure which one she wore, but it was heavy and cloying and made me think of dark boudoirs, crystal chandeliers and black satin dresses. I could feel a headache coming on.

"Aren't you stopping?"

I turned sideways and peered at Naomi, who was engaged in shedding her (very stylish) long beige coat which tied with a long belt. Her hair was straightened, her outfit looked chic but not too try-hard and she was contoured to within an inch of her life.

I immediately felt drab, dull and defensive.

"What?"

No missy, you aren't getting a 'pardon' from me today.

Naomi flicked her hair back over her shoulder and she pointed at me.

"Your coat. Aren't you stopping?"

I looked down and realised I was still in my waterproof mac that suddenly looked overly practical and middle-aged.

"Well let's see, shall we?" I said archly, spinning my chair back towards my screen and tapping in my password. "I haven't made my mind up yet."

The rest of the day passed without any further in-person interactions. I kept my head down and tried to keep some semblance of control by making and ticking off to-do lists. I love a to-do list. At the end of every day, I write the next one for the following day, so that I feel prepped and ready when I come in. Sometimes, I will even add an ad hoc task that I've just completed so that I can have the satisfaction of ticking it off to help me feel like I'm one of life's over achievers. But even that didn't help me today.

Mid-morning, I received a meeting request from Kelly for Thursday. I clicked my acceptance and sat back in my chair. I felt as though everything was out of kilter and it was leaving me unsettled. I couldn't switch off the nagging worry about my job security and the figures and reports weren't providing me with any distraction.

This was going to be a long week.

I stood in the kitchen and eyed up the remaining sherry on the worktop. I was half of the mind that it was eyeing me back, warily. Paddy was always rolling his eyes at me for giving objects personalities and feelings. There's a name for it, but I couldn't recall it. For instance, I rotate which plates and bowls I use so that the ones at the bottom don't feel left out and get a trip out of the cupboard in turn. I also reward my favourite mugs with an indulgent hot chocolate every once in a while and I imagine it's like a treat for them.

Perhaps he is right, maybe I am losing it.

I drummed my fingers on the counter surface, considering. The sherry would calm my anxiety temporarily, but I didn't want to make it a habit. A coping mechanism. How do you know when you are in dangerous territory?

Just have one, for goodness' sake.

I started to reach out for the bottle when the harsh ring from the landline startled me. I felt a heavy weight settle on me and my shoulders dropped.

What now?

I headed into the lounge and picked up the receiver.

"Hello?"

"Patrick?"

I rolled my eyes.

"Hi Evelyn. No, he's still at work."

There was a pause.

"Do you need anything?"

"Patrick?"

Evelyn sounded a bit quavery. A burst of static hit my ear. Perhaps it was the line. I raised my voice and over-enunciated.

"No Evelyn, it's Mena. Patrick is still at work. Are you ok?"

I heard the faint sound of the musical countdown from Pointless kick in.

"Do you think you could..." Evelyn began.

"Yes?" I asked, trying not to let any exasperation seep into my voice.

"If you could..." her voice was swallowed up by a crackle and the line went dead.

"Evelyn? Hello?"

There was no response. I hung up and rubbed my cheek. I weighed up my options. Paddy was on a job in Chadderton and would not be back until at least seven tonight. I didn't want a re-run of our argument on Friday night, I'd already had enough confrontation today, I felt wrung out with it.

I damped down a prickle of irritation, gave my halo a quick buff and reached for my mobile and keys. I'd have to go around and see what she wanted.

I hurried up the path, waving hello to Maud, who was placing a frog with a gaudy gold crown next to a pottery meerkat on the patch of grass outside her bungalow. There was barely any space left in the enclosed section, although I had a sneaking suspicion that the barriers had been moved slightly to enlarge the enclosure.

I rang the bell and rapped on the frosted glass. There was a distinct chill in the air tonight. I pulled my cardigan together over my front and folded my arms across my chest, my keys dangling from my index finger.

I waited for a moment, expecting to see Evelyn's familiar outline emerge through the pane. Still nothing.

I leaned forward and pushed the bell again.

"Just a minute!"

Slowly, a shape appeared and made its way towards the door. The chain rattled.

I shifted my weight from one foot to the other and breathed out puffs of air. I really should have worn my coat.

Eventually, the door creaked open and Evelyn stepped back to let me in, shuffling her tartan slippers on the carpet as she moved away. I stepped over the threshold.

"Hi Evelyn, I've popped in to see you're ok, the phone line was bad," I said loudly, wiping my feet on the mat at the same time.

"Come in dear," said Evelyn, leading the way to the lounge.

I shut the front door and followed her in. The fug was cloying, I was immediately pleased that I hadn't bothered with my coat after all. I would be sweating in a moment. The news was blaring, intoning its depressing stories to the whole bungalow.

Evelyn grunted and sat in her chair, reaching for the remote to turn down the volume. I hovered awkwardly in the middle of the room. I didn't like to just sit myself down in the hallowed space that was reserved for Paddy.

"Are you all right?" I prompted, the keys jingling in my hand. "You were asking if I could do something but then the phone cut off."

Evelyn readjusted herself in the chair and grunted again as she settled.

"I want my shoebox of letters from the wardrobe," she began. "But I can't reach. They're on top of my wardrobe. In my bedroom."

I felt a momentary pang of pity for Evelyn as I imagined her frustration at not being able to potter around her own home and do what she wanted. Getting older and infirm must be rubbish.

"Fine," I said briskly. "I'll fetch them now, just a minute."

I pocketed my keys and wandered out into the hallway. The bedroom door was ajar and I pushed it open, the carpet catching on the bottom. I clicked on the light and moved towards the wardrobe.

It was a huge walnut veneer monstrosity with curved decoration work at the top. No wonder she couldn't reach it. I stood on tiptoe and stretched up, my fingertips grazing the cardboard box emblazoned with Clarks branding. I couldn't quite reach.

I opened the wardrobe door and tested my weight on the base inside. It creaked but seemed firm enough and would give me the couple of extra inches that I needed. I decided that Evelyn wouldn't mind. I stepped forward with my full weight and reached up again, this time managing to get a firm grip on the corner of the box.

"Got it!" I called, stepping out from the wardrobe and closing the door.

As I turned to leave the room, I caught sight of Evelyn's bedside cabinet. She only had one, the bed was pushed up against the wall. A large print novel rested on the top, pinned down by an outsize magnifying glass, accompanied by a small half-empty glass of water and a pot of prescription pills. It felt sad and lonely.

I flicked off the switch, pulled the door to and walked back into the lounge.

"Here you go," I said softly, and slid the box onto the occasional table next to her armchair.

Not that you'll get any thanks for it.

Evelyn patted the arm of her chair and nodded.

"Thank you, dear."

I blinked in surprise.

Wonders will never cease! Perhaps she's mellowing in her old age.

"Um, you're welcome," I managed. "Is there anything else I can do for you?"

"No, no, just my letters. You'll be wanting to get back to make Patrick his tea. He'll want looking after, after a busy day at work."

And who will look after me?

"OK then, if you're sure. Don't get up, I'll see myself out."

I turned and made my way out into the hallway. As I left the lounge, I heard Evelyn muttering to herself.

"Didn't take her shoes off again."

Not mellowed much then.

Still, I had a thank you this time which was a definite

improvement.

CHAPTER FIFTEEN

I sat on the train on my way in and stared unseeingly at the plastic wall. Typically, I had not been lucky enough to secure a seat by the window. I was uncomfortably aware of the manspreader next to me, whose right leg was firmly pressed against mine, with legs akimbo. I glanced down towards his crotch area. Didn't look that impressive to me, I wasn't sure why he felt the need to give his nether regions so much additional space. Perhaps he was over-compensating.

Naomi's last day. I certainly wouldn't miss her. She was lazy, smug and took advantage of the fact that I was apparently a useless manager. I shifted irritably in my seat. At the very least, I would save money on replacement cereal bars once her pilfering (but perfectly manicured) fingers were no longer on the premises.

But. Her departure would only hurry along my own possible departure from a job that I cared about and had devoted a lot of time and energy to over the years. I didn't do well with uncertainty and at the moment I felt as though I was standing on shifting sands, surrounded by shark-infested waters in the middle of an earthquake. It was very unsettling.

I pulled out my book and tried to focus on the sentences, but the words lurched about and skittered away. Try as I might, I couldn't pin them down and use my brain to slip into the alternative dimension. I felt like Gandalf at the entrance to the Mines of Moria without the password. I sighed in frustration and snapped it shut.

I reached down to my bag, which I had placed between my feet on the floor. Unfortunately, because of my neighbour's firmly encroaching leg, I couldn't open my own knees enough to grab the strap. I tutted in annoyance.

Shove him back!

I sat up again and looked across at my fellow passenger. He was in his early twenties, in jeans and a slogan t-shirt, with earbuds firmly twisted into his ears. He was entirely focused on the phone in his hands. He couldn't be more oblivious if he tried.

I felt a surge of irritation. I bet he never got taken advantage of. He probably casually sauntered through life, doing what he liked and not caring if he upset other people.

Selfish pig.

"Selfish pig," I muttered, giving malevolent side-eye.

There was no flicker of anything to show that he had heard me. My frustration ramped up a notch.

"I said, selfish pig!" Marginally louder.

Still nothing.

Well, that was worthwhile. Great job.

Manspreader sniggered at something on his phone and threw his head back, a lock of hair falling across his forehead.

I snapped. Without a moment's hesitation, I firmly grabbed his knee and shoved it back towards his other leg. Without releasing it, I swiftly reached down, pulled up my bag and pushed it safely onto my lap, before swinging my own legs as open as far as I could. Only then did I remove my hand and place it triumphantly on my bag.

Manspreader flinched and looked over at me with something approaching disgust and disbelief on his face.

"What are you doing?" he asked, frowning at me before looking down at the leg that was currently pushed up against his own.

Being selfish like you!

"Being selfish like you!" I retorted, unable to stop a smug smile from appearing on my face.

"What?" he asked, scowling.

"Not very convenient for you is it, having someone else's leg shoving up against you in your own personal space?" I continued, gaining in self-righteous momentum by the second.

"What are you on about?"

I could tell the atmosphere had changed around us and that our fellow travellers were avidly listening to this exchange.

"Keep your legs to yourself in future. Stop pretending you need that much space," I said meaningfully, feeling very risqué and on the edge.

I heard a surprised gasp from the seat behind.

"Weirdo," he said, with an uneasy sneer.

However, he did pivot himself around in the chair before resuming his legs open pose, but at least this time one knee was sticking out into the aisle, with the leg nearest me remaining within his designated passenger space.

I retreated my own leg back into my own passenger area. My heart was hammering and I could feel a flush in my cheeks. I waited for a moment to see if we were done.

Manspreader returned to his phone with a shake of his head.

See, stand up for yourself. Wasn't that hard, was it?

Despite my trembling hands, I felt a bit proud of myself. I took a deep breath and carefully reached down to retrieve my book, which had slid off my lap onto the floor. I manoeuvred it into my handbag and zipped it safely away.

I couldn't think why I didn't do this more often.

I sailed into my cubicle, riding on the crest of a wave of newly found self-confidence. I slung my bag onto my desk and removed my coat with a flourish. I even started to hum something tuneless but bombastic.

I pulled out my chair and sat down, reaching over to power up my PC. Mid-hum, I waggled both index fingers in an approximation of a conductor. I would get through today on my own terms. Watch out world.

"Mena?"

I abruptly stopped humming and swivelled my chair around. Kelly stood in the entrance, a quizzical smile on her lips. She was clearly enjoying the impromptu performance.

Don't look embarrassed.

I cleared my throat.

"Morning Kelly."

I lifted my chin and met her gaze full-on.

"Morning." Another smile. "I wanted to check with you about the arrangements for Naomi's last day tomorrow."

"OK," I said warily, wondering what was coming next.

"I'll be doing her exit interview at 11am, we felt that would be easier in light of... sensitivities."

I frowned. That was fine by me.

"Fine," I said.

"Have you arranged a card or anything?"

No, but I can arrange a boot in her backside on her way out the door.

I blinked. It hadn't even crossed my mind. Everyone knew that I would be glad to see the back of her and it would have been two-faced to have pretended any differently.

"No, do I need to?"

Kelly held my gaze for a beat.

"Usually the manager makes the arrangements, but it's fine, we have a stock of cards up in HR for this eventuality. I'll just write a general one and sign it from her colleagues."

"Surely she can't expect a big send-off, in the circumstances?" I blurted, feeling heat rising up from my neck towards my face.

"Maybe not, but there are things that we usually do for form's sake. Naomi has chosen to leave, there were no marks against her as far as HR is concerned. We hadn't been given any official grounds to challenge her employment record here."

It felt like a reprimand. Kelly knew that I had been trying to resolve the issues myself before taking it further with HR officially. She knew what Naomi had been like.

The flush had reached my cheeks and I could feel my frustration building dangerously.

You knew what was going on!

"You knew what was going on though," I said quietly. I had been hoping for a reasonable tone, but it came out accusatory.

"And what had been done officially about it?" asked Kelly, also aiming for a reasonable tone and actually managing it.

233

I pinched my lips together.

"I had been working on the issues and documenting everything, I was about to..."

"Well never mind," Kelly cut me off. "It's all irrelevant now. We'll give her the card after lunch and then she'll probably leave early, there won't be much point in her waiting until the end of the day. Unless she's got any outstanding tasks you've given her?"

I just wanted it all to be done with. There would be no point in making her stay when I knew full well that she would not finish her work.

"No," I pushed out between gritted teeth.

"Great. OK then."

Kelly nodded and disappeared. I sat back in my chair and swung from side to side, feeling deflated and ridiculous. The euphoria from a few moments before had totally evaporated.

I also felt let down. It sounded like Kelly was covering her back. We had had several informal conversations about Naomi and approaches that I might take to improve matters. She had never been anything but sympathetic and helpful. The atmosphere had definitely changed.

I had the distinct feeling that I was on my way out.

As if on cue, Naomi floated into our workspace, followed closely behind by her own miasmic cloud of fragrance.

"Morning," said Naomi.

This was a rare occurrence, an actual proper greeting.

"Well good morning," I replied, in saccharine tones. "Big day for you!"

Naomi swung her bag off her shoulder and turned to look at me suspiciously.

"Would you like a farewell cereal bar, to mark this special occasion?" I trilled, pulling open my desk drawer and waving my hand at the array of snacks in the manner of a gameshow hostess. "Or you could always help yourself, you know where they are."

Narrowing her eyes, Naomi looked me up and down.

"No, you're all right," she said, looking at me as if I was an exhibit.

"OK then!" I responded, pushing the drawer closed and smiling at her companionably.

"All right then," replied Naomi after a moment. She shook her head and turned to switch on her PC.

I remained where I was, smiling at her back while she settled herself.

"Oy oy! Big day today!"

Lucas appeared, like a particularly unwelcome genie. He must have seen Naomi arrive at work and headed straight over. At least with Naomi gone, he would have no reason to visit my workspace in future.

Naomi turned around and treated him to a wide grin.

"Hello Lucas! I know, last day!"

I smiled happily between them both, as if I was involved in the conversation. I was aware that I probably looked unhinged. Perhaps I was.

"Well, you'll definitely be missed," continued Lucas, smoothing down his cheap shirt with a clammy hand. "You're my favourite colleague."

Lucky you!

"Lucky you, Naomi, what an honour!" I said, without any audible trace of irony.

Naomi flashed me a look. It was obvious to anyone that she only gave Lucas the time of day because he flattered her and was somebody to distract herself from work with.

"What will you do without her Lucas?" I asked sorrowfully, peeping up at him with sympathetic eyes.

Lucas eyed me warily, weighing up my intentions.

"It won't be the same that's for sure," he said, carefully.

Taking back the reins, Naomi flicked her hair over her shoulder and took a step towards Lucas.

"That's so sweet," she said, regaining his attention.

"We'll have to meet up for lunch sometime," said Lucas with enthusiasm. "You won't be far away on Deansgate, once you're settled."

To give her credit, there was only the tiniest flicker across Naomi's perfectly made-up face.

"That would be nice," she said.

Don't be ridiculous. We both know you have no intention of seeing him ever again.

I snorted. Both Naomi and Lucas turned to look at me.

"What?" I asked in mock surprise. "Are we seriously pretending that she has any intention at all of ever seeing you again? She won't give you another thought once she leaves this building tonight."

Naomi shot me a look. Lucas glanced at Naomi.

"You won't, will you?" I pushed.

I had never seen Naomi flustered before and she certainly wasn't going to start now. The only ruffles that Naomi ever displayed were sartorial ones.

"Do shut up Mena," she said wearily.

I shrugged.

"No point in pretending otherwise," I said. "Unless you were actually planning on giving Lucas your number?"

There was an awkward pause. I couldn't actually bring myself to look at Lucas, much as I despised him. I was sure that he would be looking at Naomi hopefully, but pretending to be nonchalant.

The pause became embarrassing.

"Right," said Lucas eventually, clearing his throat. "I'd best be getting on. I just wanted to wish you well on your last day."

Normal service had been resumed.

"Thank you," purred Naomi. "I'm sure I'll see you again before I go."

"Yes, well…" Lucas tailed off, before shuffling away.

Naomi sat back down and tapped in her username and password.

"That wasn't very nice," she said.

"Why pretend otherwise?" I asked, without turning around. "And since when have you been bothered about being nice?"

"That's not like you," she responded.

"No, it's not is it," I pondered, clicking on my email and waiting for it to download.

I could feel Naomi's gaze on my back.

"Perhaps it's time that it was. Anyway, enjoy your last day."

The rest of the day passed fairly uneventfully. Naomi sauntered off for her eleven o'clock exit interview and returned shortly afterwards, casting a sly smile in my direction. I had no doubt that she had thrown me under the bus and spent most of it complaining about me. Well good for her, she wouldn't be my problem any more after today.

I immersed myself in a particularly challenging set of reconciliations and thankfully it did its usual trick of helping to distract me from my thoughts.

When lunchtime came, I decided to stay at my desk and eat my regular sandwich. Sliced chicken, grated cheese and a layer of ready salted crisps on top. I added the crisps at the last moment, otherwise the other components migrated all across my lunch box by the time I reached work. The crunch when eating it gave me an inordinate amount of pleasure with every bite, the saltiness heightening the taste. Usually, I tried to deaden any noise by pursing my mouth in a series of complicated movements and biting with caution, but today I really didn't care and crunched away as loudly as I could.

A glance over at Naomi's back gave me the impression that she wasn't appreciating my sandwich as much as I was. The occasional irritated flicker of movement belied that I was definitely getting on her nerves.

Good.

A polite cough signalled that someone had arrived at our cubicle. I didn't bother turning around. I left that to Naomi.

"Naomi," said Kelly's voice. "As it's your last day we wanted to give you this card from your colleagues."

We?

I twisted in my chair to see who had been marshalled together to attend this ridiculous show of a send-off. Lucas (of course), Andy from the cubicle next door. Two admin girls from the other side of the vending machine and that was it. I felt a pleased pang that Sarah had not bothered to attend.

"We wish you well in your future endeavours," continued Kelly, all professional sweetness and light. "Good luck!"

A half-hearted smattering of applause broke out and the card was passed over to Naomi, who rose to receive it as graciously as an award recipient at the BAFTAs.

"Thank you," said Naomi with a generous smile. "I'm looking forward to my next chapter."

More like a paragraph if your time here is anything to go by. Or maybe even a sentence.

I surprised myself with a snort and tried to cover it by coughing into my hand. Kelly frowned at me, but Naomi didn't even waver.

"Well, good luck," repeated Kelly, before turning and ushering the others away with her.

The air settled and I busied myself with my work, tapping away on the screen in what I hoped was a nonchalant manner. I heard Naomi sit back in her chair with a creak and then tear open the envelope.

"Oh, how nice," she said. "A gift card."

That must be from the HR stockpile as well. As if anyone would have chipped in for one. I pulled a face to myself.

More noises from behind me as though Naomi was

rummaging in her bag and opening and closing drawers.

"I may as well head off in a minute," she said, as though to herself. "No point sticking around anymore."

No, not really. Not that she ever actually did anything useful at any other point in her employment either. She had made a mockery of the job I loved and made the pleasure I took in my job feel tarnished too.

The now ever-present feeling of frustration and resentment began to build in me again, I could feel it forcing its way up through my chest. I swallowed a couple of times and tried to breathe in through my nose, but the air didn't seem to be getting through. My jaw clenched and the heat rose in my face.

Don't let her get to you.

But I couldn't seem to help it. Angry tears of frustration appeared in my eyes and I blinked rapidly to try and get rid of them before they trickled down my face. I didn't want her to see how upset I was. I abruptly stood up, pushing my chair behind me with the backs of my knees before turning to hurry out of the cubicle. I wouldn't give her the satisfaction.

I rushed towards the ladies and barged in through the door. Mercifully, it was empty. I ran the cold tap and splashed my face, taking in deep shuddering breaths. No wonder people did this a lot on the television, it definitely helped.

I couldn't understand why I felt so overwhelmed. These sorts of outbursts were not like me at all. Well, not like the version of me that I tried so hard to be. I was worried that if I couldn't get a handle on them, I might get myself into some trouble.

I began to count slowly up to one hundred, leaning forwards with my hands on the counter and my eyes closed. I would conquer this.

A few moments later, I cautiously approached my cubicle, trying to look unfazed. Nothing to see here, definitely not someone on the verge of a meltdown!

I straightened my back, hummed quietly to myself and strolled towards my workstation. Naomi's chair was empty, her space had been cleared. Even my old friend Daniel Craig had been removed, with four drawing pins stuck haphazardly into the fabric divider wall the only sign that he had ever taken up residence. I felt a pang as I realised that I would miss him much more than I would miss Naomi. I had got quite used to his brooding presence.

However, I breathed a sigh of relief. No awkward goodbyes and opportunities for slights and snide comments. I wasn't sure how much more of those I could absorb today or how I would react.

I pulled back my office chair and was surprised to see an envelope on the seat. I looked quickly around to see if anyone was peering around a corner and watching me. Nothing.

I reached down and picked up the envelope, turning it around in my fingers. There was no writing on the front. It could only be from Naomi.

With slightly trembling fingers I flicked open the flap and withdrew the small slip of paper inside. It was a torn piece of lined paper from one of our work notepads.

"Thanks for the cereal bars."

I exclaimed and reached down to pull open my desk drawer. My cereal bars were all gone. Another small piece of torn paper skittered around in the empty space, a crude smiley face drawn on it in biro.

Cow.

CHAPTER SIXTEEN

By the time I'd finished that day's to do list, I was on the later train home. I trudged morosely along the packed station platform. I was not looking forward to my meeting with Kelly and Sarah in the morning. It felt like everything was unravelling and any semblance of control I had over my life had melted away.

The train pulled in and there was a surge towards the doors. I hung back and waited as the beeping noise heralded the opening of the doors. There was the usual jostling as passengers disembarked and those on the platform jockeyed for position to jump on the moment the way was clear. I couldn't be bothered with all that tonight. How pathetic, a few seconds weren't going to make much difference.

With heavy feet, I hauled myself up the steps and into the carriage. The jostlers were already settling down in their chosen seats, phones out and bags stowed on the floor. I scanned the carriage for an empty seat, locating one midway along. A man in a drab and shiny old suit was hovering next to it, eyeballing the passenger who was sat against the window.

I moved towards them to see what was going on. As I approached, I could see that the person by the window had placed a large leather bag on the vacant seat and was doing a sterling impression of someone who was totally unaware of their surroundings. It was a young woman in an artfully slouched jumper in tones of beige and cream. Her lustrous golden hair fell in perfectly created waves and she would give

Naomi a run for her money in the make-up stakes.

The man gave a cough and pointedly stared at the girl, shifting from one foot to another in an attempt to draw her attention.

The girl ignored him, focusing on her phone screen with admittedly impressive front. The man knew when he was beaten. He wasn't the type to make a fuss, from his hangdog demeanour to his unprepossessing presence that much was clear. He pursed his lips and moved away towards the next carriage.

The boiling frustration that had apparently become my new constant companion began to bubble. I could feel a now familiar tightening in my chest. I approached.

"Can you move your bag?" I said in assertive tones, laced with an edge of irritation.

Yes, that's right woman, I didn't say please. You don't deserve such a courtesy.

She sighed and slightly adjusted her position, but didn't even bother to look at me.

Rude.

"You're rude," I said loudly, stating the obvious.

A slight frown flickered over the girl's brow, before she deigned to raise her eyes to mine.

"What?" she drawled, as if I was a slight irritant who wasn't worth the effort. Which to her, I probably wasn't.

"I said move your bag."

I clenched my hands into fists, but kept my face calm and set.

The girl smirked and turned back to her screen. Clearly, she thought that that would be enough to deflect me. But I was more of a worthy opponent than Mr Shiny Suit. Maybe not before now, but I was today.

"OK then, can you show me the ticket that you must have bought for your so very important bag to justify giving it its own seat?"

"What are you on about?" sneered the girl, flicking her eyes back to me.

You heard.

"You heard. That bag is not more important than me and I will be sitting down. So, I suggest you move it."

My heart was thumping by now, but I was resolute.

"If you say so," said the girl with a sardonic smile, doing the age-old mean girl up and down look.

"Yes, I do. You have three seconds to move it, or I will."

"You can't touch my property."

"You can't take up a seat with an inanimate object when I have a ticket."

"Well, I'm not moving it."

"Well, I will then," I retorted.

I reached down, grabbed the bag and thrust it into her lap. I leaned forward so that my face was just a couple of inches from hers and fixed her with my angry stare.

"Say one word and you will regret it," I hissed, all reserve having packed up and absconded several minutes ago.

Our gazes remained locked as she considered her position. I refused to give an inch and I was half hoping she wouldn't give in. I knew I had over-reacted, but there was no way that I was backing down. I had no idea what I was going to do if she didn't let me have my way and there was something slightly exhilarating about that.

The girl rolled her eyes, took hold of her bag and turned slightly towards the window.

I sat down with a thump, with the thrill of victory and adrenaline from the confrontation surging through my veins. I felt jittery but resolved. Standing up for myself and calling out injustice was a novel experience for me. I usually sucked it up and seethed about it for hours, complaining at length later to Paddy who would barely conceal his frustration.

I took a deep breath and smiled grimly. Perhaps the worm had finally turned.

The high of victory stayed with me all the way home. Bag Girl got off on the stop before mine and I took some satisfaction in making her wait several seconds before moving sideways so that she could get out of her seat. She then made a point of whacking me with her bag as she went past (accidentally on purpose of course) but I still felt that I had had the best of her overall. I was fed up of people like her lording it over people like me and Mr Shiny Suit.

I disembarked at my usual stop and emerged from the station office into weak sunlight. I closed my eyes for a second and took in a deep breath through my mouth. I could actually feel my lungs expanding this time, the tightness had eased. I shunted forward a pace as a man striding past collided with my shoulder. I turned my head to stare at him and was on the verge of my default reaction – to apologise for being in the way – when I caught myself. No.

I pulled out my mobile and selected Annie's number from the list of recent calls. As it began to ring, I trotted down the steps and began my walk home.

"Hello?"

Annie sounded frazzled and distracted. I glanced at my watch. It was probably the kids' teatime.

"Hi, sorry, is this a bad time, should I call back later?"

"No, you're ok, just give me a minute to put the…"

Annie tailed off and I could hear some complicated sounds of banging and clanging in the background followed by the noise of a cupboard door opening and shutting with a whack. The clatter of a plate.

"Oof, sorry, just dishing up the kids' food. They've got it now, they should be quiet for a bit."

"Are you sure?"

"Absolutely. The presentation is a bit slapdash but it's pizza slices and beans for Tom and finger food for Amy so I know they'll eat that without any messing about."

"No elaborate food art today then?" I asked with a chuckle, as I skirted a spillage on the pavement.

Annie laughed.

"No, that was definitely a special occasion."

A couple of months ago, Annie had sent me a photograph of the lunch she had made for Tom and Amy. She had spent time and considerable effort in creating faces out of a sandwich picnic lunch, with rolled ham for a tongue, circular buttered bread cheeks, tomatoes with raisins on top for eyes and even noodles for hair. Tom was still talking about it to this day, hopeful of a repeat performance.

"I still think I should try that for Paddy some time, but then he probably wouldn't even notice."

"Probably not," Annie agreed. "He's not the most observant soul is he."

"So how was your day then?"

I always made sure to ask first, I was too well-versed in the rules of conversation etiquette to launch straight into why I was calling.

"Oh, the usual," said Annie with a tired sigh. "Rhyme Time at the library this morning, swim tots this afternoon and lots of toilet duties inbetween. Quite fun actually, but I'm still worn out. It's amazing how much shaking jingle bells and singing nursery rhymes can take it out of you."

"I'm sure," I agreed, personally thinking that it actually sounded quite fun.

"How about you anyway," asked Annie. "In your mouth please, not on the floor! How was the dreaded Naomi's last day?"

I was impressed that she had remembered. With all the things Annie had to deal with, not to mention the sleep deprivation, she always seemed to manage to register what was going on and when.

"Oh, you know. Swanned in as usual, probably said all sorts of horrible things about me in her exit interview and then took off early with a swish of her shiny hair."

"Well, she's gone now. She isn't your problem anymore."

"No, thank goodness."

"Is it tomorrow you have your meeting with HR?"

I hadn't seen Annie since Tom's birthday party, but had kept her updated on the work situation.

"Yes, 10 o'clock. Think of me, I'm still convinced that they're going to get rid of me."

"Don't start catastrophising until you know for sure," said Annie in her most reasonable voice. "Remember what I've told you before. You can imagine the worst case scenario, then imagine the best outcome and it's usually somewhere inbetween."

"Usually," I agreed, fishing in my bag for my keys as I approached my street. "But not always and I have a very bad feeling about it."

"Well, try and keep an open mind," Annie responded, she knew me well enough not to push the positive when I was determined to focus on the negative.

"I will."

We both knew full well that I wouldn't.

"You won't believe what I did today," I said, a proud smile on my face.

"The dance of the seven veils for Lucas?"

I made a retching sound.

"Don't be disgusting, if you had actually met him..."

Annie laughed and I heard her running the tap.

"What then?"

"Today, I actually beat a Manspreader at his own game on the train. And then on the way home I had a confrontation with a seat hogger and actually won!"

"Oh my goodness, you actually took some action against injustice instead of just stewing about it? Are you feeling ok?"

I had reached my front door and slid the key into the lock.

"I'm not sure about that, but I felt very proud of myself for doing it. I thought I was going to have a heart attack at the time, but I felt good about myself afterwards."

I twisted the key and stepped into the front room, shutting the door with a flourish behind me.

"Good for you. I think it would do you good to get it out of your system now and then, instead of bottling it up all the time."

"Maybe," I conceded, throwing my bag down onto the sofa and shucking off my shoes. "Why do you think they need to do that?"

"Do what?"

"Sit with their legs so ridiculously far apart. They must realise that they're inconveniencing everyone else."

"Advertising their availability to mate in a primeval way? Ventilation? Pretending they have more than they do?"

I snorted.

"That's what I implied."

Annie giggled.

"It can't be for space reasons, I've seen plenty of men sitting with crossed legs, if they can manage that then there should be no need for aggressive leg splaying," she continued.

There was a shriek.

"No, Amy! Don't you dare!"

"What?"

"She's spitting out her chewed up tomatoes and breadsticks and throwing them over the side of the highchair onto the floor! I'm going to have to go, she's making a right mess."

I could hear Tom crowing and banging something in the background.

"Good luck tomorrow, let me know how you get on."

"I will – good luck to you too!"

But she had already gone. I stretched out my back and padded into the kitchen, placing my phone on the counter. I probably had an hour to myself before Paddy got home. My eyes flicked over to the bottle of sherry. I took a moment to consider.

Not today.

I reached over to the kettle instead and flicked the switch. I would take a shower, take the time to moisturise myself with my expensive cream, including arms and legs for the full experience, and have a cup of tea instead.

Bolstered with resolve, I headed upstairs.

Paddy sauntered in the kitchen, just as I was dishing up the southern fried chicken and oven chips. The perfect kind of comfort tea when you feel in need of a pick me up.

"Evenin' gorgeous," he chirped in a faux Cockney accent, predictably leaning past me to pinch a chip from a plate and pop it in his mouth.

"That one's yours then," I told him sternly, turning my cheek to him for a kiss.

"Fine by me," he said with a grin, before patting me on the backside. "Ooh, mini corn cobs too, we are going for the fine dining at home experience tonight!"

"Too right, don't say I don't look after you," I said, pushing his plate towards him and nodding towards the cutlery on the counter.

I reached for my own food and followed him into the lounge. Paddy managed to switch on the television with one hand and manoeuvre into his seat, all while balancing his plate in the other. If I tried that, there would be chips all over the floor.

"Good day?" I asked, sliding carefully down into my usual space on the sofa.

After the drama and excitement of the previous week, Paddy and I had soon settled back into our usual routines. Aside from a slight wariness for a couple of days, as if he was dealing with a harmless but unpredictable lunatic, we had moved past our big argument.

"Not bad," replied Paddy, shoving a piece of chicken into his mouth and vigorously chewing.

That was one of the things I found attractive about him, how he always seemed to relish his food and ate as though he was starving. I don't know why, maybe because it showed a zest for living.

"I've nearly finished that job near Shaw so I should hopefully get that done tomorrow in time for the weekend."

Like an idiot, I sat and waited for him to ask me how my day was. I was never going to learn. The Chase chuntered on in the background, with Paddy throwing out occasional, and usually incorrect, answers.

I sighed.

"It was Naomi's last day today," I prompted, looking balefully in his direction.

"Oh yes," he replied, licking his fingers. "How did that go?"

"OK. She's gone now anyway. But not before she cleared my cereal bars out of my drawer and left me a sarky note," I said, a hint of bitterness in my voice.

Paddy chuckled.

"She's got some front that one!"

And that was that. Apparently, that was all I was going to get about the big event that took place today.

"Tomorrow will be a big day," I continued.

"Anne Boleyn!" called out Paddy, stabbing a finger at the screen. "It's always Anne Boleyn," he said as an aside to me as if imparting a great secret that only he was privy to.

"So tomorrow…" I repeated.

Paddy frowned.

"Oh yes, your big meeting."

"Yes, that. It's at 10 o'clock so will you make sure you're thinking of me?"

Paddy smiled indulgently at me.

"Of course," he said.

We both knew that it wouldn't even cross his mind tomorrow morning. He would probably be listening to the radio whilst on the job in Shaw, singing along with enthusiasm in his own little world. Whereas if it was the other way around, I would clock watch all morning, set my phone alarm five minutes before and make sure to send positive thoughts as the clock struck ten.

Paddy didn't see the point in 'thinking of someone' at certain times, he didn't believe for one moment that it would make any difference at all. He was far too practical. When we had discussed this before, he had pointed out quite reasonably that he wasn't sure how "positive vibes" could make its way from one person to another when the other person was not in the immediate vicinity. Whereas I felt that it couldn't do any harm, might actually just work and at least made me feel better to think that someone else was thinking of me.

"I am pretty worried about it," I continued, furrowing my brow to show him just how concerned.

"There's no point though is there?" he said in the annoyingly patronising voice that he used when he felt I was over-reacting. "If they've decided to make you redundant then nothing that you say is going to change that. And there's no point in worrying about it now, is there, it's not going to change anything. Ronald Reagan!"

That was how Paddy's mind worked. Unless it was happening in the here and now, he could just not think about it. It amazed me that people could actually do that. I've joked with him before that he walked around with birdsong in his head and nothing else. Certainly not the judgmental, exhausting, continuous inner monologue that racketed through my head.

"Right," he said, brushing his hands together and standing up. "I'm going to have a quick shower and get changed. I'm meeting Tony at the pub."

"The pub?" I echoed.

"Yes! Quiz night?" he said, as if speaking to someone who was hard of hearing. "Remember? They switched nights this week because of the football."

"Oh right," I muttered, suddenly crestfallen. "I thought you might be in tonight, you know with what's happening tomorrow."

If I hadn't been so disappointed, it would have been funny to watch the confusion flicker across his face. He obviously couldn't comprehend how him being in the same room watching television with me tonight could possibly help with a meeting that was due to take place tomorrow.

"We've talked about it, haven't we?" he asked. "You know there's no point thinking about it all night until you know what's actually going to happen?"

"Fine."

"Fine fine, or annoyed fine?"

"*Fine*," I repeated through gritted teeth.

"Great," said Paddy who was never very good at picking up on inflections. "I'd best get ready. I'll wash up when I get back."

He disappeared into the kitchen and I heard the crash of the plate being dumped in the sink. He then leapt up the stairs, taking two at a time.

That was that then. If I couldn't rely on Paddy to be my emotional support tonight, I would have to turn to an old faithful instead. I pushed my empty plate onto the seat next to me and headed towards my bookcase.

Mildred Pierce. She was just the person I needed to invoke tonight, so that I had a good chance of channelling her tomorrow in my meeting. It was a film noir telling of a woman who became down on her luck and had to resort to waitressing to provide for her family. Her hard work and diligence resulted in a chain of successful restaurants before it all went to hell in a handcart again, but I was prepared to overlook that part. If Mildred could start again then so could I. If I had to.

I found the DVD straight away and pulled it off the shelf. Joan Crawford at her most commanding. I slid the disc into the DVD player and headed back to the kitchen, collecting my plate on the way. This called for chocolate and wine.

I grabbed a bottle of Rioja and reached for my favourite wine glass. I filched around the back of the tin cupboard until I found my hidden bar of raisin and biscuit Yorkie. I was nearly all set.

I carried my treats back into the lounge and set myself up properly. Wine within reach, blanket draped over me and chocolate on my lap. Perfect.

Paddy thundered down the stairs and swung by to plant a kiss on my head.

"Right, I'm off out. See you later!"

A moment later, the front door slammed and a gust of autumnal air swirled around the room. Fine. If Paddy couldn't or wouldn't do it, then Mildred would be my life coach.

I pressed play.

CHAPTER SEVENTEEN

I wasn't quite sure how I felt as I made my way into work the next morning. I felt apprehensive, resentful and also strangely calm despite my recent emotional outbursts. Almost as though I was a spectator in my own story, slightly removed from the action and buckled in for the ride. It was a very odd feeling.

I brooded as I stared out of the window, watching the familiar landscape rushing by. There was the house with the shed full of breeding guinea pigs at the bottom of the long narrow garden. There was the conservatory window with the full-sized cut out figure of Pedro Pascal from Kingsman, complete with whip. He was facing outwards as if placed there for the benefit of passing trains, rather than inwards for the house occupants. And there was the children's nursery with the brightly coloured hopscotch grid painted on the tarmac, leaves swirling in eddies in the corners of the playground.

That was my signal that Piccadilly station would shortly be the next stop. I gathered my bag straps together and got ready to exit the train.

I entered my building and the strange sense of detachment continued. I looked about me with fresh eyes as I appraised the reception area that I had walked past each workday for several years. As I rode in the lift, I re-read the notices and signs as if I hadn't read them all a thousand times before. As I walked onto my floor, I scanned the layout, acknowledging each familiar feature. Nothing had changed, but it felt slightly off-kilter.

I strode into my cubicle and dropped my bag onto the desk. No Daniel to say hello to this morning. I hadn't realised how that was part of my morning routine, nodding over at him in greeting (it would have felt rude not to). I shrugged off my coat and pulled out my chair, sinking down into it. My usual drive and motivation seemed to have vanished. I considered the power button on my PC, staring at it as if it might turn on by itself. That gave me an idea and I frowned in concentration as I decided to try a spot of telekinesis.

Use the force, Mena.

I bent every fibre of my consciousness towards it. Nothing. Well, it was worth a try. I leaned forward in resignation and pushed in the button.

The computer stuttered into life and began to chunter away to itself as it powered up. I fished in my handbag and pulled out my phone.

A message from Annie: Good luck! Give them hell today xx

Nothing from Paddy, although I did get a grunt off him this morning as I slid out of bed. I chose to assume that it conveyed his message of support although it could equally have been a grunt of frustration that I had disturbed his sleep.

I tapped out a quick reply to Annie: Thanks, I'll try xx

I opened my desk drawer and dropped my phone into it with a clatter. Although I supposed it wouldn't really matter now, I didn't have to set an example to Naomi about personal phone use anymore. I could leave the phone on my desk and to hell with it. But old habits die hard. I left it in the drawer.

I double-checked the meeting entry on my Outlook calendar. 10 o'clock. That gave me an hour.

I pulled my A4 notepad out of my desk tray and flipped it open to a blank double page spread. On the left page, I wrote the title "My qualities and achievements" and underlined it. On the right page, I wrote "Accounts Team structure" and did the same.

I knew how thoughts floated out of my head when under pressure and wanted to make sure I had an arsenal of supporting information if required. I frowned in concentration and began to write. I wouldn't go down without a fight.

I approached the meeting room at 9:59 exactly. Perhaps unsurprisingly, Sarah and Kelly were already seated side by side together. I had checked the meeting room diary and they had booked the room out from 9am. No doubt they wanted to get together and finalise their approach before I arrived.

I knocked firmly on the door.

"Come in!" called Kelly.

I took a deep breath, shrugged my shoulders once to release the tension and then pushed down hard on the handle and opened the door.

"Good morning," they said in stereo.

I looked closely at them both as I approached the chair opposite them. They looked calm and detached, I couldn't read from their faces what might lie ahead.

"Sarah. Kelly."

I took a seat and laid out my notepad and pen in front of me and crossed my ankles beneath my chair.

"OK," began Sarah. "As you know from our last meeting, with Naomi's departure, we have been exploring the future of the Accounts Team and engaging in deep discussion with management about how we can best serve the needs of the business."

I gazed at her, resolved not to do my usual repertoire of validating head nods, smiles and positive affirmations like a pathetic nodding dog. It was harder than I expected.

"We have spent a lot of time this week plotting out various structures and scenarios and we feel that the optimal way forward for us as an organisation is to outsource our Accounts function."

There was a pause.

"I'm sorry, I realise that this will not be the news that you were hoping for."

How arrogant!

I cleared my throat.

"Well, that's a bit of an assumption," I managed, in a clear but low voice.

"Sorry?" asked Sarah, clearly a little surprised at my response.

I clasped my hands together in my lap.

"When you first floated this possibility last week, I'll admit that I was knocked sideways and the initial thought of losing the job that I loved was pretty overwhelming. But I've had a lot of time to think since then."

This was not how Kelly and Sarah had expected the meeting to go. I could sense a readjustment of focus and Kelly imperceptibly leaned forward.

"I feel that I've worked really hard for this company during my years here. I've standardised procedures and I've worked over and above to make sure that I can be proud of what I produce and how I support this organisation."

Kelly nodded, hopefully in acknowledgement.

"I had thought that I was a valued member of staff," I continued, rising slightly in volume. "That the work I put in was recognised. I never missed a deadline or let anyone down. Ever."

Sarah broke in, no doubt in an attempt to cut off my flow.

"And no-one is disputing that technically you have been an undoubted asset to the business. However..."

I raised up my hand in a 'stop' motion.

"No."

"Pardon?" Sarah was taken aback.

"No, I don't want to hear about the 'however'. It's obvious that I'm being made redundant and if you start to list all the reasons why you feel I've failed as an employee then I'm going to stop you right there. It won't change the outcome and will just make me feel worse."

Listen to yourself! You're doing so well!

"Maybe I'm not a great manager. But it wasn't for lack of trying. And you knew," I pointed at Kelly, "that I was having issues with Naomi and you even suggested approaches to take, informally. I was trying hard. You should have told me to make it formal if you felt that was needed. I was following your guidance."

A slight flush on her cheeks was the only indication that Kelly had been affected by what I had said. But then HR people must be used to difficult conversations.

"And you," I said, now pointing at Sarah in a very rude manner (for me). "You also suspected there were problems but as long as I kept covering for Naomi and making sure the work was done, you didn't seem that bothered either."

Sarah wasn't going to take that lying down.

"You were the team leader, Mena, it was up to you to bring any issues to me or Kelly."

"And I did. But because I didn't do it formally, it didn't get me anywhere. Well, I've learnt my lesson from that."

There was an awkward pause, which I was determined not to fill.

"I'm not sure that it is going to be helpful to continue in this way," said Kelly, in her calm HR voice.

"Probably not," I agreed. "I'm clearly on my way out so there's no point in discussing it. So why don't you just tell me what's next."

Sarah tilted her head and considered me appraisingly. She was not used to any Mena other than the acquiescent people-pleaser. This would be a bit of a surprise for her.

"Well," began Kelly, looking pleased to be able to get back on script. "You have worked here for eight years, so that means that you are entitled to eight week's notice. Here is your redundancy schedule."

She opened up the folder in front of her and slid the piece of paper across the desk towards me. I glanced at the figures.

"I see. And do I get paid in lieu of notice so that I don't have to work that notice? Because you see, all of a sudden I don't feel like working here anymore. When you realise that you are totally expendable, you suddenly lose all motivation."

Kelly and Sarah exchanged a glance.

"We can arrange that," said Kelly cautiously.

"So, I can finish today and that's it?" I persisted. "I won't pretend to know how these things work as I've never been made redundant before. But I just want to point out that if I was expected to work those five weeks, you might find that I'm too poorly to come into work anyway. This process has put me through a lot of stress."

"It can be with immediate effect," Kelly confirmed, watching me closely. "This has clearly been a big shock for you and you don't seem to be yourself."

"No, I'm being myself. I'm just standing up for myself for once, which is quite a novel experience. Will I still get a card and voucher from the HR stockpile?"

My voice finally broke and my lip wobbled as the emotion of the situation finally caught up with my bravado.

"I'm only sorry that I'm leaving under these circumstances, with my perception of myself as a valued employee in tatters," I managed.

"There has never been any question that the standard of your work…" began Kelly, who had taken on the mantle of Good Cop for this meeting.

I held up my hand once again, like a robotic traffic management police officer.

"Let's not," I said, running out of steam. "It's a bit late for that. But I will expect an excellent reference for all my hard work."

I fixed Kelly with a stare and was relieved to see that she nodded.

"Fine. Just tell me what I need to do and then I'll go and clear my desk. Just be aware that if you outsource your accounts to Naomi's new place and she's in charge of them, she'll do an utterly crap job."

It was a petty last shot, but one I wanted to make. If they were disappointed in me, I may as well go the whole hog.

"OK, let's go through the paperwork," said Kelly reaching for her folder again. "We'll try and make this as straightforward as possible."

And that was that.

CHAPTER EIGHTEEN

I swear there is a sensor on my kitchen cupboards. I always seem to have my head in one when the phone starts ringing.

I shuffled backwards and reached for my mobile on the countertop. Paddy.

"Hello," I said grumpily. "How do people always know when I'm in the kitchen cupboard?"

I could hear the sound of Paddy's van in motion.

"Because you live in one? Like Harry Potter?"

He sounded as though he was shouting across a crowded pub. Nothing like talking to someone on a hands-free kit.

"That was an understairs cupboard, that made more sense," I replied, picking up a jar of pasta sauce before putting it back down again.

"Maybe space wise, but it's more practical to be in with the food if you think about it," he continued. "I know where I'd rather be!"

Are we really having this conversation?

"What's up?" I asked, not really in the mood to talk nonsense.

"I'm nearly home," he bellowed. "But I'm going to call in on nan on the way home, I managed to get her those bin liners she wanted from Wilko."

I pulled out a jar of curry sauce and reached for a tin of

chickpeas.

"So, I'll see you in about forty-five minutes then?" I prompted.

"Yes, roundabout then. I'm not going to bother having a brew, I'll just drop these liners off and come straight home."

"Right, I'll have tea ready. See you in a bit."

I jabbed my finger at the screen and put the phone back onto the work surface. That gave me an hour and a half to myself before Paddy came home. I tapped the curry jar thoughtfully. We didn't have any chicken defrosted and I couldn't be bothered with defrosting some from the freezer. Could I use tuna, was tuna curry an actual thing?

Don't be disgusting, that's a culinary low, even for you!

Fine, it would just have to be a vegetarian bean curry then. I didn't have the motivation or mental capacity for anything else. I returned to the tin cupboard and pulled out some kidney beans and a can of cannellini beans for good measure. I popped the ring pulls on both and drained them in a colander over the sink.

I sloshed a measure of oil into the large saucepan, flicked on the power and tossed in a handful of frozen chopped onions. I rummaged in the utensil drawer swearing, until my fingers located the wooden spoon. I pulled it out, along with the potato masher and tongs which decided to hitch a ride. One vigorous shake and the interlopers skittered noisily across the floor.

"Bugger off!" I exclaimed, aiming a kick at the nearest implement.

The onions began to spit and sweat in the pan. I gave them a quick swirl, before twisting open the curry jar and upending the sauce on top with a splat. I fetched the colander and tipped the beans into the pan. Another stir. I stared at the concoction.

It all looked a bit brown and orange, it needed something else.

Green always made a meal look more appetising. I opened the freezer door and pulled out a bag of frozen peas. That should do the trick. I released the clip, unleashed a torrent of mini green cannonballs into the curry and then gave it another good stir.

That would have to do. Gourmet cooking in a rush at its finest. I reduced the heat to simmer on low, covered the pan with a lid and headed back to the lounge. With any luck, it would look as though I had spent much more time on it than I actually had. With some microwaveable rice and the mini naans it might turn out to be surprisingly good.

I sank down on the sofa and tilted my head back onto the rest. I felt drained, sad and weary all at the same time. I couldn't believe that just a week ago I had been thinking about how much better it would be at work with a new assistant in place. How the stresses of the last few months with Naomi would finally be in the past and I could look forward to doing the job I enjoyed with, hopefully, someone who was on my wavelength. Look where I was now. Unemployed, no immediate prospects and with a burgeoning alcohol problem.

Look at the state of you.

I burst into tears.

Pull yourself together!

Fifteen minutes later, the worst of the storm had passed. I wiped my eyes and blew my nose noisily into a tissue. I felt a little better, as though a release valve had been activated to reduce some of the pressure. I could easily have carried on with my crying fit, but wanted to recover a bit before Paddy came home. He didn't cope very well with extremes of emotion and if he was greeted with a weeping wife as he came in the door, it would be awkward for both of us.

I reached for the remote and flicked on the television. A bit of mindless viewing should help calm me down and keep my mind off things. I scrolled through the menu. Homes under the Hammer, perfect. I selected the channel and wiped my nose again. I loved watching the transformations of unloved homes into sleek, revamped living spaces. If only we had some capital, I could maybe go into property development. I would love to have a portfolio of something, it sounds so grand. Why not have a portfolio of properties?

For a moment I allowed myself the indulgence of imagining my property empire and the resulting millions flowing into our bank account. Who was I kidding, I couldn't even manage one difficult assistant at work, who was I to think I could manage a building project?

I watched the progress on the projects and then the property reveals with interest. It was amazing how a bit of investment and a refresh could make such a difference to a knackered old house. I looked around our lounge. It could do with a paint and a bit of a clear out. Perhaps I could spend some time on it now that I was facing the prospect of being unemployed with more time on my hands.

Tears sprang into my eyes.

Remembering the bottle of sherry in the kitchen, I felt a flash of resolve. I would have a glass, so there. I felt a giggle rise inside me at the thought of me sat on the sofa with a glass of sherry, watching Homes under the Hammer. I may as well complete the sad slide into old age by wearing a twinset and pearls and sucking a toffee. There's nothing like a tired old stereotype.

I shifted my weight forwards and was about to get up from the sofa when my mobile began to ring.

Stuff it, it can wait.

I ignored it and after a beat, levered myself up into a standing position, before heading into the kitchen. I could hear Elvis singing jauntily about having a little less conversation as I grabbed a small glass and poured a generous glug into the bottom.

I took a sip. Sherry was all very well but I think I should get myself a bottle of some decent whisky. I'd feel a bit more edgy sipping that, like Mildred Pierce. Maybe I should get some ice tongs and some kind of fancy tray like they always seemed to have in my black and white films. I loved the sound of ice clinking against the side of a glass.

Elvis suddenly shut up mid-sentence. I took another sip, stirred the curry and padded back into the lounge, placing my glass carefully by my seat. I swung around and sank into the sofa with a sigh.

My phone lit up and Elvis began shouting again.

For god's sake, give me a break!

I snatched up my phone in a temper and peered at the screen. Paddy again. Two missed calls. I turned down the TV and jabbed at the dancing phone icon. As I lifted my phone to my ear with my mouth pursed ready to ask him what he wanted this time, I could already hear his voice rattling out in a stream.

"Wait what, start again!" I said, rolling my eyes. "I can't tell what you're saying!"

His words started to pour out again, shooting like panicked pebbles into my ear.

"...and she was in her chair, I didn't know what to do. The ambulance came and they're taking her to hospital, I'm about to go there now."

I was having trouble catching up with his words.

"What? Who was in her chair? Evelyn? What's happened? Is she ok?"

Obviously not if the ambulance are taking her to hospital, you idiot.

"Nan! She was in her chair and I had to let myself in, I didn't know what to do and…" he broke off and it sounded as though he choked on his words.

"OK, has the ambulance gone yet?"

There was no response, just some muffled sounds.

"Paddy! Has the ambulance gone yet?"

"Yes, it's just left."

"Right, are you still in the house?"

"Yes," he replied quietly, sounding like a small child.

"Turn everything off and lock up. Are you fit to drive, can you come and fetch me and we'll go to the hospital together?"

Paddy cleared his throat.

"Yes, I think so."

I thought quickly. I had only had two sips of sherry, I would be fine to drive if needed. I didn't like driving Paddy's van, but if I had to, I would. It would be quicker for Paddy to swing by and pick me up than it would be to park his van and switch it for my car.

"OK, lock up and come and get me and we'll drive to the hospital. I'll throw some things in a bag just in case."

"I don't think…" he began, before trailing off.

I didn't want to think about what he didn't think. My mind felt awake and I had kicked into response mode, Miss Fix-it was on the case.

"Just come and get me, OK? I'll see you in a minute."

I hung up, turned off the TV and rushed upstairs to our bedroom, suddenly filled with new purpose. Paddy's sports bag was under the bed, filled with trainers and various gym paraphernalia. I pulled it out and upended it over the bed. I dashed to the airing cupboard and grabbed a towel, a jumper and some socks, then headed back to the bedroom and tossed them in the bag.

I thought for a moment. I had an overnight stay gift set in my bottom drawer that I had never used. It had a facecloth and mini bottles of face wash and shower gel. That might come in handy. I yanked open the drawer and scrabbled around inside before locating the box at the back behind some old t-shirts. I pulled it out and threw it into the bag.

What else did people need in hospital? I exclaimed and grabbed the bag and rushed downstairs to the kitchen. Flinging open the treat cupboard door I tipped a box of cereal bars and some chocolate into its open mouth and then opened another cupboard and extricated some juice cartons.

"Damn it!"

I realised that the curry was still bubbling away to itself on the pan and quickly turned it off. It would be fine until later with the lid on.

Right, that would have to do, Paddy would be here any time now.

I zipped the bag up and took it into the lounge, where I dropped it onto the floor by the door. I probably had another minute or so before Paddy was due to arrive. I gathered up my mobile and keys and added them to my handbag, grabbed my coat and stuffed my feet into my shoes. I headed to the front door and flung it open just in time to see Paddy's silver van come up the street to our house at speed. He stopped with a jerk and I caught a flash of his anguished face through the passenger window.

I wrestled the bag onto the pavement and slammed the front door shut, pushing against it to make sure that the Yale lock had clicked. Reaching for the bag again, I turned swiftly and headed around the van to the driver's side and pulled the door open.

"Shove over," I panted, pushing the bag into Paddy's chest. "I'll drive, you look too upset."

He didn't even argue which was an indicator of his state of mind and reassured me that I wasn't over-reacting. I watched as he unclipped and started to scoot over to the passenger side.

I waited until he had passed the midway point of the front seat and hauled myself into the driver's seat, using my hand on the open door to give myself some help. It wasn't a large van, but it was higher up than my little car and always felt like I was ascending an HGV in comparison.

I started to settle and reached to close the door. A loud, indignant beep sounded just behind me and I glanced behind to see a car waiting to pass. A ratty little man with rimless glasses gesticulated at me through the windscreen and then resolutely sounded the horn again.

I had only been a few seconds at most. I felt something snap inside me and I leaned out of the open doorway and vehemently gestured up and down with my middle finger.

I enjoyed the look of shock that passed over the man's rodent-like features and flourished my finger one more time for good measure.

"Have some patience!" I shouted and slammed the door with

alacrity.

Paddy was staring at me with his mouth open.

"There was no need for that at all," I said, reaching for the seatbelt and clipping it in. "You can't just go around over-reacting like that."

I checked the rear-view mirror and was pleased to see that instead of racing past us the moment I had closed the van door, the man was still waiting behind us. I must have shown him that I meant business.

I put the van into gear and pulled away, moving carefully past the parked cars on both sides of the street.

"Tell me what happened," I said, keeping my eyes on the road and clammy hands on the steering wheel. I really hated driving this van at the best of times, never mind in the dark.

Paddy didn't reply straight away. I risked a glance over towards him and saw that he was obviously struggling to speak. I saw with surprise that a tear trail tracked down one cheek. I had never seen him cry before.

"Paddy," I said gently, looking back towards the road. "Do you know what happened?"

I heard him take a shuddering breath and he finally began to talk.

"I was knocking on the door and she didn't answer," he said, bringing his closed fist up to the side of his mouth and wiping it. "I tried a few times, but you know what she's like about hearing the door when she's watching the telly."

I nodded and indicated to turn out onto the main road.

"But she didn't come to the door. So, I used my key and let myself in. She was in the lounge and…"

He faltered and pressed his hand into his mouth again.

"And…?" I prompted.

"She was sat in her chair, like she was asleep. She had all her letters around her and I thought she'd nodded off. But when I got nearer, I saw her mouth was open and her arm was over the side of the chair and she didn't look right. So I tried giving her a shake and patted her face but she didn't move."

Paddy broke off again and turned to look out of the passenger window, blinking furiously.

"And then what did you do?" I asked, pulling to a halt behind a line of traffic at a junction.

"I didn't know what to do, I rang 999 and asked them to send an ambulance."

I reached over and placed my hand on his leg and squeezed.

"Did they tell you how to help her, was she breathing?"

I had done an all-day first aid course for work at a local hotel. The buffet had been outstanding.

"They told me to try those chest things and breathe into her mouth. But I…"

He tailed off and covered his face with both hands. I could hear him snuffling.

"It's OK sweetheart," I said, squeezing his leg again. "What did the paramedics do?"

Paddy wiped his eyes with his fingers and sniffed loudly.

"They were really good, they tried those electric shock things and did CPR and then took her out in a wheelchair."

"OK then, let's hope they got her stable. We'll find out when we get to the hospital. You know how tough she is."

I concentrated on manoeuvring my way through the traffic.

"No-one can make Evelyn do anything she doesn't want to do, not even you," I said with an attempt at a laugh.

We drove in silence for the next ten minutes, punctuated only by occasional sniffs from Paddy. There wasn't really much else to say until we found out what was going on at the hospital.

Finally, we approached the main entrance to the hospital. I leaned forward in my seat and peered out at the signs which were dimly lit by a nearby lamppost.

"Can you see A and E? Which way do I go?" I asked frantically, trying to decode the arrows and words.

"I think it's next left," said Paddy, pointing out the window.

I signalled left and pulled into the multi-storey car park. Great, just what I needed. If it was one of those spiral ramps with barriers I might just be sunk. Whether he was in shock or not, Paddy would never forgive me if I put a scrape on the paintwork of his precious van.

Our headlights swept the wall as I swung wide to go up the first ramp, which was thankfully the normal kind. I could tell by the sudden stillness of Paddy's body that he was carefully watching. I readjusted my hands on the steering wheel and craned forward to look along the row of parked cars, searching for a space.

"There's one, at the end," said Paddy, gesturing up ahead.

I breathed a sigh of relief. The space was on the end of the row and would be easier to pull into than a regular spot. I didn't feel up to the added pressure of squeezing into a difficult space at this moment in time.

After two backwards and forwards manoeuvres, I pulled on the handbrake and let out a heartfelt sigh.

"Come on then," I said to Paddy, pulling the keys out of the steering column and opening the driver's door. "Bring the bag."

After spending five minutes following a series of red signs advertising the whereabouts of the A and E department, we finally emerged into a reception area. I felt like an Amazon explorer emerging into a clearing after a hazardous expedition.

We joined the queue for the receptionist. All around the seats were filled with people of all ages and sizes. A television flickered soundlessly on the top corner of a wall, ignored by everyone. The space was filled with the tang of people, a faint smell of cleaning fluid and a distinct oppressive feeling of boredom.

I glanced at Paddy. His mouth was set in a line and he was blinking more quickly than usual, the only indicators of his current emotional state.

I squeezed his arm. He must be feeling terrible. No matter what I thought of his nan, he was very close to her and thrived off the hero worship she directed his way.

"Yes please," asked the receptionist, without looking up from her screen.

Paddy and I stepped forward and I leaned in towards the Perspex barrier. I was never sure how well they could hear behind those things.

"My husband's grandmother has been brought in by ambulance," I explained. "Evelyn Burgess."

Tap, tap, tap went the long, orange acrylic nails on the keyboard. I was always in awe of women who could type with long nails. How they could hit the right keys was beyond me, surely it made the whole process much more difficult. There was something pleasing about the staccato noise they made as she typed in her query.

"OK," she said, still not looking up from the screen. "Take a seat and someone will be along to fetch you."

"Thank you," I said, leaning in again, before taking Paddy's hand and leading him to stand over to one side by a wall.

"Are you ok?" I asked. "Do you need a drink or anything?"

Paddy shook his head and kept his eyes fixed on the double doors to the side of the reception desk. I had a vague feeling that I should be offering him a sweet tea or something.

"No, I'm fine. I just want to know what's going on."

I nodded and patted his arm again, sympathetically. We stood in awkward silence. There wasn't much that I could say or do to make the situation any easier.

I had a thought and rummaged in my bag.

"Mint?" I offered, holding out my tube of chewy soft mints.

Again, Paddy shook his head. I popped out a mint and pushed it into my mouth. Might be a good idea to cover up any remaining traces of sherry breath before I had to see a medical professional, not that two sips should be counted as any kind of impairment.

I tried to suck the mint and make it last but, as usual, gave in after less than twenty seconds. I have zero self-control when it comes to sucking sweets, I am one of life's crunchers. I chewed thoughtfully as I looked around the waiting room. I had the idea of playing a version of my train platform game, but this variation would not only involve guessing what the person was like, but what injury they had.

I started with a middle-aged lady on my left. She was easy to diagnose as her right leg was elevated on a stackable chair.

I performed a quick assessment. A Strictly Come Dancing enthusiast who had gone over on her ankle while attempting to reproduce one of the more challenging moves on this week's episode. She belongs to a library book club and makes her own jam from her garden produce. She has a secret fetish for lilac feather boas and fondant fancies.

Next. A man in his twenties sat by himself, hunched over with his head in his hands. He was wearing a baggy tracksuit and a gold chain swung beneath his bowed head. As is often the case with a man in public seating areas, his legs were splayed wide. Interesting. Perhaps he had caught a testicle in a hole in the mesh lining of his swimming shorts and strangulated the blood supply. He is a key player in his local historical re-enactment society and needs to be fit by the weekend as they have an important event in Eccles that he has been preparing for for months. Without his input they will be a squire down.

My eyes travelled over to a large elderly couple, seated beneath the muted television. This was more difficult. Both sat morosely, staring at the linoleum floor. Both showed no signs of discomfort. I frowned. This one was tricky. I was just starting to fabricate a convoluted back story about infidelity and poisoned tea when I was startled by a woman in scrubs who was calling Paddy's name.

"Patrick Frisby?"

Paddy jerked forward and headed towards her, his sports bag swinging at his side. I quickly followed.

"That's me."

The woman smiled and gestured towards the double doors.

"Could you come with me please, I'll take you through."

We followed her as she swiped her pass on the sensor and headed through to the restricted area. She walked briskly and we trotted along to keep up with her, shoes squeaking. Trolleys lined the corridor on both sides, many of them occupied by elderly patients, some asleep, some propped up. I wondered if Evelyn would be one of them and glanced at each face in turn.

We wound our way along several corridors and through multiple reception spaces and I soon lost track of which way we had come. I was worried that we would never find our way out of this rabbit warren again.

Eventually, the woman came to a stop by a small room. There was a sign saying "Relative's Room" on the outside. We were ushered inside.

"Take a seat, the doctor will be with you in a moment."

She gave another small smile, nodded and stepped out of the room, carefully closing the door. We took a seat on a low, pale green fabric sofa. In front of us, a small coffee table displayed a box of tissues and a range of fanned out leaflets. I tried to peek unobtrusively at them. "Dealing with Grief" and "What to do in the event of a loved one's death". I blanched. This didn't look good.

I looked quickly at Paddy's face, only to see him staring blankly at the wall opposite. I didn't think he had noticed. I placed my hand on his thigh and squeezed again. I couldn't think of anything helpful to say, but just wanted him to know that I was there with him and could offer comfort if needed. I had squeezed various parts of his body more in the last hour than I had done in the last month.

The door opened suddenly, causing an inrush of bleach-scented air. A doctor in blue scrubs entered the room and sat in an orange plastic chair opposite us.

"Mr Frisby?" she asked. "I believe you are the grandson of Evelyn Burgess?"

Paddy nodded, staring intently at her.

"And you are Mr Frisby's partner?" she asked, looking at me.

"Wife," I replied, nodding.

The doctor cleared her throat. I braced myself. I had a feeling that this would not be good news.

"I'm really sorry to have to tell you that I'm afraid Evelyn has passed away."

Paddy's head dropped and he covered his eyes with one hand.

"It seems that Evelyn has had a cardiac arrest. Despite the best efforts of the paramedics, I'm afraid that we weren't able to save her."

I reached around Paddy's back and clasped him in an awkward hug. He felt stiff and non-responsive.

"It's most likely that it was quick and she won't have suffered. I'm sure it was a comfort to her that you were with her. I'm so sorry for your loss."

Paddy shuddered and I rubbed his back. He muttered something.

"I'm sorry?" asked the doctor, leaning forward with an attentive look on her face.

Removing his hand from his brow, Paddy looked up.

"I think I hurt her," he said in anguish. "When I was trying the chest things. I think I cracked something."

The doctor smiled sympathetically and looked straight into Paddy's eyes.

"That's quite common when you do compressions with older people, their bones are more brittle. You attempted CPR to give her a chance, so it was the right thing to do. And it was likely that she had already passed by then, I can assure you that you did the right thing."

His shoulders sagged in relief and I hugged him again. Paddy wiped his eyes and exhaled.

"Would you like to see her?" asked the doctor.

Paddy nodded.

"I think she's ready now, I'll ask one of the nurses to come and take you in. Again, I'm sorry for your loss."

The doctor stood and smoothed down the trousers of her scrubs and then left the room. The door clicked into the frame. What a rubbish job, having to tell relatives that their loved ones had died. I couldn't even start to image how difficult it must be to deliver that kind of news when you were desperately busy trying to treat other patients at the same time.

Paddy straightened and sat back in his chair, tilting his head back against the wall.

"I can't believe it," he said, stunned. "I was on the phone to her just before, telling her I was going round with those liners. She was fine."

"Do you want me to come in with you, or would you like to go alone?" I asked, half-hoping that he would rather go by himself. I had never seen a dead body before and I wasn't sure how I felt about it.

"Will you come?" he asked, turning to look at me properly for the first time.

His eyes were lost and frightened, a small boy who wasn't quite sure what to do. There was no trace of his usual humorous twinkle and bravado.

"Of course," I said. "Whatever you need."

"I wasn't sure what to say when she asked about seeing nan, I wasn't expecting that. I'm not sure if it's a good idea to see her or not. What if she's…"

His voice petered out. I slipped my hand back onto his leg and rested it there. I couldn't say anything helpful, but I could be there by his side.

"Perhaps it will help you accept what has happened, with it being so sudden. If you see her, I mean, maybe your brain will be able to process it a bit better."

The door opened again and yet another member of hospital staff in scrubs stood in the doorway. He was young with a receding hairline and the sympathetic look on his face that I was already starting to get used to.

"I can take you to see Evelyn now, if you're ready?"

"Yes please," said Paddy, standing up abruptly.

I followed his lead and reached down to retrieve the sports bag that was no longer needed.

"This way please," said the nurse, holding the door awkwardly open so that we had to squeeze past him into the corridor.

We followed him hesitantly, this time it was only a short walk to some kind of private examination room a few doors down. The nurse opened the door reverently and stood to one side. After a moment, Paddy stepped into the room and I trailed in behind him.

Evelyn rested on the bed in the middle of the room. A blanket covered her body up to her chest, with her arms lying by her sides and her neck and head uncovered. Paddy gingerly moved towards the bed.

"Hello nan," he said quietly.

Tears sprang to my eyes and I coughed to cover the hiccup that formed in my throat. His voice was so tender, it tugged at my heart to hear him so upset.

"I'm sorry I couldn't save you," he continued. "I would have if I could. I'll miss you."

Gently, Paddy took Evelyn's hand in his own and rubbed his thumb across the back of the mottled skin.

It was strange, it was obviously Evelyn's body lying there so still, but she was no longer there. Her face looked slack and I felt as though I was staring at a mannequin of Evelyn, not the person she had been. All the life force and spirit that had made her Paddy's nan was gone. She was simply a shell.

After a moment, Paddy released Evelyn's hand and stepped back. The nurse approached him with a small envelope.

"We've removed her wedding ring, we thought you would want to take it with you," he said quietly.

Paddy automatically took it and pushed it into his pocket.

"Thanks," he managed gruffly. He looked at me. "Can we go now?"

"Yes of course," I said, thrown into a panic.

What should I do? Should I say something to Evelyn even though I felt such a strong sense that she was no longer there?

I took a pace towards the bed and looked upon Paddy's nan's face for the last time.

"Goodbye Evelyn. Rest in peace."

Rest in peace? What a stupid thing to say, you sound like you think she'll rise again like a vampire.

I flushed and turned away, taking Paddy's hand as we left the room. I felt a strange hollowness inside, sad that such a key person in Paddy's life would no longer be there for him and sad too that we would never have the relationship that I had always hoped for.

"Come on sweetheart, let's go home," I murmured, leading the way.

CHAPTER NINETEEN

It was just as well that I didn't have to go into work in the next couple of weeks. I had no idea how much admin is required when somebody dies and it all fell on me. I didn't mind, not really. It gave me something to do to keep my mind off my work situation and I wanted to feel like I was supporting Paddy.

His way of grieving was simple, quite like him really. He had a fraught night after we returned from the hospital as he began to process his shock. I plied him with cups of tea, the British balm for all ills, and sat next to him on the sofa as he periodically trembled and repeated fragments of phrases over and over and pointlessly explored things that he could have done that might have made a difference.

"If only I'd gone round earlier..."

"If I'd realised she wasn't feeling right..."

I had ordered him to bed and felt relief as he quickly fell into a deep sleep. I, on the other hand, had lain awake for some time, thinking about my last interaction with Evelyn and how strange it was that she was no longer living in the world. There would be no more inconvenient phone calls, no more spiky comments, no more slights. But instead of feeling relief, I just felt sad. She hadn't been a happy woman but she had lived for Paddy and his visits. It was a shame that she hadn't got more pleasure out of life.

My mind inevitably then moved onto the upsetting events that had taken place earlier that day. Paddy had no idea that I had been made redundant and would not be returning to the office. I would have loved to have talked to him about it and let off some steam but of course that hadn't been possible. I felt the frustrations fizzing inside my chest as I revisited what I had said. But I wasn't sorry. It was about time I started to stand up for myself and tell people how I felt.

Too right, we can't have you being a doormat for the rest of your life.

The next morning, Paddy had got up as usual and headed straight off towards the shower.

"Are you getting up?" I asked, trying to discover subtly whether he was planning on staying home or not.

"Yes," he replied, turning in the doorway and rubbing his face. "I'll only mope at home and I've got to get on with this job in Gorton, I can't let them down."

And that was it, his shutters came down and he was trying to distract himself by being busy. He had never been one for expressing much emotion, he would rather do his best to just get on with things and wait for any pain to pass.

I threw on my dressing gown and pattered downstairs. I quickly made him a coffee in his favourite mug and a takeaway flask to keep him going throughout the day. I knew that he would stop off at his favourite café en route for a bacon sandwich and a cookie.

I popped a peppermint tea into a mug for me, poured the water from the kettle and rested against the kitchen counter while I waited for it to infuse. I could hear various crashes and thumps from upstairs as Paddy did his usual trick of getting ready with as much noise and disturbance as possible.

A moment later, he thundered down the stairs and emerged into the kitchen, trailing his familiar fragrance of soap and spray deodorant in his wake.

"Oh great, thanks," he said, reaching for his mug and taking a large slurp. He eyed me in my dressing gown. "Aren't you going in today?"

There was no point in trying to explain to Paddy in a few short minutes that I was effectively unemployed. It was not the time and it suddenly seemed so much less important in the face of death.

"No, not today," I said, picking up my mug and hiding my face behind it. "I'll tell you about it later."

"OK," Paddy said, swigging the remainder of his coffee and picking up the flask.

He took me at my word and didn't give my non-attendance at work another thought.

"Do you want me to start making calls for your nan?" I asked. It sounded like I was offering to undertake a secretarial service rather than start the depressing process of notifying everyone that she had died.

Paddy frowned. It had clearly not occurred to him that arrangements would need to be made. Anything related to life admin was always left to me. I often thought that he believed that all of our activities just happened by themselves.

"That nurse gave me a leaflet with things that we need to do. Are you ok if I make a start?"

"That would be great," he said with relief.

"If you can leave Evelyn's key, I'll probably need to go round and find her bills and things so I know who to contact."

Paddy put the flask back down and pulled his keys from his pocket and quickly unwound a keyring from the bunch, before placing it on the worktop. He stared at it for a moment, then plastered a smile on his face.

"I can't believe she won't be there," he said. "It's so weird."

"I know," I said, giving him a quick hug. "It'll be difficult getting used to it. But you know how much she loved you."

"Yes, well."

Clearing his throat, Paddy retrieved his flask and made his way out of the kitchen.

"I should be home around seven again tonight. See you later."

"Have a good day!" I called after him.

Have a good day? His Nan has just died! For god's sake, what a thing to say.

The front door slammed and a moment later I heard Paddy's throaty diesel engine roar into life.

I sighed. Breakfast and then round to Evelyn's.

It was a strange sensation opening Evelyn's front door with Paddy's key. I had never let myself in before, I had only ever been admitted by the gatekeeper when she needed me to do something.

It was still early and no-one was about. The door creaked and I carefully stepped into the hallway, feeling like an interloper.

"Hello?" I quavered. I couldn't help myself.

You are ridiculous.

It seemed rude to just walk in without her permission. I quietly closed the door behind me. There were a couple of muddy marks and wheelchair tracks in the carpet from the paramedics. Evelyn would not be impressed. I skirted them and walked into the lounge. It was a bit of a mess, there were wrappers and wipes and various bits and bobs scattered across the floor. The chair and sofa had been pushed back towards the wall. I realised that this must have been where the paramedics had done their best to save Evelyn's life. It was a good place to start and the practical tasks would help me to settle.

I found some black bin bags under the kitchen sink and shook one open, the cracking sound harsh in the quiet. I worked quickly to pluck the rubbish from the floor and throw it in. As I neared Evelyn's favourite chair, I saw a number of handwritten letters fanned across the carpet. I set the bin bag down and picked them up. Each was addressed to "E" and was signed "L".

Not letters from her husband Derek then. I wasn't surprised, as from the very few stories I had managed to wangle out of Paddy, they hadn't been a happy couple. I sat myself down on the sofa and flipped through a few. They seemed to be typical love letters, full of compliments and shared references. Thankfully, no poetry.

"You dark horse Evelyn," I said, bundling them back into a pile and placing them on the occasional table.

I would ask Paddy what he wanted to do with them. I carried on with the work of returning the room back to its usual state. Within ten minutes, it looked much as it ever had done.

My mobile vibrated in my back pocket and I pulled it out and glanced at the screen. Annie. I answered.

"Hi Annie," I said, brushing a tendril of hair back from my face.

"Hello lovely, how are you doing?"

"Oh, you know," I said with a mirthless laugh.

I could hear noises in the background, cupboards being opened and closed. Annie was clearly in the middle of something. She so very rarely sat still, it was exhausting at the best of times.

"I thought I'd better check in with you about what happened with work yesterday. You were supposed to call last night with an update, remember?" she chided. "By the time I realised you hadn't called, it was too late to ring you."

Annie subscribes to the same school of thought as me, that if it is past nine thirty at night, you don't call other people. They will immediately think the worst and presume someone has died. Which was ironic when you think about it.

"No, we had a bit of a shock last night. Paddy found his nan collapsed in her house and he had to call for an ambulance. We were at the hospital until late."

I could hear something heavy being put down with a crash.

"That's awful, I'm so sorry! Is she ok?"

I realised then that I had left out an important piece of the story.

"No, she died. They think she might have been gone even before the ambulance took her away," I explained.

"Oh no, poor Paddy. How is he doing?"

"OK considering. You know he doesn't really do emotions, but I can tell he's upset. Obviously. You know how close he was with her."

It felt wrong discussing Evelyn's death and her relationship with her grandson so freely in her house. Even if she would never be returning to it.

"Yes of course. I suppose he's keeping busy today?"

Annie has Paddy pegged.

"Yup, he's gone out to do a job in Gorton. I'm at his nan's house now, sorting things out."

"So, what did happen at work? Something or nothing?"

Annie wasn't being insensitive by moving topic so quickly. She knew the relationship, or lack of, between me and Evelyn.

"You won't believe that either," I said with a wry smile. "You won't believe what I did."

"What was that?" asked Annie, clearly dying to know the details.

"I lost my job. You're not free for a coffee in a couple of hours are you? I've got some work to do here and I need to start notifying people but I'd really like to talk to you in person. I'll probably have had enough by lunchtime and it would be good to see you."

"Yes, absolutely. Do you fancy the park? The kids are in nursery today and I've started doing a forty-five-minute power walk every other day and there's that nice coffee cabin there. I'll treat you to a pumpkin spice latte, it is coming up to Halloween after all."

I love Annie. She's always good at making time for me and doing her best to help me navigate through my various messes.

"Perfect," I said gratefully. "I'll see you there at twelve?"

"Great."

We hung up on each other. Time to start sorting out Evelyn's admin. I sighed and made my way towards her bedroom.

The morning passed quickly, which was surprising considering how much of that time was spent listening to a range of massively irritating hold tunes on loop. I phoned an undertaker and then worked my way steadily in order through the checklist of organisations to inform. I felt that these would be easier to tackle as they were impersonal. I knew that I would have to start on Evelyn's address book this afternoon and start calling friends and family. I was not looking forward to that.

The alarm on my mobile began to sound and shake just as I had hung up on a Utilities company. I rubbed my neck and glanced at the clock display. I had half an hour to make my way to the park. With a groan, I levered myself up from my cross-legged position on the carpet in the lounge and shook my legs out. I should really have sat in a chair, but I still felt strange about taking a seat in the room when I had never really been invited to do so when Evelyn was alive.

Picking up my phone and keys, I wriggled into my wrap and headed to the front door and pushed my feet into my trainers.

"See Evelyn? I took my shoes off!" I called, smiling to myself.

Wait, was that rude and disrespectful? It was only meant in fun. Perhaps it was too soon. I quickly released the door lock and stepped outside, pleased to be away from the bungalow.

I began to stride down the path, on a mission to reach the park in time.

"Just a minute! Wait!"

I came to an abrupt halt and turned to see Maud scurrying out of her front doorway. She was dressed in a variation of her mushroom theme again, this time it was inverted with bobbled cream slacks and a beige rollneck jumper that strained to contain her various assets.

"Morning Maud," I said politely, waiting for her to cross the few yards from her path to Evelyn's.

She was panting slightly as she reached me, whether from exertion or excitement, I couldn't tell.

"What happened last night?" she asked breathlessly, a hand

straying towards her mouth in a gesture of concern. "I could see all the flashing lights through my curtains and there was a bit of a to-do. Is Evelyn all right?"

"I'm afraid not. Evelyn passed away last night. Paddy found her collapsed at home, but the paramedics couldn't do anything for her."

"Oh dear," said Maud in a trembly voice. "I am sorry to hear that. We weren't friendly but it's never nice when that happens."

"No. No, it's not," I agreed.

There was a pause. Maud cleared her throat.

"Is she..."

I waited. She dropped her voice to a whisper.

"Is she *still in there?*"

Maud pointed a stubby finger in the direction of Evelyn's bungalow.

"No, she was taken to hospital last night. The Funeral Directors will be collecting her from there this morning."

That was one of the first calls I had had to make. I didn't know the first thing about arranging a funeral and moving the deceased about. Thankfully, the local undertakers did and had assured me that it would all be taken in hand.

"Oh," said Maud. I couldn't tell whether she was disappointed or not. "Well let me know when the funeral is going to be. I always like to pay my respects."

The implication was 'whether they are deserved or not', but I appreciated the sentiment.

"Thank you Maud, I'll let you know. It will probably be in the next week or two. You'll be seeing me coming and going quite a bit until then, but don't worry, it'll just be me sorting things out."

"All right dear. You take care, it's always a strain arranging these things."

Maud laid her hand on my arm. I was touched and blinked away the tears that were threatening to form.

"Thanks. You too."

I patted her hand and then turned and hurried away towards the park. I hated being late.

"Sorry," I gasped as I rushed up to the coffee cabin in the park. Annie was already there, looking very fetching in lycra leggings, slouchy knitted jumper and multi-coloured striped beany hat.

"Hey you," she said, enveloping me in a hug. "How are you doing?"

"Don't get too close," I said, reluctantly rearing away. "I've just power walked and I'm probably all sweaty."

"So have I so that makes two of us," she laughed, pulling a tendril of fair hair away from her face. "You should have seen me striding along, just like those Olympic distance walkers, but much more sexy and with less waddle."

She proved her point by sashaying her hips as she walked up and down. I loved Annie. She never took herself too seriously and always made me laugh. She pirouetted to a halt in front of me.

"Right, what are you having? Do you want a pumpkin spice latte or something else?"

I considered.

"Actually, I think I need a flat white today. Would that be ok? Are you sure I can't get these?"

"Of course not, you've just gone through the wringer at work and lost a family member. I think I can stretch to a drink."

"Well, if you put it that way..."

Annie approached the cabin and ordered the drinks while I checked my phone.

I messaged Paddy to say I was thinking of him and hoping he was doing ok. I knew he wouldn't respond, but it made me feel better.

"Here you go. One flat white."

I reached for the offered cup.

"Thank you. I'm so pleased that you could meet up today. It's been quite a week."

"Sounds like it," agreed Annie, taking a loud sip of her drink. "Ouch, that's hot. I never can wait for it to cool down."

"You never could," I said affectionately, starting to walk along the path. "You always just seize the day and get on with things, I wish I could be more like that."

Annie walked alongside me with an easy stride.

"It can get me into trouble though," she cautioned, as if I was considering being more headstrong as a career option.

"But at least you make the most of every opportunity," I pressed. "You look for things and you go for them. Look at all your business ideas."

Annie laughed. We had reached a bench overlooking the boating pond. The boats had all been removed for the winter and a slight mist drifted across the surface of the water. I brushed off some fallen leaves with my free hand and we sank onto the weathered wooden slats.

"Sounds like a mid-life crisis is coming on. Although I wouldn't blame you, you've just had two life-changing events happen in one week."

I nodded thoughtfully.

"Once I sort out all the arrangements for Evelyn, I'm going to have to have a good think about what I want to do next. I suppose it's a good opportunity to reassess who I am and where I'm going."

"True," said Annie, taking another sip. "You seem to be taking the redundancy well though? I was worried that it might send you into a bit of a downward spiral. You know what you're like about what people think of you."

"It's really odd," I said, shifting my coffee cup from one hand to the other as it started to get uncomfortably hot. "I am upset about it. And resentful that they could just dump me like that. And I have had a bit of a cry about it and that comes and goes in waves. But it already feels like I've started to accept it, like it's in the past and there's no point on dwelling on it."

I filled Annie in on the meeting and what I had said to Sarah and Kelly.

"They clearly knew what they wanted to do and nothing you could have said or done would have changed that," said Annie. "Sounds like you handled that meeting like a total boss!"

"I know, I finally acted like a manager!" I laughed. "I don't know what got into me. It almost felt like I was playing a part, but it sort of felt quite natural at the same time. Well, up until the end when my voice broke and I started to get emotional."

"That's understandable. That job meant a lot to you. No-one likes to be rejected."

"Thanks," I said sarcastically.

"It's true though. But they didn't deserve you so it's their loss."

I took a sip of my drink, which was still too hot.

"Thank you," I said with meaning this time. "I think the shock of the redundancy was totally knocked out of me by Evelyn last night. It kind of puts things into perspective, when a person you've known for years just dies and isn't there any more."

"Very true," said Annie sagely. "In the scheme of things, changing jobs is a blip in your life in comparison. Not to say that you aren't totally entitled to feel upset and shocked about your job though, so don't feel bad about feeling that way."

"I just feel guilty that I don't feel more about Evelyn dying," I said. "She never had any time for me and we were never close, but I think I always hoped that we would be."

"That was never going to happen," Annie replied, matter of factly. "The only thing that touched Evelyn's heart was Paddy. She lived for that boy and nothing else really registered. No matter what you did, she was never going to be any different with you, you were a competitor in his time and affections. Look what she did to your wedding photo in her frame, cutting you out!"

I sighed. She was right.

"Shouldn't I feel something more though? I'm sorry for Paddy's loss, but I don't feel sad myself. I spent enough time with her."

"Why should you? A relationship needs input from both sides. You never got anything back from Evelyn so you can't have that connection."

"But doesn't that make me cold?"

Annie looked me full in the eyes.

"How would you feel if Paddy or I died?"

I shivered.

"Don't say that." I quickly touched the wood of the bench. "Touch wood."

"But how would you feel?"

"Utterly devastated," I said honestly. "You're my family."

"Well then. There's nothing wrong with you so stop trying to feel something you don't. If you're worried that people will judge you for it, don't. Anyone who knows you and Evelyn will know that she wasn't an easy person to be around. Don't feel you have to perform something you don't feel."

I looked at Annie with admiration.

"Have you thought about life coaching or counselling and sack off all these business ideas?"

"No chance, I can do it with you because we've grown up together. I wouldn't have any patience with anyone I didn't know. I'd get really frustrated and wouldn't be empathetic at all. You'll have to be my only client."

I smiled.

"How did you get on with the jelly baby thing?" I asked. "Did you get anywhere with that?"

"Oh that," said Annie dismissively, draining her cup. "That was a bit of a non-starter. Do you want to hear my latest?"

"Absolutely."

"A sat nav download where the accent changes according to the part of the country you're in. So if you're driving through Birmingham, it's a brummy accent. When you cross into

Wales, it turns to Welsh. And it would have to do all the regional variations as well. What do you think?"

I giggled.

"Genius. I would definitely buy that one."

Annie looked very pleased with herself.

"It's cool isn't it. I'll make my fortune yet."

"I have no doubt that you will," I agreed. "Just remember your poor, unemployed friends when you do."

"Oh, I'll find you something to do. You can do my accounts for me while I swan around my private islands having a high old time."

"Thanks a lot."

Annie inhaled quickly and slapped a hand to my knee.

"Perhaps that's it!"

"What?" I asked, puzzled.

"You know how lots of middle-class women go off from work to have kids and decide while they're off to set up their own stay at home businesses? Doing all sorts, crafts, professional services, baking, party planning, print on demand and all that jazz?"

"Not really," I replied. "I'm not very familiar with that world."

"Well, it's a thing," continued Annie, refusing to be derailed. "Why don't you set yourself up as an Accounts person who specialises in those types of businesses? Individuals, entrepreneurs, maybe even small voluntary outfits?"

"You're getting carried away now," I said warningly. "I can't imagine that they would have much disposable income to pay for an accounting service."

"Maybe not, but you could have lots of different packages available, ranging from the most basic of one-off Accounts support to more in-depth ongoing help. If you had enough of them it might make it worth your while?"

I could see the familiar light in Annie's eyes that she always got when a new idea took hold. As much as I appreciated her encouragement, I didn't have the head space to explore a new direction right at that moment.

"Maybe so," I conceded. "It's a good idea and I promise I'll look into it. But I can't go off on a flight of fancy just yet, I need to percolate on things first. Get the funeral sorted and come to terms with things a bit."

Annie refused to be deflated.

"I'll give you that. But make sure you think about it. It could be just the thing for you. You could work from home and pick and choose. Might be perfect."

"I will," I promised. "You're ace, thank you."

"Or," said Annie in a mischievous voice. "You could always set up an Only Fans account."

"Too vanilla."

"Or sign up to do foot fetish pics? I hear there's a lot to be made from that?"

"I'm not sure my feet would be in high demand. I have wonky toes, dropped arches and I'm not artistic in the slightest."

"They don't have to be beautiful feet. Can you do anything unusual with them?"

"What?" I exclaimed. "Like what? Such as?"

"Are you double jointed? Can you even get double jointed feet?"

"Er, no. I'm not. Although, thinking about it, I can pick things up with my toes. Don't you remember, it used to be my party trick in primary school? I can pick up pencils and all sorts."

"That might work. Perhaps you can take photos of your wonky toes picking up things. Might be niche but they might pay more!"

"Now you're being ridiculous," I said, but feeling better already for being silly. "Thank you for this. You've cheered me up."

"No problem," said Annie, leaning in for another spontaneous hug. "Don't let this get you down. It could be the making of you and the life you want."

For a moment, I felt a small flicker of excitement. Maybe it could.

"I'd best get back to it," I said reluctantly. "I've got to start calling Evelyn's contacts this afternoon."

"I thought Evelyn didn't have much family? I thought it was just Crown Prince Paddy?"

"Some distant cousins apparently. Not that they have ever really bothered with her, as far as I know. And she might have some friends in her address book."

"You think?" asked Annie with a sideways look.

"Annie! Behave. There might be some people who live far away that she's kept in touch with. Speaking of which, there was a pile of love letters by her chair when she died. Quite sweet really. They weren't from her husband Derek."

"Really?" Annie was intrigued. "Were they signed?"

"No, just with the initial L."

"Were they saucy?"

I snorted.

"Definitely not. Heartfelt but not racy. I only looked at a couple, it felt wrong."

"I didn't think she had it in her."

"Apparently she did. Don't judge a book by its cover."

"I suppose we are all young at some point."

We both stared at the pond, lost in thought for a moment.

"Right. I'd best be off," I stood up and stretched. "Enjoy the rest of your child-free time and I'll catch up with you later. Thanks for the company and the pep talk."

"And the new business ideas."

"And that."

We hugged again.

"You're welcome. Call me anytime."

CHAPTER TWENTY

As I walked back up the path to Evelyn's front door, my feet began to drag and my pace slowed down. I didn't want to have to call a lot of people that I didn't know. I hated cold calling, it put the fear into me and was such an effort. Having to plan what you are going to say, hoping they don't answer and then explaining who you are when they do. It was draining and one of my least favourite things.

I slid the key into the lock and twisted it. The door opened with a push and I entered the hallway, levering my feet out of my trainers. The air still held its familiar fug, but it felt as though it was already starting to dissipate. I had turned the heating down this morning and aired the rooms and the influx of fresh air was having an effect.

I headed back into the lounge and over to the sideboard. I knew exactly where Evelyn had kept her address book and I pulled open the top sliding drawer. I had seen her fetch it numerous times when she was addressing correspondence that she wanted me to post for her. She never had any stamps and always summoned me to take them to the post office, saying she would pay us back "once we knew how much it would be". She never did, the canny old devil.

The address book was resting on the top of assorted photographs, receipts and bills. The front cover showed a basketful of kittens and puppies with a large pink bow on the handle. A less appropriate image for Evelyn I could hardly conceive of, she was the least fluffy and cute person I had probably ever met in my life and I didn't think for one moment that she would have picked it out for herself. I had remarked on it in the past to Paddy, who volunteered the information that he had bought it for his nan when he was a young lad. Problem solved. She would rather cut her own head off than be irreverent about anything that her precious grandson gave her. She even kept his handwritten shopping lists in her special drawer, nothing of his was thrown away.

I picked up the book, made my way over to the window and sat down in front of it, my back to the radiator. The gentle warmth was welcome on my back. I flipped open to the title page.

There was an inscription in childish handwriting that I immediately recognised.

"Dear Nan, I thort you would like this book. Love Patrik."

I could immediately conjure up an image of little Paddy proudly offering his gift to his adoring nan. Underneath, Evelyn had written in her cramped cursive, "A Christmas gift from my Patrick, 1995". How cute.

I flicked on to the entries under A. There were only two entries, both crossed out. That was easy, if each section was similar then this might not take long at all.

I turned to page B. Of course, Burgess, Evelyn's married name. There were three entries on this page, none of them had been crossed out.

I picked up my phone and dialled the number for William Burgess. I took a breath and slowly exhaled as the ringing tone began.

Please be out, please be out.

Although I would only have to call back again if they didn't answer, so in some ways it would be best to get it over with.

"Hello?"

It was a woman's voice, she sounded like an older lady.

"Hello? Is that the home of William Burgess?" I asked.

"Yes," replied the woman, a suspicious edge entering her voice.

"It's Mena, Paddy Frisby's wife. I'm calling about Evelyn Burgess. I think that she was married to William's brother?"

I had met some Burgesses at the evening reception of our small wedding, but it was the tradition of Paddy's family to not talk about family history and relationships. He hadn't really explained in any depth who was connected with who, he had just given me a list of names to invite. I had smiled vacantly at the strangers drinking and dancing at our wedding party, not having a clue who most of them were.

"That's right," said the voice. "She was married to Derek before he died. I'm his wife, Dawn."

I had a vague recollection of a woman wearing lots of make up with her hair in a severely graduated bleached blonde bob gyrating to S Club 7 as Evelyn had looked on in disapproval, her mouth pursed.

I swallowed. This was the tricky bit.

"I'm just calling to let you know that she sadly passed away last night. We thought that you should know."

"Oh, I see."

There was a pause. I was expecting slightly more, but nothing was forthcoming.

"I believe it was very quick."

"That's good."

That's good?

I was not very well-versed in the language of bereavement, but I wasn't sure that that was the usual response.

"The funeral is likely to be in the next week or two, if you would like me to let you know the details?"

"Yes, yes, I suppose that's fine. I'll let Will know what's happened. We have got a few things on in the next couple of weeks, we're having our radiators and boiler replaced so we'll have to see. We've been waiting for months and it's already been put off three times. We can't put them off again, it might never get done, they've been absolutely useless. But let us know and we'll see what we can do."

I felt a bit taken aback. I hadn't had a definite script in my head for how this conversation might go, but if I had I knew that this wasn't it.

I had a sudden brainwave.

"Are you in close contact with Paddy's other second cousins on your side?"

"Oh yes, we meet up all the time. We've got a fireworks party next weekend. Dave has been to China Town in Manchester to get some proper fireworks, we're setting them off in his back garden this time, we still can't get the scorch marks out of our fence from last year and I told Will I'm not having it at ours."

"Right, well." There wasn't much I could say in response to that. "Would you mind letting your side of the family know? Only they don't really know me and I think it would be better coming from you."

I could almost hear Dawn puffing up with the responsibility of being the matriarch delivering bad family news.

"I suppose I could, yes," she confirmed. "Not that we were that close with Evelyn you understand, but she was family.

Actually, we have a family WhatsApp group, I'll pull that up and tell them on that."

How strange that people seemed to feel the need to keep saying that they hadn't been close with Evelyn. That had been fairly obvious from the lack of contact with her family over the years.

"That would be a great help, thank you."

And one less thing for me to have to do.

"That's ok Tina. I'll let them all know."

I rolled my eyes but couldn't be bothered to correct her.

"I'll be in touch with the funeral arrangements when I have them."

She hung up and I sighed with relief. That was a chunk of calls taken care of in one fell swoop. I reached across to the occasional table and grabbed a pencil, placing careful ticks against the names.

The next few entries that weren't obviously family turned out to be old work colleagues from Evelyn's days at a textile factory. One had died and two hadn't been in touch with Evelyn for years. I felt a bit silly telling them about Evelyn's death, but I had no way of knowing from the address book whether they were still in touch or not.

There was only one entry under G. Laurie Graves. The phone number recorded next to the address had no area code listed next to the main number. I wasn't sure if it was a man or woman, but they apparently lived in Norfolk. I quickly googled the code from the town location and dialled.

The phone rang out and I was about to give up hope of an answering machine picking up when someone finally answered.

"Hello?"

It was a deep and pleasant voice, it sounded like an older man. There was a touch of authority about it.

"Hello, Mr Laurie Graves?"

I decided to be formal, as his voice sounded as though it was warranted.

"Yes, speaking."

"My name is Mena. I believe that you might have known Evelyn Burgess?"

"Sorry?"

I cleared my throat.

"I'm going through the address book belonging to my husband's grandmother, Evelyn. You're listed in here."

"Evelyn?"

"Yes."

I could hear him breathing on the other end of the line.

"I did know Evelyn."

"Well, I'm sorry to bother you, but I'm going through everyone in the book to let them know that she died last night."

There was no audible response.

"I'm not sure from the book who are current contacts and who aren't, so I'm sorry if I've disturbed you."

"I'm sorry to hear that," he said after a moment. "Please pass on my condolences to those affected."

"Thank you, I will. Did you know Evelyn well?"

"A very long time ago," Laurie replied. "Back when I lived in Manchester, before I moved down here. But we hadn't been in touch for many, many years."

There was a silence, not an expectant one but one that sounded reflective.

"I'm arranging her funeral. I realise it's a long way and you haven't been in contact in recent years, but would you like me to let you know the details when I have them?"

Another pause. I was beginning to think that Laurie Graves was a deep thinker, either that or he had a delayed response mechanism.

"Yes. By all means."

"OK, I'll make a note. Thank you for your time."

I hung up and pencilled a tick and the letter F for funeral next to his name. It would be good if he could make it, the numbers were looking rather small at the moment.

I quickly riffled through the rest of the address book. Only a handful of names that had not been crossed out. Either Evelyn had fallen out with a lot of people or they had died or lost touch. It was quite depressing. It shouldn't take me too long to finish up, I was starting to get the hang of this now. The sooner this was finished, the better.

CHAPTER TWENTY-ONE

The day of Evelyn's funeral dawned bright and clear a week later, with a crisp note in the air. My favourite kind of autumnal day, a day for walks in the countryside, followed by a pub lunch and a pint by a roaring fire. Not a day for a funeral. It seemed wrong to be formally saying goodbye to someone on such a beautiful day. I always felt that funerals should be held in gloomy, drizzly weather with optional fog for added misery. It would feel as though the universe was mourning your loss, as well as the mourners attending the funeral.

I sat on the bed rolling my thick black opaque tights up my legs. Paddy, fresh out of the shower with damp hair, was buttoning up his smart white shirt.

"What time do we have to leave again?" he asked, lifting his chin up to button the tricky top one.

"Ten o'clock," I replied. "The undertakers will be coming to pick us up in their car and take us straight to the crematorium."

As Evelyn hadn't subscribed to any religion that we were aware of, we had decided upon a short service at the crematorium, followed by a pub buffet lunch around the corner. There weren't likely to be many of us.

Paddy opened his wardrobe door and pulled out his dark navy tie.

"You've got your eulogy, haven't you?"

Paddy nodded over to his suit jacket, hanging on the back of our bedroom door.

"It's in my jacket."

"Great," I said, standing up and moving over to my wardrobe.

A dark grey tailored shift dress hung from a coat hanger and I slipped it off and unzipped the back. It was my go-to dress for interviews and formal occasions, but it was the first time that it would be used for a funeral. Hopefully, I would be using it for job interviews soon.

I pulled the dress over my head and wriggled around to reach the zip and pull it up. Thank goodness it still fit, despite the week of comfort eating chocolate and a generous glass of red wine each night.

"How are you doing?" I asked casually, as I wrestled with the top part of the zip.

"Fine," he replied, knotting his tie. I always loved to see him dressed up on the rare occasions he did, he always looked like a different version of himself. Like the film version of the novel. "Better once today is done with."

Paddy had kept himself busy this past week, working long hours at his job and going out to the pub most evenings. His favoured method of dealing with upset was to distract himself and not allow himself to dwell on things and it seemed to work for him. He was always able to move on from emotional situations a lot more quickly than I could.

I, on the other hand, had spent most of the week arranging the funeral and the wake at the local pub and it surprised me how quickly the time had been swallowed up. There was no time or mental capacity to even think about jobs, but maybe that had been a good thing. A bit of a break before starting up again might help me to make a fresh start.

Paddy had taken my redundancy news quite calmly. He pointed out that we would be ok for a couple of months and to see what happened. Whereas I was more prone to imagining us on the street in rags, he was much more practical and less dramatic. Just as well, I suppose, to have a counterweight to your own personality excesses in a relationship.

"Could you…?" I backed up towards Paddy.

He reached over and deftly zipped me up in one smooth movement. I turned and gave him a hug, laying my head on his chest. He hugged me back for a moment before patting me once on the shoulder and reaching for his suit jacket. His dark hair matched perfectly against the black of his suit.

"And the pub is expecting us at about twelve?" he asked, sliding his arms into the sleeves and shrugging it on.

"Yup," I confirmed, trying to find the holes in my ear lobes with my delicate hoop earrings. "We've got the side room to ourselves and the buffet will be ready at half-past. I've catered for twenty but I'm not sure we'll have that many. It's whether your Burgesses come or not, we'll have to see. I couldn't pin them down."

I could tell that Paddy was feeling nervous. He was effectively the host of the funeral and I could tell that he was struggling a bit with the responsibility. Thank goodness there wouldn't be many of us.

"I'll see you downstairs," he said, opening the door and moving out towards the landing. "I'm just going to have another coffee before we go."

"OK, I'll be down in a minute."

He thudded down the stairs and I took a deep breath. Even

the thought of a buffet lunch wasn't inspiring my usual sense of anticipation. My limited experience of funerals meant that I also had a nervous flutter in my stomach, worried that we would somehow get something wrong and cause offence.

I would be relieved when today was over.

Evelyn had left a note about her own funeral, which made everything much more straightforward. She had specified her preferred arrangements and the costs were all covered, which was a relief. Particularly in my current precarious financial situation.

I had had no idea how much funerals cost and had blanched at the list of coffin options and prices displayed in the funeral director's premises. Unsurprisingly, Evelyn had selected the most cost-effective wood and accessories package. I was with her on this one, what was the point when it would all be cremated anyway? I had already decided that I would want to be cremated in cardboard or something similarly sensible when my time came. Or bury me in a willow box and feed the trees, I wasn't interested in shiny wood and polished brass handles.

The sleek undertaker's limousine pulled up at the front of the crematorium and we awkwardly climbed out, feeling out of place. We had followed Evelyn's coffin along the winding road through the cemetery, past rows and rows of graves of people who had gone before. A reminder of so many lives that had ended. We both felt subdued.

I spied Maud stood over to one side of the chapel entrance. She was dressed in grey polyester today, with a lilac shaggy overcoat to keep her warm. I felt inordinately pleased to see someone I actually knew and headed over to speak to her.

"Morning Maud. Thank you for coming."

She nodded her head.

"Well, I always feel it's important to pay your respects," she said. "Evelyn was my neighbour for many years."

The undertakers began to remove Evelyn's coffin from the back of the hearse and we watched in silence for a moment.

"No flowers on the coffin?" she asked.

"No, Evelyn said that she didn't want any, she felt they were a waste of money."

Maud nodded again.

"She wasn't one for ornamentation, that's true. Not like me, I like a bit of ornamentation."

Having seen her front garden I could certainly attest to that. I wondered whether her own coffin would be adorned with her beloved pottery figures when the time came.

"Will you be coming to the pub afterwards for some lunch? It's at twelve at the White Hart just around the corner. You'd be welcome."

"No thank you, I'll be getting back after the service. I've got an important delivery coming today and I don't want to miss it. I'll have to be home for one o'clock. It's come all the way from China."

I could guess that it would be another asset for her display.

"Well if you change your mind, just come along."

Evelyn was now being carried up the front steps and into the chapel. We stood awkwardly until I caved in first.

"Excuse me, I'd best go to Paddy."

I walked across to the other side of the entrance, where Paddy was talking with some Burgesses (I presumed). I recognised the bleached hair of Dawn, who was accompanied by three other people, a woman and two men. They turned to look at me as I approached.

"Hello," I said, feeling as though I should behave as some sort of hostess. "Thank you for coming."

"Thank you for coming" was as popular a choice from the funeral phrasebook as "you must be very proud" seemed to be at weddings.

I looked at Paddy for direction as to who was who. Before he could speak, the bleached blonde lady spoke.

"You must be Tina," said the woman that I presumed to be Dawn.

"Mena," I corrected, shaking her hand. I waited for her to introduce herself but she obviously seemed to think that I should know who she was. "You must be Dawn?"

"Well, yes," she responded, as if it hadn't needed confirming.

"Is Will here?" I asked, looking at her companions seeing as further introductions were not forthcoming.

Honestly, Paddy's family were odd.

"No, he had to stay home. They're delivering the boiler today. Plus, there was no love lost between him and Evelyn really, he wasn't close with her at all. Not the way things were with Derek."

I glanced at Paddy, but he didn't react to this bald statement.

"So, you've come with…" I prompted.

For goodness sake, it was like trying to get blood from a stone.

"This is Dave and his wife Julia and his brother John."

I shook hands and said hello. I still had no idea how they were all related and frankly had given up caring by now.

"Well, you're welcome to come to the lunch after the service. It's the White Hart, you can follow us if you don't know where you're going."

Dave's face lit up. I could identify a fellow buffet lover at a hundred paces. I felt slightly warmer towards them. Any buffet aficionado was a friend of mine.

"Time to go in?" I said, looking at Paddy meaningfully.

"Right, yes," responded Paddy, making his way up the stairs, closely followed by the Burgess contingent who walked along in the accepted funeral walk of hands clasped in front and head slightly bowed.

We entered through the chapel reception area, which was fitted up with a large LED screen displaying Evelyn's name and dates. It was much more high-tech than I was expecting. Not being used to churches and their formalities, I had been anticipating calligraphy notices and worn leather hymn books.

We filed through into the chapel and Paddy and I headed to the front pew on the left. The quiet sounds of other people filtering into the room and taking seats was just audible over the soft background music. I turned in my seat to look behind.

Aside from the Burgesses, I could also see Maud sat on her own near the back, perusing the order of service. Another couple I didn't recognise sat on the opposite side of the aisle, whispering together. The lady wore a felt beret at a fetching angle over her shoulder-length iron grey hair.

A flurry of activity at the door caught my eye and I looked over to see Annie hurry in and take up a seat at the very back. She held Amy on one hip and had a firm hold of Tom's hand. Tom spotted me and called out "Auntie Mena!" before being fervently shushed by his mum. I smiled and gave a small wave. I hadn't been expecting them to come today and hadn't specifically asked Annie, seeing as she hadn't had a relationship with Evelyn and had enough to fill her days with.

I began to turn back around to face the front when I noticed a man come through the door and sit next to the doorway, on the opposite side to Annie and her brood. Again, he wasn't someone that I recognised. He was small, stooped and bald aside from a fringe of hair that reached around the back from ear to ear. He wore a thick, expensive-looking navy winter coat over a dark suit. He looked like a Reginald.

I swivelled back to face the front. Thirteen people, including us. It seemed a sad gathering for the end of someone's existence on this earth, but I supposed it was better than just the two of us.

Paddy sat straight-backed, staring ahead at the lectern.

"Are you ok?" I whispered, squeezing his arm.

"Yes," he replied, softly. "Just a bit nervous."

"It'll be fine. Just think of Evelyn and how proud she'd be of you today. You know that that's all that matters to her."

He nodded and patted my knee. I felt for him. He was much more comfortable wearing his happy-go-lucky persona, this funeral would be difficult for him.

A hush fell as the officiant, I think that was what he was called, approached the lectern from the side of the raised platform and cleared his throat.

"I would like to welcome you all to this service today, celebrating the life of Evelyn Burgess."

I looked over to the coffin, resting on a trestle. Poor Evelyn. It suddenly hit home that she was really gone. I bowed my head.

The short service was over. Paddy and I stood and followed the other attendees out the back of the chapel and into the fresh air. I made a beeline for Annie, who was standing by some kind of gardening station, complete with hose, buckets and a compost bin.

"Hello! I didn't know you were going to be coming today," I said, leaning forward to give her a hug without crushing Amy on her hip at the same time.

She hugged me back awkwardly.

"I couldn't leave you to do it on your own without some support."

"I've got Paddy," I protested.

"Yes, well. Like I said, I couldn't let you do it without some support."

I play punched her on the arm that wasn't holding Amy.

"I'm sorry about the kids, I was going to come without them but then they've both got a temperature today and nursery wouldn't take them. Sam couldn't come as he's got a site visit in Chorlton, so I'm afraid you've got the three of us."

"Hi kids," I said, squeezing Amy's pudgy little hand and tapping Tom on his head.

Tom clamped his arms around Annie's leg and hung on for dear life.

"I know some people don't approve of kids at funerals," whispered Annie. "But personally, I think it's important that they know about the circle of life and that death isn't a mystical thing but a very real part of life."

"Lion King!" crowed Tom.

"Yes, that's right, the circle of life," said Annie, looking down proudly at her son.

"Thank you for coming, it's lovely to see you," I said. "You'll come for lunch at the pub won't you? Lots of finger food for the kids and there'll be tons. Not a very big turnout as you can see. It'll feel like more of a send off if you come."

"If that's ok with you, of course we will."

Out of the corner of my eye, I saw Reginald shuffling awkwardly behind the Beret Lady.

"Just a moment, I need to do some of the formalities. I'll be right back."

I hurried over to Reginald and gave him a smile of welcome.

"Hello, I'm Mena. I'm married to Evelyn's grandson."

I held out my hand, which he shook.

"Laurie," he said in a low voice I recognised from the phone.

His hand was soft and dry. I had to stoop a little to make eye contact with him.

"Oh, Mr Graves," I said, realising who he was. "I'm so pleased you could make it. Thank you for coming." There it was again. "You live in Norfolk, don't you?"

"Yes, that's right," he said, clearing his throat.

"It's been a long journey for you. Have you come up this morning?"

Look at you, queen of small talk all of a sudden.

"Yes, I set off early. I'll be heading back in a moment, I just wanted to come and say goodbye to Evelyn. Help to put her to rest, so to speak."

"You're welcome to come for lunch? It's only round the corner."

"No thank you," he said, with a brisk nod. "I appreciate the offer, but I won't. Evelyn was the person I knew and now I've said my farewell I'd like to head back home."

He rubbed the side of his nose with his index finger and looked a little lost.

"Of course, whatever you feel is best." I paused. "But before you go, would you mind if I check something with you?"

He looked up at me and furrowed his brow. I opened my tote handbag and reached inside.

"I don't suppose these belong to you?"

I extricated a small bundle of paper and handed it over to him. I watched as he gingerly took it from me and peered at the writing.

"Letters?" he asked, carefully leafing through them.

"After I spoke to you on the phone, I thought you might be L," I said gently. "I brought them with me just in case. I know that she would like you to have them."

"Yes. Yes, they were from me a very long time ago. I can't believe she still had them after all this time," he said, moist around the eyes.

"She was reading them the night she died," I said. "I'm sorry if that's upsetting for you, but I thought you might like to know. They obviously meant a lot to her."

He pushed the letters back into a neat rectangle and clasped them firmly.

"Well, I'm surprised," he said. "I believed that the strength of feeling had all been on my side. But then I suppose you can get more sentimental as you get older and wonder what might have been."

I was dying to know their story. I kept quiet, hopeful that he would tell me what had happened.

"She chose her path and I eventually found mine. Perhaps if we'd both been braver we might have had a different outcome, but we'll never know that now. It's a lesson that we learnt far too late, to take the chances we're given and not be put off by initial obstacles. Too late for us, anyway."

I sensed somebody approaching us and I hoped that they would stay away until we had finished our conversation. No such luck.

"I'll be off now then," said Maud, inserting herself into the conversation by physically stepping between us. "I must get back for my parcel."

Laurie took a step back. I shook her hand.

"Thanks for coming Maud, we appreciate it."

She nodded at each of us in turn, before setting off at a brisk walk along the main cemetery road, determined not to miss her delivery.

"Are you sure you won't stay?" I asked Laurie, trying to draw him back into the conversation. "I'm sure my husband would like to meet you."

"No thank you," he said. "I'd like to go now. It's already been a long day. Thank you again for the letters."

He tucked them into the voluminous pocket of his heavy coat.

"It doesn't always do to remember regrets," he continued. "It can stop you from appreciating the life you have created for yourself."

He absent-mindedly patted his pocket and walked quickly towards the car park, head down. I watched him for a moment, affected by his words. I didn't know what had gone on between him and Evelyn, but it was obviously something that had deeply touched them both. How sad that they would never get to meet again in this life. But then life is rarely like a romance film where everything gets resolved before the grand finale.

Paddy appeared at my elbow.

"The next people are arriving," he said. "We should be making a move."

"Right," I said. "I'll get everyone moving off towards the pub." I checked my watch. "We'll be slightly early but I'm sure that's fine."

"Who was that?" he asked, gesturing towards the car park.

"Apparently, he used to know your nan many years ago, must have been before she met Derek. He moved to Norfolk and hasn't seen her since. It was nice of him to come all that way."

"He couldn't even stay for lunch?"

"No, he had to get back. He needed to get on."

In more ways than one.

"Come on, let's show everyone where they're going."

I tucked my hand under his arm and we led the way towards the cars, leaving Evelyn behind.

I manoeuvred my tray of drinks carefully onto the table I was sharing with Annie, Tom and Amy. As was my usual habit, I had my tongue stuck out in concentration.

"Don't go into waitressing," said Annie, reaching over to take her glass of white wine. "You'd put the punters off with that thing sticking out of your mouth."

"I can't help it," I said, dishing out two fruit shoots for the kids and popping the lids open. "I genuinely can't concentrate otherwise. Paddy says I mustn't ever do a reality TV show where you need to complete complex tasks as that's all anyone will be able to see."

Annie snorted.

"Can you imagine if you went on Master Chef and you were carrying your tray through to the posh judges with your tongue sticking out. Not the done thing. Although," she said, taking a sip of her wine, "the chances of you going on Master Chef with your repertoire of cupboard meals is pretty unlikely."

"Don't be rude," I said, pretending to be affronted as I laid the empty tray beside me, propped against the wall. "My meals may be unconventional, but they are nutritional and tasty."

"So how come your takeaway bill is so high?" Annie asked, with her eyebrow raised.

"Because everyone needs to slum it every now and again," I said with a wink.

Tom was engaged in colouring in an activity sheet that had been helpfully provided by the pub. Amy sat in state in one of the pub's grubby highchairs, with a wotsit in one hand and a stick of cucumber in the other. I looked over at Paddy, who was sat drinking a beer with the Burgesses. Dawn threw her head back and cackled loudly. I wasn't sure that that was the done thing at a wake, weren't we all supposed to be sat morosely, sharing reminiscences of the deceased? Again, I felt hamstrung by my lack of experience, although on reflection, I was pleased that they hadn't featured largely in my life before now.

The older couple had also come along to the pub. It turned out that they lived opposite Evelyn and had been given the funeral details by Maud. I had a sneaking suspicion that both had just come along for the food, as they sat with plates piled high, enthusiastically tucking in. They hadn't volunteered much about Evelyn apart from their proximity to her bungalow. Still, it was better than wasting the food.

"Thank you for coming," I said again to Annie, as I lifted my own wine glass in tribute. "I know you have enough on your plate without coming to Evelyn's funeral."

"Oh, it's fine," she said, breezily. "I knew it would be a big day for you today, you've had a lot to deal with sorting it all out on top of everything else. I thought it would be nice for you to have me to talk to over lunch, especially if Paddy was on family duty."

I looked over again at Paddy. For someone who didn't seem to be that bothered about family connections, he seemed to be getting on like a house on fire with his distant relations. Or perhaps that was the effect of the beer, seeing as they seemed to be getting through the rounds at a surprising rate. Almost as quickly as Dave was getting through plateful after plateful of buffet.

"It certainly is," I said. "It would have been awkward on my own."

"Eat some more food please, Tom," said Annie in her mum voice. "At least one more sandwich and a carrot stick and then you can have some more sausage rolls."

Tom pulled a face but shoved a plain ham sandwich triangle into his mouth and chewed enthusiastically. He was a sucker for sausage rolls, you could almost make him do anything for one. A bit like Paddy and a takeaway.

"So how are you feeling now?" Annie asked, popping a mini vol-au-vent in her own mouth.

"Relieved that it's done and a bit deflated, if I'm honest," I said. "I think I was using it all as a bit of a distraction from having to think about my own situation, but I won't be able to use that as an excuse now."

"Nope," agreed Annie, licking her finger and thumb. "From this point on, you need to think about yourself. But don't go rushing into the first thing that presents itself, this is your big chance to think about how you want your life to be. Full time or part time? Remote working or office-based? Freelance or employee? It's not every day we get a chance to do that."

"Not every day we get forced to have to do that," I replied, in a sarcastic voice.

"No," said Annie. "But that's your reality so embrace it."

"Are you sure you haven't been reading a coaching manual?" I asked, pulling a face. "Are you swotting up on it each time before you meet me?"

"Very funny," said Annie. "I can't help it if I'm naturally wise and clear-sighted. You should be grateful that I'm bestowing my gifts upon you."

I smiled.

"I certainly am, please continue to do so, wise sage."

"I'll think about it," she said, reaching over again to hand Amy a small box of raisins.

Amy crowed with excitement and tipped them out onto the tray in front of her.

"I wish I got so excited about raisins," I commented.

"You get that excited about those chocolate truffle balls you like," said Annie, taking a bite from a flaky vegetable samosa.

"That's not exactly the same thing," I protested. "Not quite as good for you."

Annie shrugged.

"You have to go where your excitement leads you," she intoned in faux oracle tones.

"True. And I promise I'll take the time to do that, starting tomorrow."

"Good. Because if today tells us anything, life is over before you know it and you don't want your last thought to be 'oh I wish I'd eaten more of those truffle balls'."

"I don't think that will be my last thought to be honest," I said with a wry smile. "I think I've done my best to eat as many as is humanly possible during my lifetime so far."

"Well, something else, such as 'I wish I hadn't wasted my entire working life working in dead-end jobs where I'm not appreciated' then."

"You know that little man I spoke to after the service?"

"I hope you aren't changing the subject," warned Annie, licking the cream off the top of a mini fruit scone.

"Turns out he wrote those love letters to Evelyn."

"No, really?"

Annie's eyes widened in surprise.

"He didn't look the type!"

"Well to be fair, neither did Evelyn. But something clearly went badly wrong there. He seemed almost bitter about missed opportunities. It got me thinking that I need to be more assertive and be less of a people-pleaser."

"Absolutely, but good luck with breaking that habit," snorted Annie again, moving onto the jam.

"Do you mind? That's disgusting."

"You should see me eat a Crème Egg," she threatened.

"I have and that's disgusting too. But I've decided that I'm going to start listening to my inner voice a bit more and start standing up for myself. I think it's trying to get me to be more myself, although it can be a bit mean sometimes. I've been doing it a lot more recently, saying those thoughts out loud and I've actually been quite proud of myself. It hasn't been the end of the world."

"Perhaps that's what you need to do, learn to speak your feelings instead of bottling them all up and having a meltdown. Sounds like a good idea, as long as you don't start saying mean things to me."

"I'll try not to," I said, taking another sip of wine.

"Anyway, I've got something for you," said Annie excitedly, putting down the rest of her scone and rummaging in her yummy mummy bag.

She produced a fancy pen and a notepad with a flourish.

"What's that?" I asked curiously. Aside from my lucky pen, I wasn't exactly a stationery person and Annie knew that.

"This is to help you make some big decisions. Look."

She passed the notepad over to me. It had a botanical background with a title in the middle of the front cover.

"Mena's plans for world domination".

I smiled.

"This is for me?"

"No, it's for another Mena. What do you think, silly? It's to help you plot out where you want to go and who you want to be. It's got all these handy sections for you to work through and space for plans of action."

I felt overwhelmed.

"Thank you, that's really helpful. You're the best."

I reached over the table and clasped her hand.

"Now use it to become the most fabulous Mena that you can be, even more than you are now," she said sternly, before releasing my hand and picking up the rest of her scone to take a bite.

"I will."

CHAPTER TWENTY-TWO

I helped Paddy out of the taxi and leaned back in through the passenger window to pay the fare.

Paddy lurched towards our front door, before propping himself up against the frame.

I hurried to open it with my keys and helped him through the doorway and manoeuvred him onto the sofa. He sat slumped with his chin to his chest.

"Come on you, let's get you upstairs to bed with a glass of water," I said sympathetically. "It's been a long day."

I slipped his shiny black shoes off his feet and placed them side by side before reaching to pull him up by his hand.

"No," he protested feebly, trying to stay where he was.

"Nope, you're not sleeping on the sofa tonight, you'll wake up all stiff in the morning. Off to bed, you need a good night's sleep."

I wound his arm around my shoulders and dragged him along to the stairs.

"Come on, up you go."

To his credit, he did his best to haul himself up by the banister and we managed to shuffle up a step at a time. Once in the bedroom, I slipped off his suit jacket, undid his tie and quickly unbuttoned his shirt. Paddy tried to help by unbuttoning his trousers and then standing there like a scarecrow as I hurriedly pulled them down and helped him to step out of them.

I peeled back the bed covers and he collapsed onto the bed in his jockey shorts and socks.

That would have to do. I took his water glass and went to refill it in the bathroom.

"Here you go sweetheart," I murmured, smoothing his hair back from his forehead and kissing him on his brow. "Have a good sleep."

He was snoring before I'd even finished collecting up his discarded clothes and hung his suit up in the wardrobe.

I quickly changed into my own pyjamas and headed out of our room, quietly closing the door behind me. I padded downstairs and clicked on the kettle.

What a day. I exhaled and placed both hands on the countertop, dropping my head and stretching my back out. It had been emotional and tiring. Still, the wake had gone better than expected, with Paddy enjoying the reunion with his family, as well as several pints and chasers.

I made a cup of tea in my favourite mug and headed back into the lounge, settling down in my usual seat. I pulled my blanket over me and rubbed my eyes.

Annie was right. There was no time like the present and I couldn't keep putting it off. I reached down into my handbag and pulled out the notepad and pen that Annie had given me.

"World domination," I chuckled, shaking my head.

Trust Annie to aim high. I would be happy with a settled, quiet life thanks very much, where worries were limited and I had a sense of fulfilment. But I knew that I needed to make some changes and this was as good a place as any to start.

This was my chance to look for opportunities and take them. Create my own opportunities if necessary. But one thing was sure, I was no longer going to be a doormat people-pleaser. Well, not as much of one. I would start listening to my inner voice and look out for myself. Life was too short.

About time!

I opened the notepad, unscrewed the lid from my new pen and considered the first page.

World, prepare to meet a new Philomena Frisby.

I began to write.

Printed in Great Britain
by Amazon

38258373R00185